Praise for M.A. Wardell

Advance Praise for *Mistletoe and Mishigas*

"Sheldon and Theo's opposites-attract, Beauty-and-the-Beast chemistry grabbed me from the first chapter and never let go. Their past traumas are handled deftly with Wardell's now-signature humor and care, creating a love story both steamy and sweet, with an HEA steeped in personal growth and full acceptance of the other. Wholly delightful and full of Hanukah spirit—Wardell's voice jumps off the page." - Anita Kelly, author of *Something Wild and Wonderful*

"Poignant. Nuanced. Deeply emotional. Sharply witty. Wardell has woven a tapestry of humor, healing, and love that comes together in a beautiful way that left me devouring the words and hungry for more while still deeply satisfied in what can only be described as a story that explores the way two people, in all their perfection imperfection, can complement one another in ways that transcend the basic "love conquers all" concept found in romance novels. This story has the spicy sweet flavor of his debut, with a deeper and more delicate hand that speaks to his absolute skill as a craftsman of stories that will fill your heart with joy. I am in awe of this author and can't wait for even more. - Jay Leigh author of *Whisper into the Night* and *Checking Out*

"Wardell has outdone himself and this *might* be better than Teacher Of The Year. There. I said it. I had very high expectations because I LOVED Marvin and Olan's love story and have raved because TOY was my book of the year. Wardell does not disappoint with Mistletoe & Mishigas. This is a deeply poignant MULTI-holiday romcom with lots of heart and heat. This book has every-thing: fake dating, snow storms, "pretend" kisses, a holiday decorating montage, Jenga towers made of chairs, and a cat named Janice." - K Sterling, author of *The Nannies of New York Series*

Praise for *Teacher of the Year*

"A winning love story with just the right amounts of thoughtfulness and playful energy." - *Kirkus Reviews*

"A love letter to queer educators, *Teacher of the Year* is a warm hug—and spicy treat—of a novel! M.A. Wardell expertly crafts characters who tug at heartstrings while validating our deepest needs. A laugh-out-loud, happy-cry, swoony-sigh read, prepare to meet your new auto-buy author!" - Courtney Kae, author of *In the Event of Love*

"The quick wit, delightful humor, and emotional depth of M.A. Wardell's prose come together in this debut novel that explores the nuanced relationships between family, friends, and coworkers while navigating a budding romance and balancing the demands of others. This refreshing take on such universal topics resonates throughout and the author's voice, reminiscent of Alexis Hall, creates a gem of a story that has stuck with me months after reading." --- Jay Leigh, author of Whisper into the Night

MISTLETOE & MISHIGAS

Teachers in Love: Book 2

M.A. WARDELL

To anyone who's never seen themselves reflected in a love story.

Author's Note

Dear Reader,

Sheldon and Theo burrowed their way into my heart and soul. I truly fell for them while writing their story. I hope you will too.

Mistletoe and Mishigas is an open-door romance intended for mature audiences. The characters in the story are consenting adults, and there is explicit, on-page sexual content, explicit language and adult situations.

The actual term for a Jewish matchmaker is "shadchan," but after the 1964 film version of *Fiddler on the Roof*, in which a character named Yente serves as a matchmaker, the word "yenta" became synonymous with the role of matchmaker. Hence the use of "yenta" as matchmaker in the lexicon and Mistletoe and Mishigas.

While Sheldon and Theo get into plenty of mishigas, there are also serious issues. Here are the content warnings if you need them: Parental abandonment because of homophobia, active combat flashbacks, PTSD from combat, PTSD episodes, a car accident (not on the page), infidelity (not by the main characters), and negative self-body image.

As always, if these are triggers for you, please take care of yourself and proceed with caution.

All my best,
  M.A. Wardell

ONE

Sheldon

News of my ex-boyfriend's engagement should have ruined my morning, but I have exactly one day to prepare a new classroom for a gaggle of first graders. It was a surprise school transfer. That I got *yesterday*. The Sunday after Thanksgiving. Which is fine, it happens all the time. What doesn't happen all the time? Finding an invitation to your ex-boyfriend's wedding hidden by your wombmate-turned-roommate in the kitchen junk drawer. Oh, and the wedding is on Christmas Eve. How tacky.

Will either of these facts drag me down on this beautiful, sunny late-November morning? No way. I'm living my best when-they-go-low, we-go-high fantasy.

The drive to Lear Elementary is two minutes shorter than my commute to Faye—which was only ten minutes. That's only eight minutes. First-grade math for the win! Thank you, compact Portland peninsula! We've got lobsters, 3,500 miles of coastline, and a sunrise we get to see before the rest of the country. Take that, other Portland!

The crisp autumn air mixes with the ocean breeze as I survey the almost empty school parking lot. Bigger than Faye, Lear sports a generous playground with newer equipment, including swings, multiple slides, and a climbing structure with ropes that snake across the area, creating a lovely space for children to play and explore.

With a bounce in my step, thanks to Lady Gaga's criminally overlooked "Christmas Tree" blasting in my earbuds, and my fabulous purple Converse to match my nails, I strut into Lear Elementary School, ready and focused. Pulling a classroom together in a day might sound unrealistic, perhaps impossible. Still, with how efficiently I work, I'll be done and home in time for Thanksgiving leftovers and snuggling on the couch with Janice, my tortoiseshell cat, who detests everyone and everything in the universe. Except me. Because even though Janice's resting bitch face rivals Medusa, for some reason, she adores me. Time to bang this classroom out and get home to my kitty girl.

How did I end up being transferred the day before Thanksgiving? Naomi and I were in the kitchen, my Pop Divas playlist blasting as we tried to out-sing each other while peeling apples and potatoes and preparing for our small Thanksgiving, when my phone cried out in the middle of Kelly Clarkson's "Underneath the Tree." The name of my now-former principal Gianna DeGarmo flashed on my phone. My heart thumped a little too quickly, and it only escalated when I answered.

"Sheldon, I know this is last minute, but I need you to transfer to Lear. Their classrooms have grown far over the limit, and well, with you and Rebecca each only having nine students and no more on the horizon ..." She wasn't asking, and there really wasn't any respectable way to say no. Switching to a new school within our district is common, but I adore Faye Elementary. The community accepts me. I can be myself there. All of me. Something I don't take for granted.

Leaving the bubble of Faye makes my head woozy, but I'm confident I can win this new community over in no time. Lear Elementary needs Sheldon Soleskin, which means it's time for a mid-year new-classroom-setup moment.

An older white man with a kind, round face and a long red and green scarf that engulfs his head greets me at the front door with a comforting smile. Even though this man resembles a young Santa

Claus, I still proceed with caution. Men, straight ones in particular, always make me slightly uncomfortable. They ramble about sports (only tennis for me, thanks to Rafael Nadal and his short shorts) and beer (when I'm interested in drinking urine, I'll let you know).

"Sheldon?" The man's arms open, and his eyes, bright and wide, sparkle like tinsel under a spotlight. "Thank god you agreed to transfer. I could just hug you! May I?"

"What?"

"Hug you?"

"Oh, um, sure."

Before I know what's happening, he gathers me up in an embrace like we're long-lost relatives. His gray beard scratches my forehead like pine needles. How have I found myself in this after-school special-family-reunion reenactment?

"What if I said I wasn't Sheldon Soleskin?" I squeak, still swaddled in his warm bear hug.

"Oh, you're a feisty one, aren't you? Just what we need here at Lear." He pulls away but still holds me in his arms. "I'm Kent Lester. Principal. And a hugger. I hope that's okay. Gianna gushed about you." He grips my shoulders as he surveys his new teacher. "I'm beyond thrilled you're here. Welcome to Lear."

I'm so close to this man that my chest tightens. Does he know I'm queer? Does he care? If he doesn't know, it won't take long. Most people figure it out within two minutes. One if they have perfect vision and hearing. As Naomi says, "Sheldon, you're gayer than a unicorn in drag riding on a rainbow float at the Pride Parade." And usually, I own it. Right now, wrapped in the woodsy smoke coziness of Kent Lester, I close my eyes and attempt to quiet my inner saboteur. Not everyone thinks I'm too much.

As he pulls back, I have to ask him, "Has anyone ever told you—"

"I look like a young Santa," he finishes my sentence. "Practically everyone."

"It's uncanny."

"The kids are all convinced I'm Santa's younger brother. But I'm Jewish, so I'm more Santa Klutz." He laughs from his belly.

"Come, let me show you the space," he says and immediately trips over the doorstep. "I'm fine. I'm fine." He waves away my outstretched hand and shakes his head.

Kent leads me down a long hallway lined with bulletin boards filled with children's colorful work. There are papers that have lost their staples and flutter like butterfly wings in our wake as we pass. I imagine these walls lined with festive decorations made by little hands in the coming weeks. Snowmen and wreaths and elves, oh my!

Lear is a newer school, and it shows. I spot a water fountain with a fancy bottle filler and think about how my skin will shine and glow from all the hydration provided by the fresh, clean water. Everything sparkles and glimmers under the bright lights, there are no splotches on the ceiling, and the floor has no dings or missing tiles. Lear gives off major upgrade vibes, and I'm not mad about it. Glancing down at the freshly waxed floor, I notice my reflection as we walk. I give shiny-floor Sheldon a little wave, mouthing, "Hey, you!"

At the end of a long corridor, near what I'm surmising must be the building's finale, we round a corner and slam into a dead end. Kent, walking in front of me, glances back to speak, but before words escape his mouth, he crashes into a door. Before I can ask, once again, he says, "Fine, I'm fine. Just not the most gracious goose."

The single door, slightly ajar, beckons me. An empty room looms.

"All right, technically, this isn't a classroom. But since we only got the go-ahead to add another first-grade classroom last week, I had to think creatively. This has been our physical therapy room, but we've moved them out to a portable with some other services. I know the room seems a little ..."

"Bleak?"

Kent chortles. "Yeah, you could say that." There's a distinct echo where Kent's laugh reverberates against the walls like a pinball.

With gray walls and a gray tile floor, the entire room resembles an abandoned warehouse. Or a prison. The only thing missing are bars on the windows. Soft November sun pours through the line of naked windows along the far wall, illuminating the vast emptiness. My brain imagines the transformation that will happen over the next few hours. It's giving very Drag-Race-unconventional-materials-design-challenge energy. If those queens can craft Met-Gala-worthy outfits out of twigs and berries, I can certainly do this. Tomorrow, the space will be bustling with first-grade children. My lips turn up at the thought of greeting their smiling faces.

Dust bunnies have made homes in the vacant corners. I think of my students and how I might make a game out of naming the bundles of fluff before sweeping them up. "This one is Henry, and oh look, Sheila, sorry sweetie, you've got to go!" There's a small kidney table smooshed into a corner and some boxes that need moving. That's it. Late autumn air creates a chill in the room, and I really hope the heat kicks on soon because my scrawny body doesn't produce much. My new class, an amalgamation of students from the two other overstuffed first-grade classes, joins me tomorrow. I take a deep breath and smile, reminding myself that the universe called me here. The entire day lies ahead, and we only need basic amenities for the first day. The kids will help me tomorrow.

Chin up, Sheldon Soleskin! If anyone can do this, it's you!

I take a final survey of the room, clasp my hands, and, doing my best Maria Von Trapp sing, "Let's start at the very beginning."

Kent's eyes go sideways, and a wide grin overtakes his broad face.

"Yes! A very good place to start," he sings back. Sharing a mutual love of Julie Andrews with my new principal was certainly not on my radar. I cock my head and smile.

"How about furniture? *That* would be a great place to start."

"We have everything you'll need in the basement," Kent says. "There are tables, desks, chairs, and shelves. Anything down there is up for grabs. Let me show you."

We return to the hallway and walk to the entrance, where Kent unlocks a large metal door. We carefully navigate the path down to the basement, the flimsy stairs creaking beneath our feet as spiderwebs attack my face—I do *not* feature silk webbing as part of my skincare routine, thank you very much, spiders of Lear. Brushing them aside like the schoolyard taunts of my youth and ignoring the acrid stench of mildew, I discover myself facing a tower of furniture. Pieces of wood and metal jut out in all directions, making it hard to decipher what treasures lie within.

"Perfect! It's definitely a Jenga moment, but this will get me started."

"I'd love to help, but an emergency meeting at central office beckons. Theo, our custodian, is knocking around. He can help with the furniture."

"Awesome. Theo. I'll find him," I say as if I'm methodically checking items off a list.

My new classroom, about a good city block's distance from my current location in the bowels of Lear, isn't that far. Unless you're carrying a classroom's worth of furniture and have the muscle mass of a flea. My people do not come from sturdy stock. We prefer to *be* carried over doing the carrying.

"Listen, Theo's a great guy but can be … a little frosty. But I'm sure you two will get along like two little elves." Kent wipes something from his face. "Technically, he's more Abominable Snowman, but anyway, good luck!"

With that, Kent Lester abandons me in the depths of Lear to gather furniture for my new first-grade classroom. I refuse to dwell on the fact that I'm alone in a scary school basement. Instead, I tilt my head toward the furniture because this classroom isn't going to set itself up. I manage to grab two chairs, one in each arm, nod enthusiastically to the universe, and wrangle them up the stairs.

Back in the classroom, and already out of breath, I place the chairs down and sit on one. The powder-blue contact paper on the bulletin board next to the row of windows reminds me of the lettering on the wedding invitation I wasn't supposed to find this morning.

I was rushing to get dressed so I could get to Lear and the button on my favorite steel joggers—that I wear constantly because they show off my best … *assets*—popped off. I went for the sewing kit in the junk drawer where I discovered Naomi's poor attempt at hiding the invitation.

"Naomi! When were you planning on telling me?"

"Bean, I'm sorry!" Naomi's called me "bean" since we were babies. She's exactly two and a half minutes older and has always been half an inch taller. "It came on Halloween, and I didn't want to ruin your Glinda the Good Witch evening. Before I knew it, Thanksgiving came, and—"

"You should've told me."

"I know."

She gazes at me with those puppy dog eyes that, well, mirror mine, and I'm a puddle of eggnog. It's impossible for me to be upset with her. She's the only family I have.

"Why Christmas Eve? Timothy knows how much I love Christmas," I muffled into her shoulder.

"I know. I'm so sorry, bean," she said.

"Well, are we going?"

"Um, excuse me. That invitation is addressed to Sheldon Soleskin and guest. And guest. I'm not your default guest to his tacky Christmas-Eve wedding."

"Actually, you are literally my default date. Since the womb."

Naomi and I have been each other's plus one more times than I can count. Whenever one of us needs an escort, it's easy and comfortable. It's a best-friend-twin right and responsibility.

"Do you even want to go?"

"Are you kidding? There's no way I'm letting Timothy think I'm still devastated. And after last year? This will be my Christmas-Eve do-over fantasy moment."

"Sheldon, you are still devastated."

"Yeah, but only slightly."

"We don't have to go. Who cares what Timothy thinks?"

She's right, but my face flushes at the thought of Timothy thinking I'm not over him. Is he only being polite, inviting me? Maybe, but not going would show weakness.

"Of course I'll go with you, bean, but it's still a month away. You never know, maybe you'll meet someone?"

"Listen, there are many things I would love for the holidays: the ability to put muscle on this scraggly body, a pay raise for every teacher in the country, Rihanna to release a new album. Finding a boyfriend isn't high on my priorities."

"Well, your default date will be ready if needed. Walker's on call on Christmas Eve, so I'm yours."

Walker Stevens—a gorgeous emergency doctor giving total McSteamy energy—and Naomi met six years ago when he began working at the hospital. He's one of the most patient and understanding humans on the planet. He understands Naomi and I are a package deal. I need to make sure to get him something extra sparkly for Christmas! Maybe I can find a crystal-encrusted stethoscope.

"And Sheldon, I was only trying to protect you."

I attempted a smile. It's what she does. But finding the invitation, while already rushed and frazzled, momentarily threw me off my game. A sour tang overtook my mouth. It was a very taken-a-bite-of-spoiled-yogurt-I-forgot-to-check-the-expiration-date feeling. It took three and a half minutes of meditation, followed by a mini dance party to Gwen Stefani's "You Make It Feel Like Christmas," to center myself. There's nothing a little Gwen can't fix, and I'm in no mood for negativity. Not after last Christmas, when Timothy dumped me. On Christmas Eve. Now he's engaged. Less than a year after we ended.

As I stare out the window at the gorgeous view of the staff parking lot, the last leaves clinging to a mighty oak remind me that change is imminent. Don't fight it. Sure it may be overcast and dreary, but the sun is hiding behind those clouds.

The sound of a motor snaps me back to reality. No, not a motor —someone aggressively clearing their throat, slicing into my peaceful, momentary wallowing moment.

Shaking my head, trying to fling unsettling thoughts away, I turn to see an extremely tall, portly white man standing in the doorway with a scowl on his face. Fantastic, another straight man, and I'm not getting Julie Andrews-loving hugger vibes from this one. Towering over me, he's well over six feet tall. He wears a dark navy uniform resembling scrubs, black sneakers, and has a mammoth set of keys dangling from his belt. This is clearly not a high-fashion moment for him.

Hands in pockets and eyes on the floor, it appears he'd rather be anywhere but here. His face bunches up like he's smelled something foul, and I almost consider whether I should be fearful. He's tall. Big. He almost fills the entire doorway. His demeanor sends my spidey senses tingling, but when I catch his eyes, there's a glint of something I recognize. I'm not positive, but maybe sadness.

"Hi. I'm Sheldon, the new first-grade teacher."

Silence.

"This is my classroom. I'm totally supposed to be here."

He blinks.

"Are you Theo?"

Nothing.

"The custodian? Kent told me you might be able to help me carry some furniture up from the basement. I already brought these two chairs up."

I motion to them, trying to give my best Vanna White flourish. Apparently, he doesn't get the reference because he doesn't speak, and instead emits a noise, a groan that rumbles from his throat and erupts from his lips as "Mmmh." Verification that he's the elusive Theo.

Clearly, he isn't used to the effervescent fabulousness of Sheldon Soleskin.

There's a distinct chill in the air. Usually, I could warm it up like the gooey center of a cinnamon brown sugar Pop-Tart.

But that's clearly not happening today.

TWO

Theo

On my way to work, I stop at the gas station like I do every morning for a small black coffee. It's lukewarm and slightly bitter. Like me. It'll pair nicely with the leftover white chocolate pistachio babka I baked for Thanksgiving.

"Morning, my Theo. Sunday shift, eh?" Roberta says from behind the counter.

With crimson nails filed to points I'm not sure the purpose behind, Roberta's friendliness and propensity to chat can be off-putting. She annoyed me profusely when she began working at the Fill'er Up two years ago, replacing Maulik who had rarely uttered a word unless absolutely necessary. God, I miss that bastard. But I've adjusted to Roberta. She means well.

I nod at her and pull my lips into something resembling a grin.

"How was your Thanksgiving?" she asks.

"Fine."

"Come on, Theo—turkey, mashed potatoes, football. You must love football, right?"

Because I'm built like a linebacker, people assume an infatuation with football must be pulsing through my veins. The reality is that all the cheering, screaming, and revelry at games gives me a fucking headache.

"Not really."

"A solid guy like you?"

Solid. It's a word people use when they don't want to say fat. My frame might be solid, but everything on it, not so much. Some people can eat whatever they like and not gain a pound. I could eat nothing but carrot sticks and still pack it on.

Because I don't know what to say, I do my best to smile. I remind myself. Roberta means well.

"There's that beautiful smile. Give me your phone. Let me take a picture for your momma."

Last year, on my parents' yearly visit for Hanukah, in her typical fashion, my mother talked Roberta's ear off. Stopping for a coffee with my mother and father should've been simple, but nothing is ever simple with Sylvia Berenson. She started by thanking Roberta for being kind to me. For making sure I had fresh coffee every morning. Like Roberta came in and brewed the carafe only for me. They bonded over single adult sons who live far away, have no marriage prospects, and about never having grandchildren. I stood there, tail between my legs, embarrassed, once again, by my mother's ability to overshare about her son with the world.

"No."

"Your momma would love it."

My mother would actually adore a photo of me. She'd relish seeing me, even in my drab uniform, but she would nag me to smile bigger: "Theo, you have a beautiful face. I love that punim. Now, smile."

"Sorry, but no," I say to Roberta, trying to be as gentle as possible.

"All right, all right. Maybe tomorrow, grumpypants."

Roberta smirks, and I swipe my credit card quickly to assist my escape.

"Are your parents coming for Hanukah?"

I nod. They always come. Their yearly pilgrimage north from

Florida to "visit the cold" as Abba says. I'm pretty sure somewhere in the Torah, it says that when you retire, you must move to Florida and constantly kvetch about the heat. Also, you must hound your child to marry and produce grandchildren. My mother's biggest wish? For me to have a husband. Or at least a boyfriend. Good luck.

"I don't even care if he's Jewish!" she said last year.

"Sylvia, be careful what fakakta messages you send to the universe," Abba warned.

Part of me wants to have someone. Not even for me. For them. They want it so damn bad. My stomach begins to gurgle. Maybe I should grab a glazed donut to shut it up.

"Bye, sweetie. You have a wonderful Sunday. Don't go working too hard, ya hear me?"

Even though it makes my cheeks ache, I do my best to give her another smile, squinting and turning my lips up the slightest bit.

The drive from the Fill'er Up allows a single song and today the shuffle gods deliver "We Will Rock You." I pound my fists on the steering wheel along with the drum kicks until Lear comes into view. Thankfully, the school parking lot sits vacant. In my book, an elementary school should be empty on a Sunday, especially after a holiday, but there are always teachers who can't stay away. Because of Thanksgiving break, the school has been scrubbed and polished already. Toilet paper and paper towel rolls are fresh, trash cans are emptied, and there's time before my only big scheduled task, buffing the cafeteria floor. The wax I applied Wednesday before I took off for Connecticut should be ready. Using the buffer is oddly soothing, with its whirring motor and intense vibrations making my entire body hum.

Crumpling into my chair, I glance around my custodian closet. Slightly larger than an actual closet, there's room for cleaning supplies, surplus paper products, and various tools I might require in a pinch, including my ancient toolbox. The school district's maintenance team handles serious issues, but I tackle smaller projects around the school with that box. There's an oversized sink big enough for buckets and the occasional moldy milk crate. Shelves of cleaning supplies and paper products line the walls, and with no windows, the scent of bleach and pine never truly escapes. I fucking love it.

I recline in the old teacher's chair I saved from the trash with a little WD-40 and prop my feet up on the busted milk crate I keep for this sole purpose.

Leaning over to the long dusty shelf I installed, I press play on the old cassette player I scored at Goodwill for five bucks. Everybody wants their digital music, and LPs are apparently back if you're a hipster. I have a box of old cassettes, and I'll gladly play them until the tape wears out.

Some soft crackling welcomes the layered harmonies of Freddie Mercury squeaking through the tinny speakers as "Fat Bottomed Girls" prompts me to nod along gently. It's one of my favorite songs. Maybe he was singing about fat-bottomed boys too. When the drums kick in, losing myself in the familiar melody, the edges of my lips turn up. The earthy smell of the desert. A tent in Kandahar province. Parched. Painting on a brave face. A faint humming wanders over from the other side of the barracks. Absorbed in the music, eyes closed, I fail to notice when Kent appears.

"Theodore. Good to see you." Kent Lester gets away with calling me by my full name because he's the boss. And a stand-up guy.

"Kent."

"Did you have a good Thanksgiving? You spent it with Christian, right?"

I nod. My parents always hound me about missing holidays. If guilt were an Olympic sport, my mother would be the Jewish Michael Phelps. But Florida is a plane trip, and with limited time and money, spending the day with my best friend and his wife is easier. And less stressful. My mother demanded to be put on speakerphone for a good twenty minutes of Thanksgiving dinner; luckily, after we were deployed together ten years ago and with as many years of friendship, Christian understands how Sylvia Berenson works. Thanksgiving with him and his wife Anna is like being with

—

family. Plus, like a damn monsoon, my parents will crash-land here in a few weeks.

"Well, good. I'm still stuffed from my brother-in-law's famous deep-fried turkey. Some people think shoving a turkey into a deep fryer is blasphemous. Those people are wrong." Kent laughs, his guffaws bouncing off walls in the small closet, prickling the hairs on the back of my neck.

"Mmmh."

"Listen, there's a new first-grade teacher. Starting tomorrow but setting up the room today. We're using the old physical therapy room. If someone comes looking for help, well, please help."

"Got it."

"Well, I'm off to central office," he says, turning to leave and stumbling over his own damn feet. Kent may be an amazing boss, but he's about as graceful as a doe on ice. "I'm fine! Bye, Theo! Stay safe, and I'll see you tomorrow."

Sunday after Thanksgiving is usually silent in the building. On paper, this should be an easy day. Buff the floors. Check supplies. Go home. Now this? Always one to take my medicine quickly, I head down the hallway to get this over with.

When I walk in, I spot him. Sitting in a chair, staring outside like he's searching for the meaning of life. Buddy, it ain't in the school's parking lot. I clear my throat, and he turns to me. His face comes into view, and there's a rumble in my core, a seed of emotion, and when I notice the disruption, it pisses me off. He's so … compact.

"Hi, I'm Sheldon, the new first-grade teacher."

I want him to stand so I can truly assess his height, but this guy probably barely comes up to my chest. I could probably throw him in my back pocket like a ragdoll.

"This is my classroom. I'm totally supposed to be here."

His hair is tightly clipped around the ears but full and bouncy on top, and a bright copper. My eyes squint from the brilliance emitting from his head before wandering to the dimple on his left cheek. This man, sitting here, appearing lost. My jaw stiffens.

"Are you Theo?"

15

God, I wish I weren't.

"The custodian? Kent told me you might be able to help me carry some furniture up from the basement. I already brought these two chairs up."

He motions to the chairs with a flourish like he's waiting for me to award him a medal.

"Mmmh." It's all I've got.

I assess the state of the room (desolate) and the state of the young man (slight). I'm going to have to do something I will absolutely regret.

Help.

Helping leads to conversation, and something about this guy's face tells me he likes to chat. Most teachers do. *But that damn dimple.*

Begrudgingly, I nod toward the door, summoning him to follow.

We walk down the hall toward the basement. I'm not sure if he'll notice my limp. It's not as evident as it was right after the incident, since the surgery and six months of intensive physical therapy, but it's there. Permanently. If he's aware, he doesn't say anything.

"Theo. Is that short for Theodore? Or do you prefer just Theo? Because Theodore is distinguished. Very. Wait, Ted? Oh my gosh, does anyone call you Teddy? Or, let me think of a new nickname ... T-Boz! We can have a 'No Scrubs' fantasy. I totally know the No Scrubs choreo."

What in the actual fuck? I make a fist in my pocket and peer at him. Why would he think I'd like a nickname like Teddy? I'm not soft. Or cuddly. And talking annoys me. When people talk. When I'm asked to talk. No, thank you. Kent neglected to mention that the new first-grade teacher was a man with a dimple who can't shut up. "Theo."

"Theo. Just Theo. Okay. Well, as I said, I'm Sheldon. Sheldon Soleskin. Not at all like Bond. James Bond. I mean, look at me. Clearly, not James Bond. Not even James Bond adjacent. Probably more Bond Girl material," he says and winks. This sprite just winked at me. He puts out his hand, and for the love of god, his fingernails are painted. Purple. The paint glimmers and catches the fluorescent light. Is he expecting me to shake his hand or kiss it? I stare at it for a moment before he pulls it back and continues jabbering away. "The kids call me Mr. Soleskin or sometimes Mr. S. My sister calls me bean. Or Shell. Mostly bean. Because I'm smaller. And younger. Two and a half minutes. Younger. Not smaller. Only half an inch. Anyway, it's sweet. Mostly. Anyway, you can call me Sheldon. Unless you want to create your own nickname for me."

He pauses, waiting for a reply, so I say, "Um. No."

What kind of name is Sheldon? I turn around, and my eyebrows squish together. Trying to understand this creature, with his lanky limbs and skinny jeans, hurts my head. Who the fuck wears skinny jeans to set up a classroom? And why won't he stop talking? My temple prickles, but I shake it off like a wet dog.

When we reach the basement, I give him another good look over as he assesses the furniture. I'm unsure how much help this guy will be in moving anything heavy. He can't weigh more than a hundred pounds soaking wet. And now I'm imagining him soaking wet. It's only been ten minutes, but Sheldon Soleskin already irritates the hell out of me.

"Uhhhhhhh."

"You okay?" Sheldon asks, forcing me to roll my eyes.

"What?" I ask, nodding toward the furniture.

"What, what? What do you mean, what? What do I want? I mean, I'd really love an iced mocha right now. I know it's November, but I could use a creamy, frothy chocolate mocha. When it's zero degrees out, I ask for extra ice just to confuse them." He throws his head back and giggles. "Negative degrees out? Give me my iced mocha. It's almost Christmas, so throw in some peppermint and sing 'Santa Baby' to me. And while you're at it, I'd love a boyfriend. Or at least a date to my ex's wedding. On Christmas Eve. Who does that?" he asks, shaking his head and pausing for a moment, probably to catch his breath. "Not like Timothy was ever cruel, but it feels like he's trying to rub my face in it."

I close my eyes and pinch my face. Confirmation: he's gay.

I nod toward the mangled stack of furniture.

"Oh, you mean what *furniture* do I want?" Sheldon lets out a little laugh. My stomach shifts, and a gooey feeling stirs.

17

"Yeah."

"Well, I need tables. Let's see, twenty-four kids divided by four, that's six tables. Is that right? We don't do a ton of division in first grade. And twenty-four chairs. Maybe a few extra. You always need more chairs. Let's say twenty-six chairs to be on the safe side. We don't want a musical chairs last-one-out situation. I've already carried two up, so twenty-four. Twenty-four more. Hey, that rhymes!"

He puts his arms out and does a little dance, his neck jerking back and forth while his legs jump and run in place. Without stopping, he continues, "Anyway, a few shelves for books and supplies. There's a kidney table in the room. I'll use that as my desk and work area for small groups. So, I think that's enough for now."

I open my mouth, then close it. In addition to the talking, he's a ball of energy. The way he talks and talks and then talks some more makes my brain spiral like a tornado raging inside my head. Watching his mouth moving and twisting and words spewing out, I need to make it stop. Make Sheldon stop. I wait and say a silent prayer that he'll give his body and mouth a rest.

"Chairs."

"Huh? Yes, chairs. Let's start with chairs," he says, finally ceasing his ridiculous dancing.

Stretching out an arm, long and narrow, he reaches toward the bottom of the pile. The flickering fluorescent light bounces off his ginger hair, almost blinding me, but my reflexes kick in. The base of the pile stares at me, with heaps of metal and wood above it, and my eyes widen, my pulse hurries, and the mere thought of the chaos, the twisted mess, clanking, crashing, and bodily injury to this petite man-person pushes me to move faster than I've moved in a long time. Bounding toward him, I wrap my hand around Sheldon's arm.

His wrist resembles a twig—frail, fragile, and slender—so my much larger hand encircles it completely, fingers overlapping my thumb. His skin, warm and brassy, almost translucent against my rough, calloused hands, sends a jolt of energy that travels straight up

18

my arm, into my chest, and finally settles into the gooeyness churning in my stomach. What the fuck?

"What's wrong? I need chairs."

"Top."

"Excuse me? That's presumptuous," he says, his eyes widening. "And totally wrong, by the way."

"Top."

I raise my voice louder than I should and nod toward the top of the furniture mountain. I'd moved too fast, and the fluctuating pain in my leg surged like lava.

I wince from the discomfort and say, "The top."

"Oh. Oh! Listen, I'm a little frazzled today. Clearly. I'm sorry. Yikers. We almost had a dramatic take-me-to-the-hospital moment." He wipes the sweat from his forehead, and even his eyebrows are red. "Anyway, how, um, how do we get the stuff at the top?"

I stick my left index finger up and remove my right hand from his wrist. How long was I holding it? He doesn't flinch or seem to mind. I take that as a good sign.

I leave this elf alone in the musty basement to fetch a ladder. Sheldon Soleskin already has me feeling off-balance. My head is swimming in foggy clouds. I've done a bang-up job stuffing those pesky emotions way down where they can't bother me, and now he comes raring in, yanking at feelings I'd rather keep at bay.

Returning from my closet upstairs with the treasure in hand, I find Sheldon sitting on an old bench propped up against the wall. Unlike before, left to his own devices he appears almost sullen. I do my best to smile, but I worry it comes off more like an infant passing gas. He jolts from his stupor when he sees me, shaking his head and painting that cheerful mask on like he's ready for battle.

"Of course. A ladder. Thank you, Theo. Yes. We need a Home Depot moment. Or Lowes. Orange or blue uniforms. Which do you prefer?"

I stare at him and bite my lip.

"Okay, let's do this," he says with a smile, and damn that dimple.

I could fill it with lemony hummus and dip crackers in it. Or lick it out with my tongue. *Get a grip, Theo.*

I carry the ladder over and open it, kicking the legs to check for sturdiness. Feelings bubble up I'm not used to. Useful. Needed. And I'm certain I don't care for it. Or Sheldon Soleskin.

THREE

Sheldon

Theo's a giant. After he prevents the entire pile of furniture from falling on me, in the interest of not causing myself bodily harm I decide to take a breath, slow down, and let him take the lead. He's got this.

Standing on the second step from the top as Theo's strong grip holds the ladder's base firmly in place, I begin tugging with all my might. My arms strain from the exertion, and I'm not sure wearing this cute, chunky, baby-blue cardigan was a smart idea. But even with all the force and effort my bony little arms can muster, none of the chairs near the top budge.

"If I crack a nail, I will not be happy, Theo. There's no time to repaint before my first day here." Pulling as hard as I can, I ask, "Are these chairs fused together or what?"

"Get down."

My eyes go wide. It's the first time more than a single word escapes his lips. What would I have to do to provoke an actual conversation? Sweat begins to drip from my forehead. The school's boiler gurgles and pops in the corner, and the basement feels more like a sauna every minute we're down here. I pop my sweater off so I don't pass out because I do not care to be a damsel in distress with this guy. My black tank top tries to come off along with my sweater, and I'm momentarily quasi-shirtless before yanking it down. Theo lets out a sharp huff when I lay it over a bookcase, and I worry my naked torso has somehow offended him.

"Sorry, I'm sweating like a queen about to lip-sync for her life," I say, using the front of my shirt to wipe the flop sweat from my forehead. "Aren't you warm?"

"I'm fine."

He seems to be putting a lot of energy into being ornery, but there's something about how his eyes shine, at least when he's not looking at the floor, that makes me suspect he might enjoy helping me. Maybe I need to ramp up my patented Sheldon Soleskin charm to crack his shell and make my first friend at my new school. Befriend the school custodian. Challenge accepted.

Slowly, making sure I don't tumble, I descend the ladder. When I hop off the last step, I tilt my head up and smile. Theo brushes past me and begins to climb.

Watching him clamber up, there's no denying he's a bear of a guy. Teddy really would be the perfect nickname for him. Although I'm not getting cuddly vibes, more of an eat-your-face-off feeling. No, thank you. I'm very happy with my face in place. Oh, another rhyme!

The rusty ladder gently creaks and shakes as he lumbers up. The limp I thought I noticed in the hall is confirmed as he approaches the top. I'm tempted to ask him about it, but we're clearly not in lets-chat-about-personal-aspects-of-our-lives territory. Yet. Not knowing how to help, I put my hands near the base to steady it, unsure if my minuscule frame will make any difference, but trying my best to offer the ladder emotional support.

I peek up. With all the climbing and reaching, Theo's dark navy uniform top has come untucked from his pants. The glimpse of his stomach poking out makes my lips turn up. Round, with a smidge of sandy brown fuzz. What would my fingers feel like grazing Theo's belly?

Focus, Sheldon. *Chairs.* "Can you get it?"

Theo extends his long arm, and I swear—like an eagle

stretching its wing in flight—his hand reaches and grabs a chair's leg jutting out from the mess. He plucks it out like he's removing a toothpick from Jell-O.

"I loosened it for you," I announce.

Theo peers down at me. Drops of sweat tickle my forehead, and my hair feels damp and tacky. Theo raises his chin, and for a split second, I almost see the muscles in his cheeks begin to move. My face lights up like Rudolph's nose, and I shout, "Go, Theo!"

With my spontaneous cheer, the poor lug momentarily loses his balance, and he begins to wobble. Not wanting a Theo-falls-on-me-in-the-basement moment, I scramble to action. My hands shake and shift up to his calves, but instead of steadying him, he teeters further. The ladder begins to shake, and I wince, waiting for him to come tumbling down like Humpty-Dumpty.

But he doesn't. I crack one eye to see him holding the first chair in his left hand, with his right latched on to another that's still stuck in the jumble. He's stabilized himself with absolutely no assistance from me.

"That was close," I say. "You scared me for a second."

Sweat drips from his forehead, but he shows no signs of distress. He rolls his eyes and hands the first chair down. When I grab the chair's leg, my fingers brush his. They're almost twice the size of mine but also calloused and dry. He could use a good moisturizing regime, especially in the dry Portland winter season. Maybe I could convince him to do a moisturizing manicure with me. I'll pack my kit and see if I can squeeze him in during one of my preps. He strikes me as a clear-polish kind of guy.

If Theo's annoyed at the contact, his steady face reveals nothing. I place the chair on the floor and nod at him to continue. We work like this for the next half hour, removing chairs, Jenga-style, in silence, one at a time, until we've dislodged enough for my classroom.

"Okay, let's carry the chairs up, and then we can come back for the bigger stuff," I say.

I take a chair in each arm, feeling rather proud of my ability to carry two at once. Before I ascend the stairs, Theo takes a chair, stacks it on top of another, then repeats and ends up with two in each of his thick arms.

"Showoff."

He dips his head, but the crinkles around his eyes give him away. His shaggy, sandy-colored hair, matching the fuzz on his stomach, tangles near his eyes, and I wonder when he last had a proper haircut. I'm no hairstylist, but I could at least clean it up for him. Even with that mop swaying around his face, his large frame and height make it hard for him to hide. Being teased seems to bring Theo a sliver of pleasure, so I add "make Theo smile" to my mental to-do list of ways to make the world a better place.

We carry up all twenty-four chairs, working up a sweat despite the almost freezing temps outside. Theo lifts the large table like it's a feather. My eyes are drawn to his neck. He's swimming in sweat and glistening, the physical labor taking its toll on his body. And his shoulders. And arms. His biceps stretch the deep navy uniform to its limits. I can almost hear the fabric screaming as it fights against his meaty muscles like he's a thicker Hemsworth brother. My head grows hot and flushed.

Theo's stocky arms flex again as he holds the table aloft, waiting for me to move. I do my best not to stare, but small drops of sweat on Theo's shirt draw my attention, and the smell of leather and perspiration tickles my nose. He's waiting. I blink away my stare and rush to lift my end.

"Oh, damn, this is heavier than I thought."

My lanky arms feel numb. Facing Theo, the morning catches up to me, and I suddenly feel light-headed. The breakfast bar I ate on my drive to school feels too far gone and clearly inadequate. All this exertion is way more than my regular Zumba routine in the living room. I am so ready to be done with hauling furniture from the depths of the building. Manual labor is not part of my school setup dream. I want to finish the room and get home to relax for a hot minute before school tomorrow.

"It's the wood."

"The wood?" I ask, suddenly feeling overheated.

"The table. It's solid."

"Right. Sorry, Theo. Clearly, I'm not as strong as you, and it's a sauna in here. Aren't you hot?"

Even though he's clearly sweating, Theo simply shrugs.

"Okay, how are we gonna get this up the stairs?" Extremely narrow, the stairway to the first floor doesn't seem like these tables will fit. "The furniture got down here somehow, and I know we'll get it up," I say.

As we approach the first steps, Theo turns, forcing me to go up first. Is he doing this to hold the brunt of the table's weight or to try and take control of maneuvering? Either way, my weak muscles rejoice.

My relief quickly fades. Being at the top of the table doesn't dismiss me from actual hard work. I can barely manage to keep my fingers gripped on the edge of the table. This huge, solid, brute of a guy, and I'm the one yanking and pulling.

"You good?" he asks quietly as if the veins on my neck about to launch out of my body and hurl into deep space aren't a clue.

"Yup. It's fine. I'm fine. Everything's fine."

After a few steps, he begins lifting and turning, and slowly the table's weight transfers, and maybe I won't actually die a tragic death here on the stairway of Lear Elementary School. When we're about halfway up the stairs, the light from the hallway beckoning, Theo speaks.

"Good job."

I wasn't prepared for him to grace me with his deep voice, let alone praise me. My stomach flinches, my sweaty fingers slip, and I almost drop the table.

"Whoa," he shouts.

"Got it. I've got it," I spit out, gripping the piece of furniture.

He gives one more push, and we breach the door, the table shooting out like a child zooming down a slide.

"We did it!" I cheer.

"Mmmh." His grumble sounds faintly favorable.

"That wasn't so bad," I say with sweat stinging my eyes, and the moment the last word escapes my mouth, the lacquered wood slips from my hands and crashes to the floor, barely missing my foot.

"Oops."

Theo's lips curve ever so slightly, a ghost of a smile emerging. Do I amuse him? Maybe in a straight guy taunting and teasing way, but hey, a smile, even a partial one, is a win in my book.

We return to the basement until all six tables are deposited in the middle of the space. My arms and legs resemble jellyfish, and I'm not sure I have much left in me to set up the entire classroom. Exhausted and hot, we both collapse on opposite tables, tired, and sweaty.

"You're amazing, Theo," I say with a huff. "I couldn't have done it without you. Clearly. I'd have chairs and nothing else. I don't suppose you want to stay and help me set the room up?"

I lift my head to see him peer at me. Any hint of softening is gone, and his eyes squint. He pushes himself off the table and bellows, "No."

He exits the room, and I let out a huge breath. Theo, helping me put a classroom together? I'm lucky he showed up at all. He's an interesting guy. Step one: befriending the custodian, complete! They hold the keys to everything. Literally. Theo may take some time to warm up to me, but I know we'll be buddies. Alone, with hours of room prep ahead of me, I pop in my earbuds, cue up RuPaul's underrated "Christmas Party" album and get to work.

FOUR

Theo

After yesterday's shift, today feels more like a Tuesday than a Monday. Helping Sheldon shlep furniture was definitely not part of my plan. The guy is a peanut. There was clearly no way he could do it himself. It was admirable how he tried to keep up with me. What is it about smaller guys and their need to prove themselves?

It took me two hours to finish the floors after helping Sheldon. The floor buffer felt like a deep tissue massage for my sore arms after all that lugging. I was glad to have some peace and quiet for a bit. And by quiet, I mean the ridiculously loud motor of the buffer moving in circles repeatedly, calming my frazzled mind. With my earplugs lodged in tight, it was more of a soothing soft hum.

No talking. No helping. No questions. No skinny jeans, purple sneakers, and matching nails. No black tank tops clinging to damp bodies. It was downright meditative.

But also, that damn dimple kept flickering in front of my eyes.

"Happy Monday, my Theo!" Roberta's voice slaps me awake before I can sip my coffee.

"Morning, Roberta."

"Whoa, 'Morning, Roberta?' You're chipper today."

"Not really."

"Now, don't go and ruin it for me. Let your lady be happy for a minute."

My cheeks begin to pull and stretch as my lips curl into a smile. Roberta's nails click-click on the register as she rings me up, and this foolish smile takes up real estate on my face.

"There we go. Now you have a marvelous Monday, Theo, ya hear?"

"You too, Roberta."

When I arrive at school, a sky of muddy clouds covers the empty parking lot. December is right around the corner, and the crisp air means I'll be dealing with snow soon enough. Shovels, snowblowers, and endless mopping of wet boot-tracked floors await me. Unlocking the school, disabling the alarm, and getting the building ready for the day brings a brief lightness to my feet. I feel a little taller.

An hour or so before breakfast begins, I head to my space. My first real task of the day is breakfast cleanup in the cafeteria. It's a bit like swimming upstream because in a couple of hours it starts all over again with lunch. Even if every student picks up every wrapper and every lid, which never happens, the floors will be sticky and covered in a mystery goo that's equal parts food and saliva. I'll mop, but I'll need to sweep first. Pushing the broom—making small piles into larger ones before sweeping them into the dustpan —soothes me.

Putting my feet up, and pressing the play button, the lead guitar rips through my small space. When Freddie's voice joins in, "Now I'm Here" unravels with a cascade of drums and layered harmonies, and my head begins to sway and bop. The magic of only a voice, lead guitar, and drums creating an entire wall of sound never ceases to amaze me. I'm transported to sunshine. Dry heat. With my coffee long gone, my mouth becomes parched and cracked.

"Good morning! Theo? Theo? Hello?"

My eyes creak open to Sheldon, who's wearing a baby-blue button-down shirt with rolled-up sleeves, light khaki pants, a dark brown belt, and his purple sneakers. He looks ridiculous. I want to slam the door in his face, but that would require getting up. In his hands, Sheldon holds not one but two coffees. He extends his left hand. My chest tingles at the gesture.

"Thank you for all your help yesterday. You made a really difficult task doable. Was I here until dinnertime, creating the perfect learning environment for first graders? Yes. Did I ruin three nails while doing it? Also, yes. But those are easily repaired." He holds his hand out in front of him and surveys his work. "Theo, I couldn't have done it without your help. So, thank you. I didn't know how you take your coffee, so I just got you black. But I have cream and sugar in my room if you feature a more light and sweet moment, and I'm happy to run down the hall and get you whatever you like."

I open my mouth, but all that escapes is, "You ..."

"I know, I didn't have to. But I wanted to. To thank you," he finishes. He moves quickly, as if I might lunge at him, and places the coffee on the desk near my cassette player. My eyes linger on his long, lanky arm, smooth and hairless. A few freckles dot his wrist. Where else might they hide on his body? The muscles in his wrist flex as he reaches forward like he doesn't want to come too close—and why am I staring at his arm? His hand approaches, and I stir, swiveling my chair slightly, which emits a loud creak.

"Anyway, like I tell my students, have a wonderful day, make it your best yet!"

I want to say something. Thank him. But the words get stuck in my mouth like thick molasses. He pulls his hand back like a child not wanting to get nipped by a dog. I'm not that scary, am I? He turns to leave, and I'm aware of my heart pounding in my chest like a drum. Can he hear it?

"Absolutely adore Queen, by the way," he says with a wink. Then he's gone.

My eyes and throat slam shut. Thoughts scramble in my head and bounce off my skull. The knot in my stomach reminds me to breathe. The song begins to fade with Freddie's layered voice pondering love.

Opening my eyes, I stare at the coffee for a minute before rolling over and picking it up. Nutty, rich overtones travel up my nostrils, and I close my eyes before sipping Sheldon's gift. It might only be a simple cup of coffee, but it triggers thoughts of the last time an almost-stranger gave me a gift.

My fingers find their way to the ring of dozens of small keys latched to my belt loop which bang and clang when I walk. The limp seems to make them louder. More aggressive. The keychain, lost in a sea of dull metal, momentarily eludes me, but my fingers find it, as they always do, and rub the worn plastic, royal blue, almost purple. I trace the outline of the crown, the capital Q, and the rubber bends under the pressure of my hand.

After breakfast, lunch, and making my rounds to empty bins and fill soaps and sanitizer, I return to my closet where I can be alone. The clock above the door reports there are seven minutes until the drill. Seven minutes to breathe. Like every school, fire drills are critical and mandatory at Lear. Kent provides me with a list of all the dates and times and whether the drill will blare the damn alarm or not. Thankfully, the first half, before the December holiday break, happen without the racket of incessant blasting noise. The children need to practice evacuating without the harshness of the sound, and I'm grateful for those silent drills as much as they are. My eyes dart to the clock, and now, with only five minutes left, I open the drawer in my desk, pull out my earplugs, and walk outside to wait.

"All right, good job. Kindergarten over there, first grade, next to the goal post ..."

Kent takes the safety of his students and staff seriously. As he should. There's never been a fire at Lear, but we need to practice evacuating the building in a timely manner. The state requires ten drills a year. With winter lasting anywhere from late October through early April in Maine, Kent knows we need to get at least half the drills in before the new year. This is our last scheduled drill before next spring. I'll be relieved when the damn thing is over. Kent made a point to show me how he uses a fat black marker to check one of the drills off the list he keeps on a sticky note tacked to his computer.

"Nice job, first graders. You followed me without talking. I knew you could do it. Everyone pat yourselves on the back."

Sheldon and his class stand with the other first-grade team and their classes, waiting for Kent to account for everyone. He'll then give the signal that it's safe to return.

I'm standing by the swings. Where I always wait. Far from everyone. Far from the commotion. Even the controlled chaos can be triggering.

With my earplugs planted deep, everything bubbles like I'm underwater, and voices wash over me.

My thumb traces the large Q on my Queen keychain. Over and over. Around with just a dip for the tail. Repeat. I take deep breaths. In through my nose and out through my mouth like I'm blowing a candle out. I read about the birthday candle trick as a way to reduce triggers. Even though I thought it was babyish when I discovered it, right now I'm grateful for the strategy. It will be over soon. We'll be back inside. Safe. Quiet. Even when no alarm blasts, I always wear my earplugs as a precaution. It's just easier.

After a few minutes, hands go up, hands go down. Kent whispers to various teachers and then signals for everyone to return. My lips part, and I feel wetness behind my eyelids.

It's over. My PTSD can take a breath. For now.

Sheldon leads his class through the soccer field abutting the playground. As he passes me, I look away, but out of the corner of my eye, I notice he shoots me the tiniest wave. He doesn't speak, which feels like an early Hanukah miracle. Probably because he's trying to be a good role model for his students. He definitely strikes me as the goody-two-shoes type. A rule follower. Most teachers are.

My fingers flinch on my keychain, and before I can stop myself, I'm waving back like a doofus. Sheldon smiles, and that annoying dimple returns. Why the hell did I go and do that?

FIVE

Sheldon

This first day feels different from other first days of school. After dropping my students at the cafeteria with my patented "Eat Your Lunch, Munch, Munch" song, I skip back to my room to catch my breath and gobble down a power bar.

A voice shouts, "Sheldon!" It belongs to Becky Mason, one of my new first-grade teammates. "Come have lunch with us."

"Us?"

"Jolene and me."

"Did you say Jolene?"

"Yes, Jolene. And she's heard every joke in the book and had the song sung to her a million times. She's a good sport if you don't overdo it," Becky says. When I don't reply, she adds, "You're singing it in your head now, aren't you?"

"Guilty. I'm most definitely singing it in my head. Actually, I'm picturing Queen Dolly in her full sequin glory, three wigs stacked on her head, propped on a stool, and strumming along."

Becky giggles and says, "Come to my room, A-27." She points toward the basement door.

I grab my bar and dash to Becky's room, where she sits with another young white woman. Jolene, unlike her namesake, does not have locks of auburn hair. Both she and Becky have blond hair tied up in messy buns. They both wear chunky sweaters, Becky's in blue and Jolene's in orange, over black leggings. I fear I've stumbled into some sort of Stepford Wives First-Grade reenactment. Becky and Jolene appear to be a matched set.

Once again, I'm the odd man out. The only man. The only queer man. Where are all my gay teachers? Is that too much for a guy to ask for? Since I've literally only worked with women and the rare straight man, apparently, yes. But Becky and Jolene's harmonious demeanor rubs me exactly the right way. Early-ed teachers are my people; I'm confident I'll fit in here.

"Hi, I'm Jolene. Welcome to Lear!"

"Jolene's classroom is next door." Becky nods to the left. "Sheldon, listen, I know we're down the hallway, but we're here for you."

"Thanks," I say, peeling the wrapper on my peppermint-stick flavored protein bar.

"We're so happy you're here," Becky says.

"Yeah, we each had over thirty. It was getting a little wild," Jolene adds.

"Oh, wow, that's a lot. Well, thrilled to be here. Faye is fantastic, and I'll miss my teammate, but you two seem amazing. Do you mind if I ask, are there any other ..."

"Male teachers?" Becky says.

"Gay teachers?" Jolene adds.

"Well, I was going to say redheads." I give them a broad grin. "But yes to it all."

Jolene glances at Becky. "Well, Ruth Parrish, the PE teacher, we have our suspicions about her," she says.

"You can't tell if she's a redhead?" I ask.

"Oh my god, you're a hoot," Becky says, then adds in a whisper, "No, if she's gay." She rolls her eyes. "It's a terrible stereotype. PE teachers and all, but she's in her fifties, single, and never been married as far as we know."

"Interesting. Well, you know you can never assume anything about anyone. There's no one way to be queer, and people surprise you all the time," I say, trying my best to explain in a friendly way. "And Kent, well, he seems … jovial."

Jolene grins. "We call Kent our unicorn principal."

"We love a unicorn fantasy," I say.

"I've worked at three other schools and never experienced an admin like him," Becky says with a nod. "He goes on coffee runs, covers our classes during report card season, and buys us pizza during conferences. Deluxe pizza. He's simply the best."

"He hugged me. I'm not used to that."

"Principals hugging you or men in general?" Becky asks.

I know my new teammates assume I'm gay. When you're small, slight, and called "ma'am" over the phone when you order takeout, it comes with the territory. The assumption isn't mean-spirited, and there's a blessing in it. I rarely need to come out to new people. Instead, I only need to confirm what they already suspect.

"Both."

Becky and Jolene shoot each other a perplexed glance. Tickled by confusing them for a second, I don't make them squirm long.

"Right now, the thought of a man hugging me gives my stomach a too-much-Mexican-food-before-a-big-date feeling."

"Right now?" Jolene asks.

"Yesterday, I found the invitation to my ex-boyfriend's Christmas-Eve wedding. We broke up last year. On Christmas Eve. Who does that?" I bite my bar and mumble, "'Packed with flavor' feels like a stretch."

"Are you kidding?" Becky asks.

"No, it tastes like sweetened Styrofoam. Oh, you mean the wedding. Sadly, no. My sister hid the invitation in our junk drawer, and I found it yesterday."

"Oh, hell, Sheldon. That's horrible." Jolene pats my back. "Does your sister know you found it?"

"Yeah, we're good. Naomi was trying to protect my feelings. I get it."

"My sister once hid a winning lottery ticket from me, but it turned out she only won five hundred dollars, not five million. She was behind on her portion of the rent, so the joke was really on her," Jolene says.

"Living with siblings is not for the faint of heart," I add.

"I wouldn't know," Becky says absentmindedly.

"She's married." Jolene points to a glorious J.Lo-sized diamond on Becky's ring finger, "And her husband's gorgeous. And a lawyer."

"Sorry—" Becky grimaces.

"What deal did you make with the devil? Do you have to give him your firstborn? Is this a Rumpelstiltskin situation?"

"You're a riot, Sheldon. And I just got lucky, I guess." She leans over and pats my hand. "You seem okay about it, all things considered."

"I'm fine. I just wasn't expecting it. The invitation. The wedding. On Christmas Eve. It feels like a dig."

"I mean, you could always not go. Make up some excuse. It's Christmas Eve. Aren't you going to spend the holiday with your family?" Jolene offers.

"Yeah, except Timothy knows I'd never do that. Naomi is the only family I spend holidays with."

I've only just met my new teammates. Regaling them with a dramatic "parents shunning their children" story feels unnecessary.

"Oh. Would she go with you?" Becky asks.

"Definitely. And she'd be a fantastic date. But I'd much rather show up with a handsome guy on my arm."

"Obviously. Some gorgeous man-candy would be the best revenge. What happened with your ex anyway? I mean, only if you're comfortable. And feel free to swear away," Jolene says, skittering to close the classroom door.

"The short version: Timothy wanted to bulk up for the summer because, well, he's gay. He joined a gym, again gay, and started working with a personal trainer to 'maximize his results'—his words, not mine. He worked with a trainer named Dwayne who was drop-dead gorgeous, and 'completely heterosexual.' Well, turns out he wasn't straight enough to keep his dick out of Timothy's mouth."

"Ouch. Well, *that* will make you never want to work out again," Jolene says.

"Can I get an amen?" I reply, lifting my hands to my lord and savior, RuPaul.

Last Christmas Eve, as I wore my gorgeous red cashmere sweater and stood under the mistletoe in my apartment entryway, Timothy dumped me. All my insecurities slammed into my heart as the words poured out of his mouth. From the moment we met—me waiting for the bathroom at the coffee shop, him coming out and handing me the key, me fumbling with the key because it was wet, and then him waiting for me to come out of the bathroom to assure me it was only water and definitely not pee on the key—it felt like the perfect meet-cute. Too good to be true. Timothy is classically handsome, with dark brown hair and eyes and a jawline sharper than a good Vermont cheddar. Guys like Timothy don't usually go for me.

I know I'm a lot to handle, but I'm also not going to hide who I am. I mean, it really wouldn't be possible. But I felt pretty good about myself. Until Timothy left me for an ultra-hetero personal trainer with more muscles in his pinky finger than my entire body. Do I have the balls to go to his wedding? Maybe. But right now, facing Timothy and Dwayne, who could stunt double for The Rock, feels overwhelming.

"Well, I should get back to my room. I've got to read over the math lesson before they come back," I say, gathering my trash and heading for the door. "You'd think first-grade math would be a breeze, but well, not so much."

"Okay, we'll see you at pickup," Becky says as I turn to leave.

I stare out my classroom window. The wind whips the trees, attempting to shake the last stubborn leaves of fall. I'm not sure why Timothy invited me, but the thought of him thinking I'm either a) not over him, b) not big enough to attend, or c) all of the above is not happening. I whip my phone out of my pocket and thumb a text.

Sheldon: Hey stranger! The big day is in less than a month! Hope you're excited. I'm mailing the RSVP tomorrow. Can't wait.

My chest puffs, and a small smile erupts on my face. If Timothy had any thoughts about me being too devastated to come to his Christmas-Eve wedding, now he knows better. Basking in my own pride, I almost miss the vibration signaling a reply.

> Timothy: That's wonderful, Shell. I was really hoping you'd come. Can't wait to see you and Naomi.

Of course, he assumes Naomi will be my date. No, sir.

> Sheldon: Actually, I'm seeing someone.

> Timothy: Oh. Well, great. Can't wait to meet him.

Crap. My chest tingles at the ginormous hole I've dug myself into.

The rest of my first week at Lear whirs by in a blur. It may not be September, but there are many first-week-of-school parallels. We still start by establishing a cohesive classroom community and working hard to settle everyone. Rules are created. Routines are modeled, practiced, and then practiced again.

"If we can't walk correctly in the hallway, we'll have to go back and try it again."

The class does their best to listen, follow directions, and meet my high expectations. They're a sweet group, showering me with whimsical drawings and adorable notes after the first day. Martha, a little girl with bright red hair that makes mine appear more tangerine, appears to be ecstatic that her new first-grade teacher is a fellow ginger. Each day, the drawings feature my short hair in the brightest orange crayon she can find. Somehow, the classroom placement gods (that would be Becky and Jolene) have granted me a Norah, a Noah, and a Nolan. Unrelated, they all have blond hair, blue eyes, and look like triplets. This makes it really challenging for me to call them by the correct name. And then there's Brodie.

Brodie, with his jet-black bedhead hair jutting in every direction. Brodie, who never seems to hear me, let alone listen, and most definitely resembles a lost little lamb. Brodie, who literally cannot sit still. If I told him his sweet little life depended on him not moving for more than thirty seconds, he'd be a goner. Here lies Brodie: He couldn't sit still to save his own life. Brodie, who—during my read-aloud on Tuesday—licked my shoe. Licked. My. Shoe. Yes, my Converse are purple, but no, they're not grape flavored. Brodie, the only child I was "warned" about by both Becky and Jolene (he was Jolene's) in the entire group. Brodie, who has already burrowed a soft spot in my heart.

"Friends, this is one of my favorite stories," I say, holding up my well-loved copy of *Where the Wild Things Are*.

After recess, they still seem to be having their own wild rumpus. Nolan and Noah try to continue the apparent wrestling match they started outside, and Kylie spins on the rug like a top, trying to expel the last remnants of her energy. I know reading a story will work. It's my magic trick. No matter how restless children are, they'll almost always sit quietly, relax, and enjoy a story. Brodie is at my feet, twirling my shoelaces as I begin. I need to find him a proper fidget, but for now, I'm simply ignoring the behavior and hoping he's not tying my shoes together.

Not two pages into the story, when Max begins making mischief as if taking it as a challenge to create his own, Brodie drops my laces, stands up, stares at me, and bolts for the door.

"Brodie, do you need the bathroom?"

Silence. He turns away from me, and I fear he's going to leave the room. Skipping over quickly, I shut the door and put my hand out. He glances at it, then scans my face. I'm not sure what he's looking for, but he takes my hand and I lead him back to the rug and the rest of the children.

"Why don't I sit on the floor? Brodie, you can sit next to me," I say, releasing his hand. He does as I ask, but more lays on my knee than sits.

I'm able to finish, but managing a squirming Brodie, along with the rest of the class, and reading the story feels like juggling every ball in one of those giant ball pits at McDonald's. By the time I put them on the bus at the end of the day, I'm toast.

Most nights, I head home, microwave a frozen dinner, and crash on the couch way before my usual ten o'clock bedtime. At some point, Naomi prods me to go to my room, and like a drunken zombie I mosey under the covers with Janice and pass back out. Tonight, after a week of school, my stomach craves something more substantive than frozen processed carbs.

"Naomi, wanna order takeout?"

"Pizza or Sushi?"

I flip my eyes up and momentarily stare at her.

"Okay, pepperoni or sausage?"

"Deluxe. I want to drown myself in super-deluxe sauce and cheesiness."

"That's my bean."

She flops down next to me on the couch, sending Janice bolting away from her perch on the back of the sofa. Naomi takes out her phone, opens the food delivery app, and thumbs an order while I stretch my neck, fruitlessly trying to work the cricks out.

"All right, ordered. Now tell me what's going on before I run myself a bath. My shoulder's bugging me," she says, rubbing the right one. "Rough time adjusting to the new school?"

A few head rolls and cracks, and Naomi begins massaging her neck.

"Wait, did you hurt yourself?" I ask, moving my hand to take over. My fingers struggle against the tough muscle.

"Not really, more aggravated it. I lifted a patient this morning, and I think I might have pulled something."

"Are you sure you're okay?"

"I'm fine. Walker did an exam. Just an aggravated muscle."

"Make sure you throw some Epsom salt in the tub."

"Yes, Sheldon, I'll use salt. Now tell me about school."

"Go start your bath and come back. We'll have our brother–sister after-school special conversation while it runs."

Naomi darts into the bathroom, and moments later, I hear the water begin to rush into the tub. We don't do secrets, but I also don't want to burden her. Only two minutes older, you wouldn't think Naomi would be such a big sister, but she's always taken care of me. After my parents disowned me, we escaped to Portland and became even closer, which I didn't think possible. I worry about putting all my stuff on her. I'm really good at putting on a happy face for the world, but no matter how much sunshine comes beaming out of me, I'm terrible at hiding anything from her.

"Okay, we've got twenty minutes," she says, setting the timer on her watch to measure the time of our building's old plumbing. "Now spill it. School or boy related?"

"I mean, I'm trying really hard to be a big boy about Timothy. It's still a month away. That's a problem for another day." I wave away thoughts of Christmas-Eve nuptials. "Right now, switching schools mid-year is tougher than I anticipated. I'm taking two groups and meshing them into a new cohesive class. Lear is fantastic. The principal, amazing. My new teammates, wonderful. I mean, an actual human named Jolene. Can you top that? But am I the only man?"

"Of course, and I'm assuming the only queer person?"

"Actually, I'm told the PE teacher might be."

"Naturally."

"Anyway, it's not that. I'm used to being the only queen. The kids, well, they're kids. It will take time, I know that, but this one boy, Brodie, he's testing me. A lot. I know it's probably out of his control, and I adore him already, but he takes that much more energy on top of everything else."

"Okay. Let's talk it out."

Whenever either of us has a problem, talking it out is our solution. We sit and talk until we come up with a few possible solutions. Having a twin sister means having not only an instant best friend but a therapist from birth. When the bullying ramped up in middle school, Naomi was my first defender. Both mortified and elated at needing my sister to stand up for me, there was simply no stopping her.

41

"What do you think the issue is with Brodie?"

"I'm not sure. He's a cute kid. He seems sweet, but there's something else going on, and I'm not sure what."

"Hmmm. Well, it's a big change. Can you ask his old teacher about him?"

"I did. Jolene said he did the same thing with her. They were hoping a fresh start might help him. Maybe a male influence. Clearly, I'm not fitting that bill," I say, cocking my head.

"I still can't believe you work with a woman named Jolene." She pulls the blanket over her feet. "Maybe Brodie needs time to adjust to you."

"Maybe. But I can't chase him around all day."

"Have you talked to anyone else about him? The guidance counselor? Your principal?"

I shrug.

"Bean, you have to ask for help. You can't solve the world's problems solo."

"I know. I'm new. I don't want people to think I'm causing problems."

"Asking for help isn't causing problems. Promise me you'll ask."

"Okay, okay. Tomorrow."

"Promise?"

"Yes, Naomi, I promise. Now, go soak your shoulder."

The next morning, as I lead the class in a rhythmic game of knee slapping and clapping, a game I taught them in hopes it would engage Brodie, the boy in question stands up, walks to the door, and —without looking back—darts into the hallway.

I rush after him, instructing the children to continue the game as I wipe my clammy palms on my pants. If I chase after Brodie, the entire class will be alone. There's no one to ask to watch them unless I call the office. My breath quickens in the doorway as I search for the small boy. After a few panic-filled moments, I spot him down the hallway. His shaggy black hair sways from the wind he's creating with his speed.

"Brodie! Can you please come here and chat with me?"

I don't yell but try to combine calmness with the increased volume required for Brodie to hear me. My voice doesn't seem to register with him. For a moment, I wonder if he might have a hearing problem, but my gut tells me it's more of a listening issue. His head darts around, seemingly searching for something. Without warning, he takes off like a bullet and smashes right into a giant roadblock. Theo.

SIX

Theo

The absolute bane of my existence? French toast sticks for breakfast in the cafeteria. Makes my right eye twitch. Maple syrup oozing out of tiny plastic tubs pooling in sticky, goopy messes on the floor. Wrappers, lids, and straws all get stuck in the syrup and fight me as I try to pick them up.

Disgusting.

After mopping up the mess with a little elbow grease, I put a warning tent out and hope the kids avoid the slippery spots.

I finish and head out into the hallway back to my space when, with the full force of a bull in a fight, a child-shaped blob rams right into me.

"Whoa. Slow down."

The kid gapes up at me with furrowed eyebrows. He's pulled back from my bad thigh where his face slammed, but still feels awfully close. Throbbing radiates outward, and I wince from the pain. Eyes darting from my face to the wall to the ceiling to the ground and back, the kid appears confused, disoriented, or both.

Nothing. He doesn't speak. Forcing me to talk a lot more than I like. "Where are you supposed to be, kid?" My forehead begins to sweat as my core temperature climbs.

Sheldon's head pokes out from his classroom. Lips open, eyes blinking quickly, sweat dripping from his forehead. No dimple in sight. I almost feel sorry for him. Almost.

"Theo, that's Brodie. He's mine. In my class. He's having a tough morning. Can you bring him back to me, please?"

I'm the custodian. I'm here to clean. Not to wrangle children. But this kid, when I glance down at him, he looks up at me with wide eyes and panting breath. I recognize his expression from the battlefield. He's petrified. Without thinking, I ask, "Wanna help me?"

Brodie doesn't answer but nods slowly exactly two times.

"He's coming with me," I say without looking at Sheldon, but loud enough for him to hear.

Listen, I didn't ask for this kid to crash into me right before my break. He clearly doesn't want to be with Sheldon, and I can't say I blame him. Maybe he needs a break from the commotion of the classroom. He seems quiet, and I can handle someone who enjoys silence as much as I do. Maybe he'll actually be helpful.

Back in my closet, I motion for the kid to sit down on the milk crate near my swivel chair.

"Brodie, right?"

A nod.

"I'm Theo."

Another nod.

"Listen, if you're gonna hang with me, you're gonna help me. Okay?"

Brodie glances to the ceiling, appearing to contemplate my question for a moment, and then replies with a double nod.

"You're in luck. We take our fifteen-minute break now."

I lift my coffee cup up, now cold and clammy, but I'll slug it down anyway.

"Coffee?"

Brodie looks at me like I've just asked him to drink a bowl of acid.

"Got it."

Kent flies in, bracing himself on the doorframe, head bent over, panting. His dress shirt is untucked, and one shoe is untied. As a fellow big guy, I sympathize with his current state.

"Brodie. You're here." He catches his breath as he speaks, and I wonder if I should fetch him some water. "Mr. Soleskin called the office and said you'd gone with Theo. I'm going to bring you back to class."

Brodie gets that wild look in his eyes again.

"He's gonna help me for a bit."

"Oh. Um. Okay. It's your break. What if I …"

"We're good. I've got coffee, and well …"

"How about if I get Brodie's snack?"

Brodie nods, and Kent exits, slipping on his dangling shoelace but catching himself right before a fall.

"Fine, fine, I'm fine," he says, facing the hallway.

"After our break, we'll check the floors for scuff marks. Then reload paper towels. You up for that?"

Brodie nods. I respect his silence. I sip my coffee, and while it somehow got colder than room temperature, the nutty smell comforts me. Even though I crave routine, working in a school, things happen. Kids happen. Apparently, Brodie happens. We sit quietly, staring at each other, until Kent returns holding a fabric lunch bag covered in dinosaurs.

"Okay, Brodie. Mr. Soleskin knows you're with Theo. You can have your snack and then help him for a little bit, but then you've got to return to class. Sound good?"

A nod.

"Theo, you sure you're okay with …"

"Yup."

"All right, I'll leave you to it. If you need anything, call the office."

I nod at Kent, and when he turns his back to us, I give Brodie a wink. He tries to wink back, but both eyes close, and a pained look washes over his face.

"Don't hurt yourself, kid."

I finish my coffee, and Brodie eats his cheese crackers with only the faint noise of the world outside entering our space.

"Let's get to work."

We walk the hallway searching for scuff marks. Nobody makes them on purpose, but something about shoe soles making contact with the tile floor creates the perfect storm for their production. No matter how much I clean, wax, and buff the floors, the damn dark marks appear. I give Brodie an old broom handle. The bristles have been removed and replaced with a tennis ball. He holds it proudly, his arm extended and raised triumphantly. If he bops me with that ball on a stick, I might roar. But he doesn't. He raises and lowers it, and the hint of a smile overtakes his little face. Watching him march like a drum major, I can't help but feel a little taller as we tramp down the hallway together.

"What happened?"

I stop in my tracks, his squeaky hoarse voice catches me off guard.

"What do you mean?"

He points to my left leg. My limp.

"Old war injury."

"Does it hurt?" His eyes squint as he examines my leg, trying to figure out what's wrong.

"Sometimes. But not usually," I say. And then, spotting a smudge on the floor, I point. "There."

There's an offending mark, as if someone took a burned stick and dragged it across the white tile.

"Take the ball. Push it on the mark. Hard."

Brodie takes the stick in his hand and gently rubs it on the smudge. Nothing happens.

"Here."

I put my hand out, and he hands it over. Pushing the stick, I make a show of it, pretending to use more force than I need.

"You gotta use elbow grease."

Brodie scrunches up his forehead and nose.

"Hard. You gotta push hard."

I hand the broom-ball back to him, and he pushes it on the scuff. Nothing happens.

"Harder."

He leans into it and appears to give it all he has, but the mark's stubbornness exceeds his.

"Again. Keep at it."

Brodie continues, and eventually, the cursed mark begins to relent. When the first pieces of dirt lift off, he pauses for a second and looks up at me, eyes bright and wide, before returning to it. This kid kills me.

"Good job," I say because even I can't be an ass to that punim.

We spend the next half hour searching for scuff marks. Each time Brodie spots one, he immediately goes to town scrubbing away and then looks at me, eyes glowing when he's cleaned it like he deserves a fucking medal. When we've cleared the entire front hallway, we head back to my closet to return the broom-ball and stop at the water fountain near my door. The kid's forehead shines with sweat, and I worry I'm overworking him.

"Drink."

Brodie puts his mouth in the stream of water and laps it up like a dog on a sweltering July afternoon. I stand and watch. I wasn't trying to adopt a puppy today, but this little tyke seems eager to help.

He pushes my cart of paper products down the hallway. The front left wheel squeaks every few seconds, and I stop him so I can refill paper towels in every bathroom. Working alone is my preference, but spending my morning with this kid isn't the end of the world. He's mostly silent and listens to me. By the time we finish, it's almost lunch.

"Chow time."

Blank stare.

"You gotta eat."

He blinks at me.

"Want me to take you?"

A nod.

Brodie seems to enjoy hard work. And quiet. And the smell of industrial-strength cleaning products. I like the kid.

We walk into the cafeteria, and everyone's already sitting and eating, so I bring Brodie up to get his tray. There's no talking. Just a series of nods between Brodie, Delores, and me. Delores, our proverbial "Lunch Lady," with her gray uniform, hair net, and plastic gloves, hands him a tray with a hamburger, chips, an apple, and a cookie on it. He takes it and looks at me.

"Sit," I nod toward the table where his class eats.

Sheldon floats up and down the aisle, making sure everyone's containers are open, and kids are doing more eating than talking. In those checkered pants. Does he want people staring at his ass? Wait. Maybe he does.

Brodie walks over, plops down on the end of the bench and rips into his burger like a wild dog. Good.

I need to clean up in about twenty minutes, and I'd like to eat my own lunch first, so I head for the exit, but not before Sheldon jogs over and stops me.

"Theo, thank you."

His lips turn up like a balloon, slowly rising, creating a panoramic vista on his face. Today, when his smile peaks and that ridiculous dimple appears, an insult grows in my throat, but before it forms and weasels its way out, something extinguishes it. Sheldon gives me a quick wink and returns to helping his students, opening containers and cutting hamburgers in half. He is gliding up and down the aisle like one of those ice skaters on TV. The ones with the sparkly outfits and teeth whiter than fresh snow. And it hits me. Like a goddamn Mack truck. Sheldon Soleskin is utterly adorable. Asshole.

SEVEN

Sheldon

After spending the bulk of his morning with Theo, Brodie is polite, listens, and follows directions. What sorcery has Theo performed on him? Brodie barely speaks to me, and I'm, well, magnetic. Not connecting with one of my students isn't part of my fabulous-first-grade-teacher plan. After the last of my charges boards the bus at the end of the day, with muscles tightened, I head to his closet.

When I walk in, Theo's sitting in his chair with his back to the door. "Bicycle Race" plays from the ancient cassette radio on Theo's shelf. Anyone who adores Queen this much can't be all bad, right?

"Theo, thank you again for your help with Brodie. I don't know what you said or did, but you really saved me this morning."

He stands and approaches the doorway, appearing to prepare for his after-school routine. I've seen him vacuuming the rugs, wiping down sinks and water fountains, and prepping the school for the next day. His eyes search mine. I'm definitely postponing his work and need to make this as quick as possible. With how Brodie has been escalating, I'm desperate for help, and I'm not above a small groveling moment. Even with Theo.

"I know you're busy. I ... I don't want to bother you, but I'm wondering if you could tell me what you did. With Brodie. How did you get him to calm down and, well, listen?"

Theo opens his mouth and then closes it. Come on, friend, we were on our way to speaking in full sentences. Let's not retreat to this no-talking nonsense again. Why won't this ... this ... Shrek speak to me? Maybe if I were more of Princess Fiona, he'd warm up to me. Running my hand through my hair, I open my mouth to prod him. But before I can speak, he does.

"Nice flower."

"Excuse me?"

"Nice flower."

He nods toward my head. The flower behind my ear. After Quiet Time this afternoon, Alison presented me with a beautiful mistletoe flower she'd crafted from construction paper and way too much glue. It's not uncommon for me to be showered with colored paper and glue creations. It's sweet. To celebrate the festive season, I put out photos of poinsettias, amaryllis, and mistletoe. I'm man enough to wear paper bracelets, crowns, and, yes, even flowers. And after my day, I'm not in the mood for Theo Berenson to belittle the pure gesture of a child. I take a deep breath, trying to calm myself. When I open my eyes and see this tall lug staring back at me, my mouth suddenly has a mind of its own, and the words explode like a cannon being shot across the sky.

"A student gifted me with her treasure, and appreciating the love and kindness it was presented with, I put it behind my ear. And maybe it looks silly to you, but I like it. It's cute. I'm cute. And I'm not ashamed to admit it. I'm sorry, I forgot I was wearing it. Yes. I'm wearing a flower. Because I'm gay. A homo. A queen." I put my right hand out and dramatically drop my hand, going limp in the wrist. "That's why my ex-boyfriend dumped me for Dwayne, his straight personal trainer, who clearly isn't that straight! And now I have to watch them get married. Alone. Because who in the world would want a complete flamer like me?"

The monologue flies out of my mouth like lava, and the minute I finish, regret washes over my pale face. I open my mouth to apologize, and once again, Theo interrupts me.

"I'll go."

"Go? It's your space, Theo. I'll leave."

"No, I'll go."

"Where?"

"With you." He pauses. "To the wedding."

"Why on earth would you do that?"

"Why not?" He shrugs, and his broad shoulders hoist up near his ears.

"Theo, that's very sweet, but no. It's bad enough that I'm going at all. I'm not taking a straight guy, to boot. That would be beyond pathetic."

"Annoying," Theo grumbles, his eyebrows furrowed.

"Excuse me?"

"Dense," he mumbles, his eyes on the floor.

"What are you talking about? Can you speak in a complete sentence, please?"

"Why. Are. You. So. Dense?"

"Me? Dense? You're kidding, right? I'm actually very smart. Teaching first grade might seem simple, but it's actually more complicated than most people think. The math alone, I mean, sometimes I have to read the manual multiple times before teaching the lesson, but I get it eventually, and my students learn, and—"

"No. Why do you assume?" Theo interrupts. He looks up, and his eyes go wide.

Oh. This was a twist I did not see coming. "Wait, you mean you're not straight?"

Silence. He looks up and attempts a smile.

"Oh. Oh! Well, I mean, Theo, I had no idea. I ... I mean ..."

He looks down, and my head feels dizzy. I assumed he was hetero from the moment he first growled at me. He's so ... grouchy. Towering and burly in his uniform and with that low rough voice, he almost always sounds like an idling motor. My brain begins to process all this, and my stomach tumbles and rumbles before something else, maybe embarrassment, splashes over me.

"Theo, I'm so sorry."

"Sorry?"

53

"For assuming."

"Anyway, I'll go with you."

I need to think about this. Theo's, well, handsome, but bringing a stranger to the wedding probably isn't a wise move.

He continues to focus on the floor or maybe his feet, I can't tell, but he's stealing glances now, perhaps trying to gauge my reaction.

"We'll chat soon," I say, trying to take some of the air out of the situation. I came here to talk about Brodie, not have a shocking mid-season revelation thrust upon me by Theo Berenson. All I can think about is packing my bag and heading home to Naomi to talk this out.

"Also," Theo adds. "I really do like the flower."

EIGHT

Theo

Keeping quiet allows me to think before I speak. Take my time. I crave efficiency with my words. Patience in all things, but patience with my tongue above all. But something about Sheldon, the way words fly out of his damn mouth, and he looks at me, really studies me, like he's trying to figure me out. It throws me. And that dimple. I've realized not only does it turn up when he smiles, but sometimes when he's focused or frustrated. When that happens, I don't know why, but my brain can't keep up, like railroad tracks crossing in every direction. When he thought I was teasing him about that flower, his annoyance brought out the dimple, and I blurted without considering the consequences.

Why would I offer to go to his ex's wedding with him? What the hell was I thinking? Why would anyone want to take *me* anywhere? Around people. And talking. I'm a complete oaf. I need a time machine. I need to rewind and undo it all.

And it's not about folks knowing I'm gay. I couldn't give a rat's ass. Kent knows I'm gay. I told him when he hired me. He said, "Good for you. We welcome and accept everyone here at Lear. Thanks for telling me." Then he pulled me into a huge hug. I stood there, rigid as a tree, unsure how to react. Also, my guess is that most of the staff here do not care about who I'm sleeping with. Or not sleeping with, really.

People suspect that because I'm built like a tank, I'm some burly straight guy. Does it annoy me? Kind of. But people annoy me in general. I can count on one hand the number of people I've had conversations with about it: Kent, my parents, Christian, and Ricky. I guess Sheldon now too. So that bumps it to six. One hand and a finger. Sheldon's the extra finger.

Being a veteran probably adds to the assumptions, I suppose. When I enlisted, "Don't Ask, Don't Tell" was in full effect. Being a quiet guy, I kept to myself. Nobody asked, and I didn't tell.

Technically, they couldn't do anything about it as long as nobody knew. Which really made no sense. We had to remain closeted. Not tell. Not do anything. But we were young men. We found ways.

Ricky's beautiful face floats into my head. His dark brown hair. In the right sunlight, auburn tones emerged if you looked at him from the right angle. He had a smidge of freckles on the bridge of his nose. There were exactly fourteen freckles, but you had to get close to count them. Really close. And he smelled like the ocean, which made no sense because he was from Kentucky, but he did.

When Ricky plopped down next to me on our deployment flight, blinking rapidly, his chin trembling slightly, there was no choice. With such a long flight, I knew I couldn't put my headphones on and ignore the poor kid. And he was a kid. I mean, we were both young, him twenty and me barely twenty-four. Ricky had such a baby face. When I first saw him, I thought there must be a mistake.

"Are you new, kid?"

"Uh-huh."

"Sit. Name's Theodore Berenson."

"Theodore."

"Theo. Call me Theo."

"Sorry. I'm a little anxious, is all," he said with a southern drawl that melted my core like butter on a warm biscuit.

"What's your name?"

"Ricky. Ricky Joven."

Even trembling in his seat, Ricky Joven was the most beautiful creature I'd ever seen. His dark brown eyes were pools of hope staring back at me. His hair was buzzed like mine, but the soft texture made me wonder what it might have looked like longer. The moment he sat next to me, I was consumed with an incredible urge to shelter Ricky Joven from any harm.

When he grabbed my hand to shake, I was done for. His skin on mine, the heat made my face flush. How were his hands so soft? Slightly embarrassed at my rough, calloused fingers, I pulled my hand away quicker than I should have. But it didn't matter. I could see it in his eyes. We both felt it.

We talked for hours. Well, Ricky did most of the talking, but more words came out of my mouth than I was used to. He was so ridiculously handsome. By the time Ricky fell asleep eleven hours into the twenty-four-hour flight, his head rested gently on my shoulder. Unable to sleep, I listened to his soft breathing through the night as we soared above the clouds.

"We're landing." I shook him awake as we began our descent into Bagram.

Ricky's eyes were suddenly wide and his breathing quickened. He grabbed my forearm.

"Stick with me," I said. "I'll keep you safe."

His brown eyes shone as they locked on me. "Thanks, Theo."

And then he briefly returned his head to my shoulder, but this time, he wasn't sleeping.

If the other folks in our company knew what was going on between us, they didn't ask, and we didn't tell. We never spoke about it until after, but Christian knew. After everything. Ricky and I kept things fairly hushed, and privacy was fleeting at best. We shared a bunk, him on top, me on the bottom. We found ways. In the middle of the night. Tapping on the metal of our bed. Passing a notebook back and forth. Playing footsy under the table in the mess hall. It wasn't much, but it was everything.

"Teddy! How are things, honey bear?"

One of two people on the planet allowed to call me "Teddy," Mom typically phones me on Thursday evenings. It's always been her thing. She says she doesn't want to intrude on my weekends, but the joke's on her. My weekends are spent cooking while jamming to Queen. Of course, she doesn't know that, and I'm not telling her.

"I'm good, Mom."

"Good. Very good. Sweetie, how's the knee?"

Even though my injury and subsequent discharge happened almost ten years ago, she still asks me about it every time we speak. Every. Single. Time. It's what Jewish mothers do.

"Fine, Mom. All better. I've told you."

"Okay, okay, I just worry about you and that limp. You're on your feet all day. And you live alone."

"I get breaks, Mom. Lots of breaks. And I like being by myself."

"I know, but remember what the doctor said …"

"Mom, I'm fine. Really. How are things with you and Abba?"

"Oh, you know your father. He's crafting potions in the basement. This year he's trying kombucha. We can bring you some at Hanukah. If it's drinkable."

Each year, my parents come for Hanukah. The entire eight days. According to Mom, "If we only see you once a year, we're going to get our fill." They drive up from Florida, where they finally settled like all good Jewish retirees. They found a liberal community in Boca Raton and are sure to let me know how open and accepting everyone is down there. "If you ever wanted to move." Because I'm sure there are so many gay single men in Boca under the age of sixty-five.

"Sounds good. Kombucha is tasty."

"Now, don't bite my head off, but you know I have to ask. Are you seeing anyone?"

"Have to ask? Is it commanded in the Torah?"

My parents would love nothing more than for me to have a boyfriend. Be married. Provide grandchildren. On my thirty-fifth birthday, she'd talked about hiring a yenta and she hadn't yet managed to drop the subject.

"There are yentas for everyone now. Even the gays," she proclaims.

"Mom."

"Jean, one of the ladies I play mah-jongg with, makes matches and has a solid track record. Eighty-five percent success rate. That means marriage. She said since you're a faygeleh, she won't even charge us full price."

"Mom, you can't say that," I say, rolling my eyes.

"What? Yenta? Okay, we'll call her a 'genta' instead. A gay yenta!"

"No, Mom, faygeleh. It's derogatory."

"Is it? Well, I'm reclaiming it. You're my faygeleh, and I adore you to bits." I can hear her feet pacing on the parquet floor of their lanai. "And you're thirty-six, and we've waited long enough for you to find someone."

"You! You've waited. Don't drag me into this mishigas," my father shouts, likely from the lounge chair with the impression of his body in it.

"We're your parents, and we want you to be happy," she says.

"I am happy," I grumble.

"And looked after. Nobody knows you better than us, Teddy. We know what a sweet man you are, even if you try your darndest to hide it. You're closer to forty than thirty now. It's time for help. Don't worry, your Abba and I will pay for everything."

As she speaks, my mind wanders. Standing at the kitchen sink, I spot a bluebird with feathers brighter than the September sea perched on the birdfeeder attached to the neighbor's window with a suction cup. It pecks and eats and flits back and forth on the rod underneath the seed compartment. Not a care in this world, the bird finishes its meal, turns its tiny head from side to side, and then, I swear, peers right in the window at me.

"Actually, I'm seeing someone."

"Wait. What? When did this happen?" The excitement in her voice rushes through the phone, prying me from the bird's stare. She pulls the phone away and shouts, "Abba, Theo met someone. Baruch Hashem!"

My father's voice is distant, but I can hear a faint "Oy" before more mumbling.

She lifts the phone back up to her face. Her voice trembles with glee. "Oh, bubbeleh. What's his name? Can we meet him? He'll come to dinner on Hanukah. I need to start thinking about a gift for him. What size does he wear? What are his interests? Besides my handsome son, of course! What does he do? Tell me everything."

"There's not much to tell. Um, it's kinda new."

"Well, tell me something. This is such a mitzvah, Teddy. What's his name?"

I have to think fast. If I'm going to be Sheldon's fake boyfriend for a wedding, he can be mine for the first night of Hanukah dinner with my parents. Tit for tat. With his bubbly personality and ridiculous dimple, he's a parent's dream. And if having him around stops this yenta nonsense, at least for a while, it would be worth it. I'll have to grin and bear it—him. And maybe find a way to get him to shut up.

"Sheldon."

"Sheldon? Hmm. Is he Jewish?"

NINE

Sheldon

"He did what?" Naomi asks as I tell her about Theo's offer. "The custodian? At your school? I thought we didn't like him?"

I *may* have relayed some of Theo's less-than-charming, beast-like nature to Naomi. "We didn't. I mean, I never said I didn't like him, but ... he was difficult. And cranky. And he still is. He doesn't talk much. He kind of snarls when he speaks. But he's actually helped me with Brodie. He's not a cruel person. He's just, I don't know ... irritable."

The left side of Naomi's lip curls up, and she cocks her head in an I'm-not-buying-your-bullshit, twin-brother way.

"So, you're going to take the custodian, a bear of a man—your words, not mine—to Timothy's wedding. A man you don't truly know."

We stare at each other, both at an impasse.

"It's not for three weeks. Obviously, we'll know each other better by then."

"And how, pray tell, is that going to happen?"

"I don't know. Maybe we can write our life stories and study each other's dossiers."

"I mean, that's a start. But if you're going to convince Timothy and everyone else that you and the custodian are a couple, you're going to have to do way more than that."

"Why do you keep calling him 'the custodian?'"

"Because he's the custodian. At your school."

"His name is Theo."

Naomi has a propensity toward snobbery. One time, we took the train to Chicago to visit Walker's family because she wanted an adventure, and I detest flying. We booked a small sleeper room on the train. By small, I mean microscopic, but it was cute and provided an almost-as-close-as-when-we-were-in-the-womb experience for us. We had to walk through the coach section to get to the café car for meals, and Naomi kept referring to the people in coach as "the poors." The poors. I know she was only joking, but I still reprimanded her pretension. We can barely make our rent some months between our two paltry salaries, and the only reason we could afford the minuscule room on the train was because Walker's parents paid for it. I'm not sure if she's being a snob about Theo, but if so, I'm stopping that nonsense right now.

"Okay. Theo. You're going to have to do more than write up some facts about each other. Nobody's going to buy that. Especially if he's so H squared." Huge and hetero. "People will see right through it."

"So, what do I do?"

"You've got to actually date him."

"Um, did you pour something extra in that ginger ale? I'm not dating Theo. He's, he's a boar. And he's so, so ... tall. He looks like a football player. And not the one who runs and catches the ball. He looks like the one who smashes people to the ground."

"Who's being the snob now? And what do you know about football?"

"Fair and noted."

"I don't mean date as if you think something will actually happen. Go on some pretend dates. As friends. Spend time together. Get to know each other. It's the only chance you have to convince anyone you're actually boyfriends."

"Pretend dates?"

"Yes, like practice. For the wedding. Think of Theo as your student."

"I teach seven-year-olds."

"Okay, think of him as your large, brutish *adult* student. Think of it as a teaching challenge. You're going to have to teach him how to be your boyfriend. And if you can pull it off, you'll have a tall, beefy date to flaunt in front of Timothy. I'm sure there's something there you can work with."

Naomi might be on to something. Theo *was* gentle with Brodie. Almost warm. And I bet he would clean up well.

Plus, I love a challenge.

TEN

Theo

The quiet piano intro to "Spread Your Wings" gives way to Freddie's voice, a high hat, and then the guitars come in. Before the chorus explodes, I hear Sheldon's voice. "Okay."

I lean over to lower the volume.

"Okay?"

"You can be my escort. To Timothy's wedding."

Standing in the doorway to my closet, Sheldon wears a shirt with tropical flowers in pinks and purples and reds, and oh my gosh, my eyes might bleed if I stare too long. And I'm not staring. For fuck's sake, who wears a tropical shirt in December? I'm immediately regretting the offer.

"Escort? Are we teenagers going to a cotillion?"

"Fine. Date. You can be my date. As friends. I mean, I know we're not really friends, but we'll go to the wedding as friends. Except, it would be amazing if everyone thought we were actually dating. Boyfriends. So, *we'll* know we're just friends, but everyone else will think you're my boyfriend." Sheldon tilts his head and winks at me. God damnit, he's got to stop winking. "But only for the wedding. And you don't have to do anything that makes you uncomfortable. No touching or kissing or anything physical. Unless you're okay with that. We can cross that bridge when we get there. Pretend boyfriends. It will be our very own Debra Messing's *Wedding Date* fantasy. Such an overlooked classic. Anyway, would that be okay with you?"

Once again, word vomit flies out of his mouth. When he talks, my eyes home in on his lips. No touching. No kissing. Pretend. His mouth moves, and I imagine what his lips might feel like. The bottom lip is slightly fuller than the top, and when he closes them, which doesn't happen for long, it almost looks like he's pouting. Except I can't imagine Sheldon Soleskin ever pouting.

"Um, okay."

"Really? You mean it? Theo, thank you!"

He steps forward, and I'm not sure what I'm supposed to do. High-five him? So, I stand and put my hand out for a shake, and he grabs it. Warm and soft, his hand feels like he hasn't done a hard day's work in his entire life. He doesn't shake my hand but instead pulls me in, which takes more effort from him given our size differ- ence, and wraps his other arm around me. Friday morning, and I'm standing in my custodian closet with Sheldon Soleskin's slender arm wrapped around me. His hand barely reaches my shoulder blade, and he pulls his head back and glances up at me with a soft grin.

"Boyfriends hug."

His face is close to mine, and for the first time, his warm breath reaches my nose. It smells like a fresh candy cane. Was he sucking on a peppermint stick before he came to work?

"But we're pretending," I say.

"Right, well, friends hug, and if we're pretending to be boyfriends, we've got to at least be friends. I won't do it again. Hug you. Without asking, I mean. Sorry about that. Consent is critical. We good?"

Bam, and just like that, Sheldon's back to making me cringe, and I truly have to find a way to get him to stop filling the air with his voice all the time.

"Yeah. Good."

He steps back and turns to leave, but instead, hands me his phone.

"Put your number in, and I'll text you."

I take his phone and thumb my number in. As I hand it back to him, I notice the case. A light purple, with a giant rainbow across the back, and there's a unicorn flying over the rainbow with sparkly glitter adorning the horn. It's quite possibly the gayest thing I've ever seen.

"Nice case."

"Thank you. I will take that as the compliment it was meant to be. Now, I have your number."

He smiles, that damn dimple reappearing, and then punches something into his phone. My phone vibrates in my pocket. When I pull it out, Sheldon's message stares back at me.

> Sheldon: This is Sheldon. You look dapper today.

My eyes roll up the minute I read it and land on Sheldon's smirk, and a growl escapes my lips.

"What? You do. Did you tuck your uniform top in on purpose? Do your hair different?"

"No, and no."

"Well, anyway, now we have each other's digits. I'm going to text you this weekend about hanging out."

"Hanging out?"

"Yes. Theo, if we're going to convince anyone we're boyfriends, we have to spend time together. Get to know each other. Think of it as practice for the wedding. I won't monopolize too much of your time, I promise."

"But Christmas is …"

"Three weeks away, I know, but we don't know each other. At all. We can't dillydally if we want to pull this off."

Three weeks of listening to Sheldon talk and talk and then talk some more. Three weeks of hearing him say things like "dillydally."

I might need to invest in more earplugs. But he's right. And if I want my parents to believe he's my boyfriend, it will take time and effort. And I need to ask him about it. I hold my breath for a moment before saying, "Okay. Text me."

I squeeze out a paltry smile. Sheldon's eyes widen, and his whole face lights up, a perfect match to his obnoxious floral shirt.

"Thank you, Theo. I'm on it."

He leaves, and I'm alone in my space. What the hell have I gotten myself into? I close my eyes and take a deep breath. My hand rubs the keychain on my belt loop, and I try my best to stay calm. I turn the volume up just as the opening piano chords of "Save Me" introduce Freddie's vocals before the whole band kicks in at the chorus, and he screams, asking to be saved. When he sings about spending his life alone, I close my eyes to halt the wetness prickling them. Sheldon Soleskin has no idea what he's getting himself into.

Because it's Friday, the line for school lunch snakes almost to the cafeteria door. Nothing quite compares to the school's pizza, with its generic red sauce and an overabundance of gooey cheese. The antithesis of gourmet, it's incredibly comforting. It's the one day a week I don't pack, and apparently, Sheldon has the same idea. Once all the first-grade children sit and begin eating, Sheldon skips up to the front to grab his tray.

"Delores, how are you on this fine Friday?"

Delores actually grins at Sheldon. And it's not fake. She appears to mean it. Delores never smiles at anyone. Ever.

"Mr. Soleskin, excited for the weekend?"

"Yes, I have a hot date."

"Oh, really?" Delores starts to prepare his tray as I stand behind him, waiting my turn.

"With my couch."

"Theo," Delores says my name, and any joy in her voice evaporates.

"Hi, Theo," Sheldon says, and for once, I'm actually grateful to hear his voice.

Delores now has two trays in front of her, one for each of us. On both trays, she plops two pieces of pizza, green beans, and then goes for the dessert.

"Boys. We have a problem."

"What's wrong?" Sheldon asks.

"You two are the last ones to get lunch, and there's only one piece of cake left."

Delores smiles at Sheldon. Clearly, she wants him to have it. Out of the two of us, I probably don't need a piece of cake.

"Mr. Soleskin, you were here first …"

"Give it to Theo."

Delores's eyes pry open, and her left eyebrow shoots up.

"Really, I don't even like chocolate cake very much. I'm more of a vanilla guy. With strawberry frosting. And sprinkles. Rainbow. Do you ever have that?"

"I'll see what I can do," she says, and then places the cake on my tray, her gloved fingers smooshing into the creamy frosting a little too much for my liking. I suppose it's my lucky day. Sheldon and I take our trays and begin walking away from Delores. I take a deep breath and hold it in, knowing I should thank him.

"Thanks."

"It's nothing. I meant it. I really do prefer vanilla. And we're friends. Friends are nice to each other."

He winks and my chest feels like there's an itch deep down but no way to scratch it.

"But if they ever have vanilla cake with strawberry frosting, save me a piece."

"With rainbow sprinkles," I add.

"Of course! Extra for me." He smiles, and that despicable dimple returns. "I'm going to eat with Becky and Jolene, but I'll text you about this weekend. We're hanging out."

"Okay."

I watch him walk toward Becky's classroom. He's wearing purple jeans. I didn't know they even made purple jeans. They don't leave much to the imagination. My eyes dart between the finger-prints Delores left in my cake and Sheldon's ass. I really do love cake.

ELEVEN

Sheldon

> Sheldon: Happy Sunday! I'm going to the light festival downtown this evening and thought maybe you'd like to join me.

> Theo: Tonight?

> Sheldon: No worries, I just thought I'd ask.

> Theo: I'll go.

> Sheldon: Really? How about 7? Yay! I'm happy to pick you up.

> Theo: I'll drive. What's your address?

At seven o'clock, I come downstairs, and Theo is waiting in his truck. Of course, Theo drives a pickup truck. Of the monster variety. The official mode of transportation for straight men. It's a dark gray to match his mood. The paint chips near the tires, and lord, how am I going to climb my petite self into this beast of a vehicle without a falling-on-my-ass moment? When I approach, Theo pops out like a jack-in-the-box and shuffles over to the passenger side. When he moves quickly, his limp seems to rush to keep up with him.

"Hey."

"Hey, yourself, handsome," I say, trying to butter him up. "Ready to see some festive lights? Have some yummy cocoa? Be enamored by the season?"

"I mean, sure. I guess so."

"Don't sound so enthusiastic."

Theo wears a rather fetching black and red flannel, dark mustard utility pants, work boots, and the cutest red beanie. Refusing to be contained, his scraggly hair pokes out the sides. He's serving butch realness for sure. He is standing beside his truck, hands behind his back, and his eyes scan the ground and only take fleeting glances at me. This is the first time I've seen Theo in anything but his custodian's uniform, and it occurs to me that Theo Berenson is actually handsome. Relaxed. Until—

"Why is your face all scrunched up?" I ask.

"My face isn't scrunched up?"

I whip out my phone, open the front-facing camera and place it before him.

"You look like you just ate a lemon."

"It's nothing."

"No, tell me."

"You're wearing …"

"What? This?"

I'm wearing my favorite soft pink and powder-blue flannel, matching powder-blue cords, Chelsea boots, and a navy puffy vest because it will most certainly be chilly being outside for a couple of hours.

"Is this too gay for you, Theo?"

I twirl and then bow, offering him my best I'm-ready-for-the-ball fantasy.

"No. Why do you always say that?"

"I don't know. It seems like my level of fabulousness, an eleven out of ten"—I check off an imaginary box—"might be too much for you. You know, Theo, if you can't love yourself, how the hell are you gonna love someone else?"

"You look … good."

"Good?"

"Get in."

He opens the passenger door for me. I wasn't expecting knight-in-shining-armor behavior from him. I stare up at the seat and wonder how I'll launch myself up there without a ladder.

"Well, aren't you a gentleman?"

I stand frozen because I can't suss out how to lift myself up, and then Theo taps a bar on the side of the truck and nods.

"That's a grab bar. Grab it."

Okay, I can do this. My fingers latch onto the bar, and I pull with all my strength until my feet begin to come off the pavement. My left foot starts to land on the step near the seat but slips on the metal, and I fall back to solid ground where Theo has placed his hand on my back to soften the blow.

"Is there a must-be-this-tall-to-ride sign I missed somewhere?"

His eyes go sideways, but he doesn't move his hand.

"Let me help."

This time, when I yank myself up, Theo gives me a little push on the lower part of my back, and when I go to sit, his hand slips just an inch or two, brushing my behind. The contact is innocent and brief, but his paws were on my bottom and immediately my body temperature rises a few degrees.

"Sorry," he says.

I lick my lips, and his face flushes red to match his flannel. Making Theo blush gives me a small rise. He may be bigger than me, but I'm starting to understand how to get under his skin. This is going to be a fun evening.

"Have you ever been to the light festival?" I say, trying to spark some sound into the quiet cab of his truck.

"Nah. Not really my thing."

"But the lights are so … sparkly. So festive. So Christmassy!"

"I'm Jewish."

"Well, they have a giant menorah. And tons of Hanukah decor. It's a holiday lights festival, and Hanukah *is* the festival of lights!"

"True."

"And I get to show it all to you."

I slap my hand on his back, and he gives me a quick sideways glance. Theo can posture all he wants, but he can't deny the magic of the holiday season. My center warms thinking about our own magical holiday evening. If Queen Mariah, the Christmas goddess, has her way, it might even snow.

"Lucky me."

"There's going to be lots of walking, and if you get hungry, there are food trucks. One sells delicious little personal pizzas. I know you love pizza."

"I'll definitely be hungry," he says, patting his belly.

My eyes linger on his hand as it rests on his stomach. A warmth rushes to my chest as I scan him up and down. I get the feeling he doesn't know it, but he's sexy as hell. All of him.

"Well, I wouldn't want you to be hangry."

"What the hell is hangry?"

"Hungry and angry. Hangry. Is that why you're a grumpy bear all the time?"

Perking up, I reach over and gently pat his stomach. It's soft, and my mind zips back to watching him on the ladder in the school's basement. The fuzzy hair covering it like moss on a damp stone. The thought sends a small shockwave up my arm and straight to my groin. Those thoughts can go right to bed, thank you very much.

"I'm not a bear."

"Theo. You literally growl at people."

"Bears don't growl. Dogs growl."

"Okay, well, you're some sort of beast."

"Does that make you Beauty?" He steals a quick glance and my face flushes, and what the heck. Is Theo Berenson flirting with me? Are we heading for our own tale as old as time?

"Obviously. Now, eyes on the road, Beast."

We drive through the city and toward the park hosting this year's festival. I glance around the truck, which, honestly, is way tidier than

I expected. Theo's a custodian, so maybe he's super neat and clean about everything. A green pine tree air freshener sways front and center. Not lavender. Not rose. Not mint passion papaya. Pine. It smells like, well, Theo's closet at school. The little fake tree dangling from his rearview mirror sways back and forth, releasing the sharp odor of imitation saplings into the truck's cab, and I attempt to find some loveliness in it.

"Mmmh, piney," I say, nodding at the freshener.

Theo ignores me, and I shake my shoulders, finally feeling the seat warmer kicking in.

"These heated seats are lovely. My butt has never been so toasty."

Theo opens his mouth, but only a cough escapes. My cheeks welcome a smile, knowing I've once again caught him off guard.

Sitting in Theo's truck, you can see everything. It's like we're gliding above the road, higher than I ever feel in my car. The pavement below seems so far, and there's something about this vantage point that makes me feel safe and secure. Maybe these pickups really are the way to drive in style? This must be what it's like for Theo all the time.

"So, tell me something about yourself," I say.

"What?"

"Anything. What's your favorite color?"

"I don't have a favorite color. I'm not five."

"Excuse me, I'm thirty-one, and I have two favorite colors."

Theo's eyes never leave the road as we chat. His thick fingers firmly grip the steering wheel at exactly two and ten o'clock.

"Don't you want to know what they are?" I ask.

"Not really."

"Well, I'm going to tell you anyway. Pink and powder-blue."

I shove my left arm in front of him, showing off my flannel. He grunts and pushes me away with a smirk.

"You know, when you growl like that, it's kind of hot."

"Noted. Never growl in front of Sheldon."

My wit and charm don't seem to be penetrating his turtle shell. He seems hell-bent on keeping me at a distance. Maybe he's one of those gays who only like super masculine straight-acting gym guys. Like Dwayne. Guys who don't wear nail polish. Guys who don't create choreo to the latest Gaga song. Basically, everything I'm not. I suck in a deep, piney gulp of air and try another angle.

"What do you do for fun?"

Again, nothing.

"Theo, if anyone is going to believe we're friends, let alone boyfriends, we're going to need to know things about each other. And in order for that to happen, you have to tell me something about yourself. Anything." I puff my chest up and employ my best teacher voice. "I'll go first. I like making up dances to my favorite pop songs, singing with my class, and decorating gingerbread houses at Christmas. Actually, the decorating usually leads to me popping an equal amount of sweets in my mouth as on the house, so I guess I really like eating. Sweets. And Christmas," I say, and Theo shoots me a quick look. "Hanukah too. Okay, now you go."

Theo exhales. His nostrils flare, but he doesn't speak. I decide to wait him out, and finally, he graces me with a thought.

"I like to … cook."

"You do?"

"Yeah." He gives me a quick glance and darts his eyes back to the road.

"Theo, that's so cool. Oh god, please tell me you watch 'The Great British Baking Show?' Could we watch it together? It's so binge-worthy. Oh my god, would you ever go on it? How awesome would that be? Listen, when you go on, and it's pastry week, remember, no soggy bottoms!"

"Excuse me?" Theo's annoyed, pinched face has returned.

"No soggy bottoms. You have to make sure the shell of your tart is crisp and flaky before you add the filling. If the bottom is soggy, all the yummy stuff will fall out when the judges go to pick it up, and you'll have a horribly embarrassing pastry moment on national television."

"I'm pretty sure you have to be British to be on that show."

"Oh. You're probably right. Well, maybe 'Chopped?' Anyway, what do you like to make? Any favorite ingredients? Do you make up your own creations or follow recipes?" I clasp my hands together, thinking about all the holiday treats Theo might whip up for me.

"I mostly make up my own. But I use recipes too."

I sit back and stare at him. There's more to this man than I first thought. That red beanie is cute as hell too. I'm intrigued and not sure what to say, which rarely happens.

"What?" he asks.

"I … I'm … surprised."

"That I cook? Most people cook, Sheldon."

"I don't. I mean, I heat things up. I boil water. I make cheese sandwiches. With the cheese that comes individually wrapped and feels cold and clammy on your cheeks." I place my palms on my cheeks. "I order takeout. So much takeout. Actual cooking is different. It's creative. It's an art."

"Maybe I could … cook for you sometime?" he says.

I open my mouth, but nothing comes out.

"Do you like Japanese?"

"Hai. That's yes in Japanese. But that's about all I know … wait, and konnichiwa—hello! Naomi and I adore sushi. She doesn't like fish, and I don't really like rice, but somehow we both love sushi."

"I could make you some Japanese."

My face lights up like the star on top of the Rockefeller tree. My tall, strapping boyfriend can cook. And he's going to make me Japanese food. Make that my fake boyfriend. But the rest still works.

"I would love that, Theo." I clasp my hands together and give him my best smile. He keeps his eyes on the road, but I can tell he feels the sunshine radiating from my face warming his entire body.

There's a large makeshift parking lot near the park. What normally would be some sort of sports ball field has been demoted by the heteros to a large area for cars. We haven't had a big snowstorm yet, and the truck kicks up gravel and dust, creating plumes of brown smoke. The park spans many acres on the most beautifully tree-covered land and overlooks the ocean. Lights, so many lights, have been hung, wrapped, strewn, and placed. The entire park glows like a child's eyes on Christmas morning. There are festive decorations, reindeer, sleighs, and a giant menorah, all covered in lights. My face crackles with excitement as I take in how everything radiates and sparkles in the cold darkness.

"Oh, Theo, look!"

I point to the giant menorah. It's massive, huge, and dwarfs Theo, and that's a feat. There are no candles on it, but the entire structure has been wrapped in gorgeous white and blue lights.

"Imagine how beautiful it will be all lit up!"

"Well, Hanukah isn't for another couple of weeks. The first night anyway."

I'm thrilled at the length of his sentence.

There's a chill from the stiff ocean breeze and I cuddle up to his left arm in an attempt to pilfer some of his body heat.

"What are you doing?"

"It's cold. This vest is cute, but well, only a vest."

"C'mere."

He removes his hand from his pocket, where I'd latched onto his arm, and puts it around me. It's heavy and cumbersome and warm and delicious. He's definitely wearing cologne because he smells like sandalwood and cinnamon. I can't remember smelling this on him at school, and I wonder if he wore it for me.

"Sheldon!" A voice shouts from the distance, and with the crowds of people gathered, I struggle to make out where it originates.

"Sheldon! Over here."

Craning my neck, but not enough to give Theo any indication that I want him to remove his arm from its perch on my shoulders, I spot a friendly, adorable, familiar face. Marvin Block, last year's state winner for Teacher of the Year, all smiles and curls, is waving his mittened hand and heading over our way.

"Marvin, how are you?" I ask, shaking his hand, spying the gorgeous Black man with him.

"Amazing, and these lights, it's so magical," he says, surveying the entire park. "This is Olan, my fiancé."

I shake Olan's hand, and he leans on Marvin. I recognize the gesture from students when they feel overwhelmed. I wonder if it's the number of people, lights, or a combination of the two.

"Nice to meet you," Olan says, eyes down.

After Marvin won the Maine Teacher of the Year award last year, he visited our school. It was a fairly short assembly. He talked a little, they showed a video about teaching and his journey, and then he took questions from the children. Afterward, Marvin spent some time chatting with the staff, and as I was the only male teacher at Faye, we connected right away.

"This is our first holiday season engaged, so it's extra special," Marvin says, snuggling up to Olan, who offers a sheepish grin. These two are relationship goals.

"Oh my gosh! Congratulations! That's so special. Mazel tov! When is the wedding? Oh my gosh, do you need help planning it? I'm fabulous with creating a sweet Hallmark movie moment. Let me give you my number."

"It's not until next summer, and my mother, well, she's involved," Marvin says, stealing a glance at Olan, who smiles back, and lord, that smile could sell toothpaste.

"Ah, a summer wedding in Maine. Classic. Well, let me know. Always happy to help create a little wedding magic." I do my best to drag Theo forward a little. "This is my … my friend Theo." I give Marvin a little wink.

"Nice to meet you, Theo," Marvin says, extending his hand. Theo shakes it but only offers a nod before doing the same with Olan, who also nods back. These two seem like two peas in a pod. The silent nodders.

"Marvin came to Faye last spring after he won the Teacher of the Year award. He probably came to Lear too. Do you remember?" I ask Theo.

He shrugs.

"Oh! Are you a new teacher at Lear?" Marvin asks.

Theo scrunches up his face and lets out a huge sigh. Sensing his mounting frustration, I swoop in and try to smooth things over.

"Theo's our custodian. He's the best. He helps with the kids. A complete gem."

"Oh, what a mensch," Marvin says, and Theo's face softens.

"Are you Jewish?" Theo asks, and I stumble a bit because I simply didn't expect him to speak.

"Proud Hebrew here!"

"Nice, me too," Theo says. His lips have turned up for the first time since we arrived.

"We're going to grab some cocoa. Wanna join us?" Marvin asks.

I shoot Theo a glance. He's biting his lower lip, and I figure his time around new people has probably reached its sell-by date, and say, "I think we're going to walk around a little first, but it was great seeing you."

Together, Theo and I head off to explore the lights.

TWELVE

Theo

Being out and about among so many people produces a quiver in my stomach. I'm not sure who I'm hiding from, but I know that—given a choice—I will always be a homebody. And Sheldon is clearly the exact opposite. He demands attention. He knows people. People want to know him. He actually craves social interaction.

Running into that Jewish teacher and his fiancé wasn't the end of the world, but we literally just got here. I was still getting my bearings and assessing the layout. And Sheldon was chilly. And I had my arm around him. Nestled into the spot between my chest and shoulder, he fit like baby Moses tucked into his basket. I may not love the idea of pretending we're boyfriends. Heck, I may not even like Sheldon very much, but I'm not about to let him be cold. That's just bad manners. My mother taught me better.

Mom. Abba. The giant glittery menorah. I've got to ask Sheldon about coming to the first night of Hanukah dinner. I'm sure he'd be into it. The guy loves people. Loves talking. My parents will eat him up.

"Look!" Sheldon shouts.

"What?" I follow his hand, pointing at the sky, wondering what I'm supposed to be gawking at.

"How do you suppose they got those lights all the way up there? I mean, a ladder wouldn't do, right? Do you think they brought in a crane? Or one of those, oh what are they called, lift things? So many lights, so high up." He wraps his hands around my arm, once again burrowing into the spot he seems to be becoming fond of. "Can you imagine living here? With all these lights and how magical it would be. I'd never leave. You'd have to live on cocoa and food truck pizza, but that's the price you'd pay for living in your very own enchanted forest."

I open my mouth, but before I can speak, he does.

"Whaddya think?"

"You talk a lot."

"Well, you don't talk enough, so I'm making up for it." He punches my arm softly.

My stomach lurches, and I have the sudden urge to sprint to my truck and bolt from this godforsaken electricity-sucking park, leaving Sheldon alone and all the damn lightbulbs to die. When he talks, he sounds so, so chipper and tickled about everything, and my ears tinge red when he smiles at me. I promised myself I'd find a way to get him to shut up, and I need to figure it out quickly because if I don't, this whole pretend boyfriend idea will crash and burn like the Hindenburg.

Look at the lights. Go home.

"Hey, I wanted to thank you again for helping with Brodie."

"It's no problem."

Sheldon and Kent decided Brodie might need an incentive plan in the classroom. He has a checklist Sheldon made for him. There's a list of tasks with corresponding pictures. If Brodie can get through all his morning activities, he can spend a little time helping me in the afternoon. For the last week, it's worked like a charm. It's not my usual cup of tea to have a kid tagging along while I work, but it's only for about thirty minutes, and the little bugger actually helps. And unlike his teacher, he's mostly silent.

"He's a good kid."

"He can be. And he adores you. Although, I'm not entirely sure why."

"Do you want my help or not?" And I swear, the moment the words fly out of my mouth, the wind kicks up, blowing his soft copper hair back. Oof.

Sheldon's nostrils flare, and his face turns beet red, matching his flip of hair. The freckles that dot the bridge of his nose and upper cheeks deepen. He opens his mouth, and he barks right back at me.

"Theo Berenson. You may be big, and you may be tough, and you may be a complete ogre, but you do not scare me. So, if you could simmer down and stop having a Coco Montrese 'I'm not joking bitch' moment, that'd be great."

Sheldon's eyes bulge out of his head, the veins in his neck protrude, and the guy actually shakes his index finger at me. Like I'm a first grader. Maybe he thinks yelling at me will change things, but he doesn't understand. I want him to be angry with me. A steamed Sheldon won't get under my skin nearly as much and that will make this whole act easier.

"Who the fuck is Coco Montrese?" I ask.

"From season five?"

I cock my head.

"All Stars Two?"

My fingers find my chin and begin rubbing.

"Drag Race? RuPaul's Drag Race?"

"RuPaul's Drag Race? Isn't that a little … cliché?"

"Honey, I'm a walking cliché, and I own every bit of it. Theo, look at me," he says, waving his hand over his torso. "For someone like me, there's no denying this."

I bite the inside of my cheek and say, "I'm hungry."

"I'm sorry, Theo. I didn't mean to shout. But you, you're really hard to communicate with. You don't say much, and you're confusing. You do nice things like help me move furniture and say you'll come to Timothy's wedding with me, but then you shut down or lash out. And with Brodie, you're kind and patient. You're sweet with him. Why can't you be sweet to anyone else?"

I take a step toward him and rest my hand on his shoulder. He blinks up at me, and I want to tell him. I want him to know. But not here. Not now. Not yet. The words get stuck in my throat like broken shards of glass. I open my eyes wide and try to convey all this to him, unsure how to mold it into words. My palm, stuck to his flannel, squeezes lightly and tries to tell him I'm sorry, but my mouth remains frozen.

THIRTEEN

Sheldon

I'm trying with Theo, but each time he does something to make me think he's not a complete dolt, he does something else to confirm he totally is. Why does he bellow like that? What's he trying to accomplish? Intimidating me? Not gonna happen. I've dealt with much worse and let it crush me. Never again.

Theo's making it extremely difficult for me to keep my cheery demeanor. I'm not buckling to him. I shouldn't have used my teacher's voice. Having a Miss Viola Swamp moment was not part of my winter-lights-festival-with-Theo plan. But I apologized. God, he's such a lug. A big, doofy, lug. I have to control my temper.

"Okay, let's grab pizza," I say. "I think the truck stands are down this way. Not too far. Are you okay to walk, or do you need to sit for a minute? I can run and grab you something and bring it back. I don't want you getting … crabby. I'm not calling you a crab. Just low blood sugar and all. I've seen it before with students. They don't eat breakfast, and the morning goes on, and before snack time they start crashing. It shows up as negative behaviors. Let me run and grab it. How many slices do you want?"

"Sheldon."

"What?"

Theo moves closer and puts his entire enormous hand over my mouth. His dirty, rough, been-all-over-his-truck's-steering-wheel, calloused fingers brush my lips, and when I try to open my mouth to protest, his palm muffles my voice.

"Sheldon. You've got to stop talking."

He doesn't move his hand, and I'm tempted to bite him.

"Okay?"

I nod, his large hand moving with my head. He pulls back, and I open my mouth but then close it before speaking. Talking is part of my charm. Or I thought it was. Once again, I'm too much for someone. How can we get to know each other and pull off being boyfriends if we don't talk? I try to speak like he does, in as few words as possible.

"Theo?"

"What?"

"Please don't do that again."

"Please don't talk so much," he replies.

I scrub my hand over my face, turn toward the vendors, and march. At this point, I want to eat and go home.

Like a beacon of hope, the pizza car comes into view. Unlike the other food trucks, this one is a car. An older, long, and low car. I don't know the make or model because all I know about cars is how to put gas in one and drive it. They've installed a wood-fired pizza oven in the place where the hatchback once was, and the pizzas are crispy and delicious. Maybe a little Italian sauce and cheesy good-ness will soothe Theo's temper.

"Four cheese slices, please," I say to the lovely woman bundled up in festive gear.

"What are you going to eat?"

Like a really tall, sly fox, unbeknownst to me, Theo sneaks up and startles me.

"I only need one slice. Three are for you. Wait, do you want four? I can order another," I pull my shoulders down and glance up at the moon. "I'll order you a whole damn pie if you want."

Theo puts his hand on my shoulder and gently turns me to face him. "I'm sorry," he says.

With his free palm, he rubs his stocky chest, and for the first time, well, ever, Theo Berenson's eyes look at me with something other than confusion or irritation. A sea of lights reflects in his pupils, and a softness emerges. I can't stay upset with him.

"See that bench over there? Why don't you go sit? I'll bring our pizza over. Want some cocoa too?" I ask.

"Sure."

He removes his hand from my shoulder, and I intercept it and give it a little squeeze.

"I'll be right over."

I know I'm a people pleaser and I want Theo to like me, but he has to give me a little to work with. Maybe all my talking scares him? I'd like to get to know him. He seems like he could use a friend. Maybe we both could.

Theo situates himself at the far end of the bench. I sit and place the tray of food between us, but the bench slopes slightly, so I pick up his cocoa and hand it to him. When he reaches for it, his fingers overlap mine. His entire hand covers mine.

"Gosh, I'm such an oaf."

"Theo, it's okay. If we're going to pretend to be boyfriends, you're allowed to touch me."

His cheeks tinge pink, and my heart slows to a crawl. Maybe I've not been clear enough.

"It's only my hand, Theo. We can even hold hands. For practice. When we go to the wedding, you might want to hold my hand. You know, to sell it."

Theo takes his cocoa, sets it on the ground, and reaches for my hand. His giant fingers around my much smaller ones look almost comical, but he's being gentle.

"See, that's not so bad, right?" I say.

"No."

"Your hand is toasty. It's nice."

This elicits a small, sweet smile from Theo, and, well, this Theo might be adorable. The warmth from his hand travels up my arm and begins to spread throughout my entire body.

"You're not an oaf. You know, you have a beautiful smile."

His face flashes red, and I worry I've gone too far.

"Okay, I won't say it again. But hasn't anyone ever told you that?"

He grunts. "My mother."

"Oh, I bet your mother adores that smile. And your whole face."

"She has this saying, 'I love that face.'"

"Oh my gosh, of course she does."

"When I was a kid, she put it on this corny wood sign in the bathroom."

And that might be the sweetest thing I've ever heard, but—maybe more significantly—that is definitely the longest sentence Theo has spoken to me since we met, and that makes my stomach do a little flip. I rub my finger across Theo's palm, trying to send him some soothing energy.

"So you'd see it every time you brush your teeth," I say. He purses his lips and nods. "Your mom sounds amazing."

I drop his hand and reach for his face, pulling it slightly toward me. His deep brown eyes meet mine for a moment before he looks down, and I rub my thumb across his cheek, the stubble from the day already causing friction.

"Yeah, your mom is right. You do have a good face."

He closes his eyes and takes a deep breath, and then, for all that is good in this world, leans into my hand—only for a second before his eyes blink open, and he jerks away.

"Will you come to dinner?" he blurts, and I'm left slightly confused.

"You can meet my mom. And Abba. That's my dad. He'll be there too."

"Um, yeah, of course. What dinner are you talking about?"

"My parents come up every year for Hanukah. We have a big dinner the first night. And the last. But you only need to come to the first."

"And you want me to come?"

"Yeah."

"I'd love that, Theo."

He turns to face me, and his brow wrinkles. He opens his mouth but then closes it.

"What? Tell me."

He takes another deep breath, staring at the ground. The pebbles around the bench reflect the light from the giant twinkling reindeer surrounding us.

"I told them I had a boyfriend."

I reach over and place my hand on his knee. "And you don't."

"Obviously."

"But why? Why did you tell them you have a boyfriend?"

"Look at me."

"I'm looking. I see a good face."

"Sheldon, I'm thirty-six. I'm, well, I'm …"

"What? You're a catch. I mean, if you'd stop snapping and barking all the time. You're a catch, Theo. You may know this, but being thick and juicy is a total asset."

"What did you call me?"

"Thick and juicy. It's a compliment. Trust me," I say, and his bushy eyebrows bunch. "So, you want me to pretend to be your boyfriend for your parents." When he nods, I continue, "This is perfect. Now we both need a date. I'll meet your parents for your Hanukah dinner, and then you'll come with me to Timothy's wedding. There's only one problem."

Theo's brows rise and disappear behind his shaggy hair.

"Meeting your parents and convincing them I'm your boyfriend is way more complicated than you accompanying me to a wedding with tons of people. Your parents know you really well. There won't be other people or, well, a whole wedding to distract them from our … our … well, lie. If we want this to work, we'll need to spend more time together."

Theo nods in one slow motion.

"Are you okay with that?"

Another nod.

"And you'll be … nice to me."

A pause, then, "Yes."

"All right, then we have a deal."

I put my hand out for a shake, and when he grabs it, I pull him in, wrap my arms around his body the best I can, and try to hug him. My hands land on his back, nowhere near each other, and I do my best to squeeze him. He's stiff and clearly uncomfortable, but within a few moments, Theo Berenson melts into my embrace, and I let out a big sigh, feeling this lumbering man finally relent, even if only momentarily.

"Now, let's finish our pizza and walk around and see these lights. And then you can take me home. And I might give you a peck on the cheek ... for practice," I tease.

His eyes widen, and I fear I may be pushing my luck.

Theo's truck hums along as he takes me home. Knowing he has a reason for this whole charade makes me feel better. I have no desire to take advantage of anyone. Even a testy boar.

"These seat warmers are fancy. My tush has never been so toasty."

Theo shoots me a quick glance.

"Sorry. For talking about my bum. Does that bother you?"

He replies with a low grumble, and we're back to this nonsense.

"If anyone's going to believe we're dating, you can't get all weird at the mere mention of my derriere."

Theo emits a low gurgle that becomes a cough that morphs into a choke and finally escapes his mouth.

Subject change: "Do you have any friends?"

"Christian."

"Wait, I thought you were Jewish?"

"No, my friend. His name's Christian. He's my best friend. Well, my only friend, really."

"Oh, got it. That's kinda cute." I give a little clap. "You're Jewish, and your best friend's name is Christian."

"Hilarious. His name's actually Todd Christian. But I call him Christian. It's a military thing."

"How long have you been friends?"

He lets out a sigh but then, after a moment, actually speaks calmly. "We met in Afghanistan. So, about twelve years ago. Two years in the service and ten since we were both discharged. He lives in Connecticut with his wife, Anna."

"Right, you're a veteran. Gosh, you must have stories. I can't even imagine."

"Nope. You really can't."

A small lump forms in my throat. I lean over and rest my hand on his forearm, wishing I could give him a big hug instead.

"Well, if you ever want to chat, I'm a fabulous listener."

"If you ever stop talking," he mumbles under his breath.

"I heard that."

Theo turns the corner, and we're a few blocks from my apartment. The night hasn't been a total disaster. How do I feel about spending more time with him? It's less than two weeks until the first night of Hanukah. Handling Theo Berenson for that amount of time should be a no-brainer. He seems to be less irritable. Well, slightly. I'm trying my best to be a charmer and not poke the bear, but even I have limits. He pulls up to the curb, and I feel my pulse quicken. I'm overtaken with a deep sense of curiosity about this wannabe barbarian.

"Well, thanks for a … fun evening," I say, and yeah, I actually had a nice time with him.

Theo shrugs. And with our night almost over, I feel him pulling his giant turtle head into his giant turtle shell, and I want to grab him and shout, "Snap out of it!" But instead, I reach over and put my hand on his knee.

"Theo, would you like to come up for a minute?"

He turns to me, and his face has gone ashen. I'm not trying to scare him. I wouldn't hurt a fly.

"To meet my sister. That's it. Promise."

"Oh. Okay."

He parks, jumps out, and walks as quickly as he can to open the door for me. I put my hand out for help, and he rushes to take it.

"Theo Berenson, you are a complete gentleman."

"Well, you're out past nine, so he must not have been a complete—"

"Naomi, this is Theo," I interrupt before she embarrasses us both by shoving her foot completely in her mouth.

Naomi's wearing her favorite pink sweats. Her hair, a tinge deeper red than mine, is up in a messy bun/pony combo. She appears to have been reading one of her steamy romances. The half-naked man and a woman in a ripped bodice stare at us from her lap. A glass of wine sits on the coffee table, half full, and she scrambles to look presentable.

"Bean, you have a guest. And you didn't text me. What if I were sitting here naked?"

"Because you sit around naked all the time? Thankfully for everyone involved, you're dressed. Anyway, Naomi, this is Theo."

Theo steps forward and puts his hand out. Naomi stands, and even with her one inch on me, he completely dwarfs her. Janice, hearing the commotion, enters from my bedroom, meows, and saunters over suspiciously, her tail curled into a salty question mark.

"There's my baby," I say. "And this is Janice, the current love of my life. Who always gives me head butts and kitty snuggles. Right, baby girl?"

I scoop her up, and she immediately begins purring and booping her nose at mine. Theo approaches cautiously. This might be bad. I've never asked if he likes cats. Even a fake boyfriend must love cats. Or at least Janice.

"Do you want to pet her?"

He bites his lower lip and nods gently.

"Right there, on her back. She loves that spot," I say, pointing to the place between her shoulders.

Theo begins stroking Janice's fur, and she continues to purr and head butt me, unfazed.

"How was the festival? You boys have fun?" Naomi asks.

"We did. Theo's never been, and we had pizza and cocoa. We bumped into Marvin Block, the guy who won Teacher of the Year and came to Faye last year—remember I told you about him? The cute Jewish guy? Anyway, he was there with his fiancé, who, by the way, looks like a model, and then we——"

"Theo," Naomi interrupts me, "did you have a nice time with my talkative brother?"

I give Theo a sheepish look.

"We had fun," he says with a shrug.

Three words. Naomi should be honored. But also, he said he had fun. With me. Little, femme, ginger, me. Is he just being polite?

"Well, I was about to head to bed. Bean, I'll see you in the morning. Theo, it was a pleasure. Don't let my brother talk your ear off."

Theo chuckles, and I can't say I've ever heard him laugh before. It's deep and throaty, and my knees shake a little.

Naomi gives me her eyes-wide-we'll-talk-in-the-morning look, and my face flashes hot as she heads to her bedroom.

"Wanna sit?"

"Sure."

As he did on the park bench, Theo plasters himself against the far end of the sofa. The blanket Naomi was using rests crumpled in the middle, creating a lumpy wall between us.

"Let me get this out of the way," I say, grabbing the knit throw, folding and placing it over the back of the couch.

"I'm going to sit here." I pat the spot beside him.

I plop down in the middle, not allowing Theo to keep too much distance. He doesn't seem alarmed, and once again his sweet and spicy scent envelops me, and I can't help the slight stirring in my belly.

"So, you had fun?"

"Sure."

"You liked the lights?"

"Yeah."

"And the pizza and cocoa?"

"Uh-huh."

"And me?" I smile and jut my face the slightest bit closer to his.

Theo sighs, and crap, I've pushed him too far.

93

"You're not awful." He rolls his eyes, but a smirk accompanies the gesture.

"What a ringing endorsement. I will put that on my dating profile: Sheldon Soleskin—not awful."

"I'm kidding."

"If that's your idea of flattery, no wonder you're single."

"I'm teasing you. Christian and I rag each other constantly."

Maybe the jibes are his way of showing affection. I'm going to have to recalibrate myself to Theo Berenson. Maybe a little vulnerability will help. I lower my voice and wet my lips. "Theo, people think I'm happy all the time and nothing bothers me, but actually, that's not the case. Sure, I'm cute. Sure, I'm chipper. Sure, I'm almost always thinking of a pop song and choreographing a dance to it in my mind. But the truth is, well, often it's a mask."

"A mask?" Theo scratches the back of his neck.

"A facade. A show."

"Why would you do that?" he asks, and then Theo gently grasps my knee. My stomach drops a little and, placing my hand on his, I continue.

"All my life, I tried to suppress who I am because I knew."

"Knew what?"

"How my parents would react. I hoped I was wrong, but I wasn't. My mom and dad are religious. And not the good kind that preaches about loving everyone and then actually loves everyone. They wanted me to 'renounce' who I am. Which, hello, look at me, not possible."

Theo lets out a little snicker.

"It's just Naomi and me now. I try to put on a brave face, but there's a lot of hurt here," I say, placing my hand on my chest. "Part of why I'm so chipper all the damn time is to make myself feel better. Maybe if I force myself to be happy, I'll believe it. I'm living my best fake-it-till-you-make-it fantasy." I gently squeeze his hand and take a breath. "But also, maybe if other people think I'm strong, they'll be less likely to hurt me."

He stares at me, and a small smile crawls onto his face.

"Now, what about you? Tell me something about you."

I take a deep breath and hope, maybe, just maybe, being vulnerable with him will crack a layer in his armor, and he'll return the favor.

"Where's the bathroom?"

Or maybe not.

FOURTEEN

Theo

Shutting the bathroom door, I immediately sit on the closed toilet seat. How could Sheldon's parents do that? How could any parents? Who cares if he's gay? My parents, for all their overbearingness, love me. All of me. Crap, I should call my mom tomorrow.

A quick survey of the room and I wonder if a purple monster exploded in here. I know he said pink and blue, sorry, powder-blue, are his favorite colors, but purple must rank up there.

"Not awful." Why the hell did I say that to Sheldon? My mother always tells me I come off as gruff and I need to work on tempering myself, but how does a porcupine soften its quills? I have no clue.

At the sink, I splash some cold water on my face. My hair looks matted and disheveled from being under a sock cap all night. Maybe if I just run my wet hands through it a few times, it will look less ratty. Or maybe not. Why do I care? Sheldon doesn't care about my hair. How long have I been in here? Probably too long. Sheldon probably thinks I'm sick. Or taking a shit. Fuck. I scramble to dry my hands and head back to him.

"There you are. Everything okay? Too much pizza?"

I'm mortified. I close my eyes and wince a little at his question.

"I'm fine."

"Your hair … looks different. Very handsome. Come here. Sit."

Sheldon pats the spot I vacated. The moment my ass hits the sofa cushion, his hand brushes a loose curl out of my face. Trying to tame it. Calm it. Wrangle it into submission.

"I'm sorry," I say, the words tumbling out.

"About what? You have nothing to be sorry about. I just want to see your face."

"No, I mean about your parents."

"Oh. Yeah. But I have Naomi. She's my soul mate for life. We'll always be together."

"That's sweet."

"Yeah, we can get on each other's nerves, but we really do love each other. What about your family?"

"Oh, well, my mom, Abba, and, well, me. That's it."

"Only child. Noted," he says and does his imaginary checkmark thing. "Do they know you're gay? Wait, are you gay? Or bi? Pan?"

My shoulders relax a little, thinking about Sylvia and Adam and how, while they might border on smothering, they really do love me unconditionally.

"Gay. Definitely, gay." My eyes fall to the floor before returning to Sheldon's face. "And my parents know and couldn't care less. They just want me to be happy. Which to my mom means meeting someone."

"Is that why you told her you had a boyfriend?"

"Yup. To get her off my back. Even for a little. She can be … relentless. She was about to hire a yenta. That's a …"

"Matchmaker, matchmaker," Sheldon sings.

"Anyway, she means well. I'm thirty-six and single, and she wants a wedding. A big gay Jewish wedding with a chuppah, stomping the glass, and all the Manischewitz wine you can imagine."

"What about your dad?"

"He's a quiet, simple man. My mom pretty much runs the show. But he's kind. And he loves me. A lot. When I told them I was gay, he didn't say much at first. But when he finally got me alone, he simply said, 'I will always love you, son.' And that was it."

Sheldon pulls his legs up and mangles them into a pretzel shape. He tilts his head, and a small grin washes over his face.

"When did you tell them?"

"After my discharge. I ... I ... was—" I stop because I'm unsure what words will convey the shell of a human I was when I returned from two years of active combat duty. Sheldon cocks his head and smiles. That dimple stares up at me, and I spit the rest out. "In a really dark place. I actually lived with my parents for almost a year."

"Oh, Theo, I'm sorry. I know we're just getting to know each other, but I hope you consider me a friend. I mean, fake boyfriends should at least be friends, right?" His neck slants and his eyebrows shoot up. "If you ever need a chat ..."

He reaches over and rests his hand on my knee. His fingers rub gently, and—unsure how to respond—I sit there, willing the words to come. My eyes begin to prickle, and I want to run back to the bathroom or, better yet, out the door to my truck. But I don't because the weight of his small hand on my knee somehow grounds me. Sheldon is really trying, and his trying makes me want to try too.

"I appreciate that. My folks are good people. They just worry about me being alone."

"Well," he says, clasping his hands together, "we need to make sure they're convinced we're boyfriends. That will buy you some time."

Time. I'm not sure all the time in the world would help me. Time confuses me. Sometimes it feels like I was boarding that plane to Afghanistan yesterday, and other times, it feels like a lifetime ago. My brain seems to twist and flip time over, and I try to remember what Christian tells me. "Dude, be present, don't get stuck in the past, and try not to worry about tomorrow."

But all this time with Sheldon. Close. His sweet breath. Those freckles. That dimple. It's fucking with my head.

"Well, I should probably get going."

It's not far from the couch to the entryway, and even with my limp I'm there in a jiff. Sheldon shadows me, his hand on the door-knob, directing my escape.

"Okay. Would it be all right if I gave you a little peck on the cheek?"

With his free hand, he points to the ceiling. A small piece of plastic mistletoe hangs from a tack. Taunting me.

"You know," he says, "for practice? We're going to have to show some affection if we want your folks to think we're dating."

Nobody but my parents have kissed me in over ten years. Not since Ricky. The thought of Sheldon Soleskin's lips on my skin makes my stomach both tingle and drop. I can't figure out why he's being so damn nice to me?

"Um, sure."

Somehow the silent room gets even quieter. My heart beats harder, faster, thumping in my chest as Sheldon leans over. I'm almost positive he can hear the pounding in my torso. He's tentative, as his lips barely brush the skin on my cheek. He adds slight pressure, and I close my eyes as my head begins to lighten. After only a few seconds, he pulls away, and I immediately wish he'd return his mouth to my face.

"You good?"

"Yeah."

More than good. Before I overthink it, I lean down and return his kiss. I try my best to move slowly, be gentle, and when my mouth lands on his cheek, all I can think is how can a grown man's skin be so damn soft. Does he shave? There's no hint of stubble. My beard begins to grow seconds after I've shaved, and most days, my five o'clock shadow appears around lunchtime. Sheldon smells like lavender and something else I can't lock down. I didn't notice before. Something citrusy. Maybe lime? Being this close to someone hasn't happened in a long time, and my heart is tripping. And now I realize my lips are still on Sheldon's face. Most definitely longer than they should be. I withdraw quickly, and he takes my face in his hands. Holding me in place. I investigate the small cluster of freckles dotting the bridge of his nose. They fan out to his cheeks. How long would it take me to inventory them?

"Contrary to what you may want the world to believe, you're a sweet man, Theo."

"No, I'm not."

"Yes. You are."

He closes the inches between us and kisses my cheek again. But this time, his soft lips land closer to mine. Still on my cheek, but only a hair from my mouth. If I moved, even the tiniest amount, our lips would be touching. But I don't.

"Well, it's late," I say, not knowing the actual time.

"Yeah, school tomorrow. For both of us."

Sheldon opens the door, and I take a step into the hallway. My head swims with thoughts of his lips. His cheek. His freckles. I glance back, and he waves. His palm only moves a few inches. It's a tiny wave from a tiny man with a huge heart. He's kind, and yeah, he talks too much, but there's no way I can rope him into the mess I've become. People who get too close to me get burned. Hurt. Worse. It's better to go it alone.

"Night, Theo. Text me when you get home. So, I know you're safe."

With heavy, damp eyes, I bolt to my truck.

FIFTEEN

Sheldon

Monday morning, walking into Lear, my lips tingle in the frosty air as they whistle "Santa Baby." The Madonna version. Obviously.

Hanging out with Theo last night—even as two people only getting to know each other to facilitate pretending to be boyfriends —was the most fun I've had out with a guy since, well, Timothy. Theo's soft body on my sofa. Standing under the mistletoe, giving him a gentle kiss on the cheek. My belly flutters thinking about taming the lion, but really he was more of a kitten in my lap.

Floating toward Theo's closet, I take a breath and paint a huge grin on my face.

"Good morning, friend!"

Theo hunches over his desk, and from the back it appears he's tinkering with something. His toolbox is on the floor, and he's holding an object, elbow out, going to town on it.

"Hello! Theo?"

I step a foot inside, and he grumbles.

"I came to tell you I had a really nice time with you last night. And … Happy Monday."

The man won't even turn around and look at me. Why is he being so chilly with me? Theo's cool as a penguin on a good day.

This approaches deep-freeze-North-Pole-frigid. No sir. I'm not having it. I march over and push myself up against his desk, attempting to divert his attention.

"Theo? I said hello to you. I told you I had a good time with you last night. Did you hear me?"

Without looking up from what I think is a dismantled pencil sharpener that he's now assaulting with a screwdriver, he mumbles, "I heard you."

My eyes narrow, and I take a breath before speaking.

"Okay. Fine. If I did something to upset you, you could tell me. I'm not a mind reader. You go ahead and be a louse. I still had a nice time last night with you. Have a good day."

Shaking my head to try and relieve the stiffness in my neck, I storm out and head to my classroom. I have no idea why Theo's giving me the cold shoulder, but his peppery pouting is not cute. I have no time to coddle him this morning.

I really did enjoy our date. Friend date. Fake date. Whatever. He was a gentleman, and I'm starting to understand there's a teddy bear hiding inside the beast. We practiced those few simple cheek kisses, and I thought he was totally into it. I even tried inching a smidge closer to his lips. If we really want to sell it, a quick lip kiss would seal the deal. Maybe it was too much too soon. Maybe being that close to me was a big turnoff for him. Maybe I had bad breath! Note to self: restock gums and mints.

Theo continues avoiding me all week. After trying to corner him after school Monday, I stop making overtures. My texts go unanswered, and I have the unsettling feeling that I'm being ghosted by a man I'm barely even friends with.

To add insult to injury, Brodie's bad behaviors ramp up. The incentive program with Theo had been helping so much, but maybe the novelty is wearing off. Or maybe the impending holiday madness is too much. Whatever the issue, he's not able to verbalize what's bothering him. Either way, I'm paying the price.

Typically, if Brodie can earn four points by lunchtime, he gets to help Theo for thirty minutes in the afternoon. He earns a point for Morning Meeting, Reading, Writing, and Phonics times if he stays safe, which means staying in the room and calm. Monday, he earned three points, but then during Phonics, he took his whiteboard and tossed it across the room, almost hitting Norah. I think he was frustrated with the word-family activity. Learning the "dge" ending can be tricky. But I'm not sure if that was even the problem because he clammed up when I asked him what happened.

That started a snowballing of issues that prevented him from seeing Theo all week, and I was trying really hard to get him back on track. When I came in this morning and said, "Happy Thursday, Brodie!" his eyes darted at me, and then he swiftly ran under his table, curled up into a ball, and refused to come out.

"Brodie, you okay?"

Silence.

"Did something happen on the bus? At home?"

Nothing.

"Buddy, I'm going to read a book to the class. If you feel like chatting, let me know."

He won't budge, so I'm ignoring him. For now.

I read a story about the invention of ramen noodles, and whenever I glance over, Brodie seems calm. He may even be listening to the story. It's hard to tell, but he isn't disturbing us, and maybe he just needs a little time. If things with Theo were better, I'd ask for his help. I'm surrounded by males who refuse to communicate with me. One is six, and the other is a grown man acting like he's six.

By lunchtime, I'm in a bit of a pickle. I can't leave Brodie alone, but I also need to walk the rest of the class to the cafeteria. As much as I hate to admit it, I need help. I call Kent and instruct the class to prepare for lunch and recess.

The December weather has finally hit us in full effect. I actually had to let my poor car warm up this morning. I taught Naomi the choreo I created last year for Queen Carly Rae's "It's Not Christmas Till Somebody Cries" while I waited for my Toyota's heat to kick in. Once Thanksgiving is over, the holiday jams take over. Oh, who am I kidding? We fire up the festive songs right after Halloween. Thanksgiving is a big Christmas appetizer in our apartment.

The frigid temps mean we have to suit up properly to be outside.

It takes longer for everyone to get into full winter gear, but thankfully, as first graders, they're mostly independent.

"What's the issue?" Kent asks, arriving at the door. The sea of winter gear and children strewn about blocks him from noticing Brodie under the table.

"Brodie has had a rough morning."

I nod to the table, and Kent nods, and heads over while I line the class up.

"Mr. Lester, I'll be back in two minutes," I say and march the class down to the cafeteria.

When I return, Kent has crawled under the table, and I'm momentarily optimistic about a rapid resolution. I head over and stand near Kent's feet. I'm not sure if I should crawl under and join them or not, so I listen and wait.

"I know you're having a hard day, Brodie, and I'm sorry. It's lunchtime, though, and we need to get you to the cafeteria. Or you could eat in my office with me. Would you like that?"

Silence. Brodie's completely shut down.

"Brodie, I'm going to count to three, and I want you to decide. Cafeteria or my office. One, two, three …"

Brodie doesn't flinch. The kid is persistent, I'll give him that. Kent lets out a sigh, and I sense his frustration simmering.

Kent maneuvers himself out from under the table. He's not a small man, and he grunts and groans as he shimmies out. He struggles to stand, and I offer him my hand, which he takes before promptly slipping, yanking me down with him.

"Sorry, sorry," he says as we stand. "Have you tried Theo?" He brushes the random floor-filth off his, I'd guess, Gap baggy khakis.

"I haven't …"

"Why don't you go see if he might be available?"

"Um, okay."

A tightness spreads through my chest as I walk toward Theo's closet. The last thing I want to do is see Theo, let alone ask him for anything. At this point, I'm mentally preparing to take Naomi to Timothy's wedding. People love when we dress up together. Obviously, we're fraternal twins, but we appear surprisingly identical.

Only our hair and our one-inch height difference give us away. And Timothy will expect Naomi. I don't need to rock the boat on his wedding day. That would be petty.

Walking down the hallway toward the custodial closet, my head feels light. Theo is so clearly not interested in being anything resembling friends. But now, I need his help. Maybe if it isn't about me, he won't ignore me. With his closet door in my sight, I take a deep breath and steel myself to face the barbarian.

SIXTEEN

Theo

Fifteen minutes until the first-grader's lunch is over. I'll need to clean and reset the cafeteria for second grade. I pick at my microwaved leftovers. The cheesy Italian meatloaf came out dryer than usual. I used the same amount of wet ingredients. Maybe the eggs were smaller than usual. I don't know. I don't really care. If I slather enough ketchup on it, the staleness will be bearable. Poking at the failure of a meal, a meal for one, my pulse throbs in my throat as I ponder what a disaster I've been this week.

What was I thinking? This mishigas with Sheldon was a huge mistake from the moment I said "I'll go." More proof that it's better to keep my big mouth shut. Talking gets me in trouble. When he was going on and on about having to take his sister to his ex's wedding and how pathetic he felt, something in me wanted to comfort him. It's the dimple. I blame that damn dimple.

Sunday night went better than I thought. Sheldon was so damn patient with me. And adorable. He really took the whole pretending thing seriously. For a moment, in his apartment, on his couch, it started to feel like … like more. When he crawled over, his face so close I could see the freckles dotting his nose and cheeks, my stomach felt like I'd been fasting for Yom Kippur. I detest fasting.

Sheldon's a good guy. And I've been ignoring him all week. My throat feels thick and heavy, and my mind scrambles to figure out a way out of the mess I've started. He'll leave me alone soon enough. I'll make up an excuse for my parents at Hanukah. My fake boyfriend is sick. The fake boyfriend that's covering for a nonexistent one. A lie to cover the lie.

I've been chewing the same bite of food for longer than I should because I've completely zoned out. Abba says it's the brain's way of escaping reality. And for folks with PTSD, escaping reality happens more often. It's a miracle I haven't choked on this damn meatloaf, and as I force my throat to swallow it, I gag for a moment as the quiet refuge of my closet is broached.

"Theo, I need you."

It's Sheldon. I haven't heard from him since Tuesday. When he stopped texting me. Because I ignored him. Like a fucking ass. Staring down at my lunch, I do my best to avoid eye contact. You'd think he'd get the hint, but apparently not. I know ghosting him is a dick move, but it's easier to rip the Band-Aid off.

"It's Brodie."

"Is he hurt?"

Adrenaline simmers in my system, and I brace myself to stand.

"No, it's not that. He's just, well, having a really rough time. He's been hiding under a table all morning. Kent's with him now, but I worry he may actually be making things worse."

"Oh boy."

"Kent asked me to get you."

I sigh. "I have ten minutes before I need to—"

"Listen, I realize you're not happy with me. Or maybe the thought of even pretending to be my boyfriend was too awful for you. I don't know exactly what I did. How would I? You won't talk to me. You won't reply to my texts. It's fine." He takes an audible breath and pauses. "I'm used to people shutting me out. God, I even told you about my parents. What a fool. Me. For telling you. Not you. I mean you for ghosting me." He pauses again, and I think he's going to leave, but he doesn't. "Why am I so easy to reject?"

The words come out like gunfire in all directions. I'm not even looking at him. He's verbally assaulting the back of my head. Once again, I simply want to make him stop talking. But I'm not even sure what to say. So I stand and face him. I open my mouth to speak, but my breath catches in my chest. Tight. Cold.

Apparently, my standing is enough to halt the stream of words flowing out of his lips. His soft lips. On my face Sunday night.

"So. Can you come?"

"Where?"

"To my classroom. For Brodie."

Oh, right. I forgot why he was here. The poor kid must be truly struggling. I haven't seen him all week. Sheldon pinches his lips together and runs his hand through his carroty, softer-than-silk hair. At least, it appears that way. If I hadn't been so vile, I might have run my fingers through it. For practice.

"Um, sure, I can come. But what do you want me to do?"

"I don't know. Talk to him. He adores you."

I shake my head and slowly lower my chin. "Nobody adores me."

"Theo, you may find it hard to believe, but I like you. And I was having fun with you. I'm not exactly sure why you've suddenly decided this, this"—he motions between us—"whatever we were doing wasn't for you, but since you refuse to talk to me, I guess I'll never know."

"It's not you."

"Um, it's always me. Timothy. My parents. Every guy I've ever interacted with. I get it. I'm small. I'm skinny. I'm gay. I mean, you're gay, but I'm like *gay* gay." He puts his hands out and shakes them like some kind of show of gayness. "But, right now, Brodie needs you."

I want to tell him it's not him. I want to tell him I love his compactness. I want to tell him his parents are ignorant and missing out on a wonderful son. I want to tell him his flamboyant femme-ness is fucking hot. But that would be a lot of words. Too many. My stomach hardens. Knots tying on knots.

"Okay. But Sheldon. It's not you." My eyes sting. He's staring at me, and I wish I could evaporate. "You're, you're …"

My throat clenches. The words are right there, on the tip of my tongue. They're caught. Stuck. And I can't dislodge them from my throat. I want to apologize. I want to make it better. Him better. Feel his lips on my cheek again. Touch his hand again. I open my mouth, and my breath catches in my chest. I try to knock the words free, but the sudden blaring traps them in.

Wah! Wah! Wah!

The fire alarm. Crushing noise and vibrations rain down on us. Muscles tighten, and my mind vibrates. Flashing. Smoke. Gunfire. Dust. Screaming. Blood.

Sheldon's eyes widen, and he shouts, "My class!" Words become echoes. His darting body becomes a blur.

Heart jolts.

Skin sizzles.

Kent didn't tell me. Why didn't he tell me? He always tells me.

My ears buzz. Eyes clamp shut.

Take cover!

Drowning.

The noise envelops me, and the world crumbles.

SEVENTEEN

Sheldon

I have to get to my class. As I sprint down the hallway, my mind races. I was just with Kent. He couldn't have known about this. He would have told me. He wouldn't have stayed with Brodie. Is there an actual fire in the school? I don't smell smoke or anything burning. We're not supposed to run inside, but the fire alarm isn't supposed to be going off right now, either. Adrenaline shoots through my body, and I will my scrawny legs to carry me quickly.

As I dart down the hallway, I can't escape the look of panic on Theo's face. He didn't seem overly upset by our conversation. If you can even call it a conversation. A conversation implies both people speaking. The alarm clearly startled him. I nearly jumped out of my skin. Even when I know it's coming, the noise shocks me, and this was definitely a surprise.

I burst into the cafeteria as the last children head out the exit door. They'll walk around to the playground and wait. The smell of today's lunch—macaroni and cheese and hot dogs—assaults me as I sprint over and catch up with my class en route. Thankfully, they're dressed for recess. The frigid temps won't be too shocking for them, but the rest of the school isn't as lucky, and neither am I. When I leave the warmth of the building, the frosty wind of an overcast

December day greets me, and I shove my hands in my pockets, searching for some semblance of comfort.

When I reach our spot near the swings, my class waits with one of the lunch aides. I don't immediately see Kent. Or Brodie. My heart begins to pound loud enough to compete with the blaring alarm, and a giant pit unfurls in my core. My eyes scan for them as sirens approach in the distance. Firetrucks (plural) circle the school. Tears sting the corners of my eyes and I take a deep breath because, right now, I need to be calm for my students. Their worried faces examine mine for information.

"Friends, we're all safe. We'll wait for Mr. Lester to tell us ...."

As if summoned by my saying his name, Kent rushes out of the building. He's grasping Brodie's hand, and the little boy is doing his best to keep up. Kent's eyes are wide and blinking profusely. A pained mask covers his usually friendly face.

He rushes over and places Brodie in the front of my line.

"A word," he says, and if Kent's eyes could pop out of his head entirely, I'd expect that to happen at any moment.

We turn our bodies away from the children, and Kent whisper-shouts over the loud sounds.

"It was Brodie. He pulled the alarm."

Covering my mouth with my hands, I shake my head and close my eyes. My head knows this wasn't my fault, but my stomach churns with dread. This may be a colossal disaster, but relief washes over me. There's no actual fire.

"I counted again, and he bolted and, well ..." The veins in his neck are visibly growing, and his eyes dart around the playground.

"Where's Theo?" he asks.

My stomach sinks even deeper, and a wave of worry crashes over me.

"We were talking in his closet when it went off. I left him to get my class."

"Crap." Kent squeezes his eyes shut. "This isn't good. I've got to go get him. He won't come out on his own."

My throat contracts and there is a massive boulder crushing my chest. Any relief I felt at the lack of an actual fire engulfing the school dissolves. Should I have stayed with Theo? But my class … I'm not sure how, but I have to help.

"What do you mean he won't come out?"

"He just won't. The alarm, it, it …"

"I'll go."

Reentering the building while the alarm blasts and firetrucks approach might not be wise, but the look on Theo's face when I ran off haunts me already.

"Are you sure?"

"Yes. Please, let me."

"Okay, but take a walkie-talkie," Kent says, shoving one at me.

Firefighters surround the building, and Kent rushes to meet them. Hopefully, they can turn the alarm off. Soon. My body shivers as I watch every child and adult stand outside, freezing, with their hands covering their ears. The thought of Theo, inside, with this noise … Why wouldn't he leave the building with everyone else?

I walk over to Becky and shout in her ear. "Watch my class. Okay?"

She nods and gives me a thumbs-up, and I jog into the school, my sweaty hand clutching the walkie-talkie.

The noise overtakes me, and I cover my ears, but it does little to muffle the incessant siren. The building is dark, except for the light from outside, which isn't much on a cloudy day. Small blinking lights in the hallway pulse with each sonic blast. When I spot the door to Theo's closet, it's wide open, just as I left it.

With no window, there is little illumination, and I don't see Theo. He's kind of hard to miss. Maybe he ran out while I was en route?

"Theo!" I scream his name with all the power and ferocity I can muster, but in this small space, the bellowing alarm almost deafens me, sucking up any noise I emit like a black hole.

I pull my cell phone out and turn on the flashlight. I sweep it across the room a few times. Nothing. My breath feels cold and dry as I gulp air and attempt to remain calm. One last scan and I spot something. On the floor. His black shoes. I squat down, and Theo comes into full view. He's under his desk, curled up into a ball. His legs and feet stick out a little, and his entire body shakes like a leaf. Holy hell.

I drop the walkie-talkie, run over, crawl on my hands and knees, and scoot to get close to his face. If I want to have any chance of him hearing me, I need to get right up next to him. His hands are clasped behind his head, with his thick forearms covering his ears. This hulking bear of a man is trembling. My brain races. How can I gain control of the situation? Clearly, he can't hear me, so I inch as close to his head as I can and place my hand on his arm. The moment I touch his skin, he flinches like a flame has burned him, and he recoils even closer to the wall. My heart aches to help him, and I don't know what to do.

Because I'm so damn short, I'm able to position myself with my legs crossed and Theo's head right next to my lap. Slowly, like I'm handling a carton of eggs, I lift his head and scoot over. Theo's head must weigh more than a bowling ball, and he's not helping me in the least bit, so it takes every ounce of strength to hoist him onto my legs. But I do it. And he doesn't fight me.

Immediately, I stroke his hair. It's the only thing I can think of to soothe him in the cacophony of clamor. His soft, sandy curls, damp from sweat, cover his face. Even in the low light, because he's only inches from my face, I notice a sprinkle of tan freckles across the bridge of his nose.

My hand travels over his hair, and I move my other to his chest. His heart pounds like a locomotive engine about to combust. My throat constricts, and I wish I had a glass of water from that fancy water fountain. I know the firefighters are outside. Kent knows we're in here. This nightmare has to end soon.

With his head on my lap, I can feel Theo's teeth chattering. I can't discern if he's freezing or burning up. I close my eyes and try and send him calm, positive energy. Right now, all I want is for this to end for him. I'm unsure how much more of this he can handle, and I contemplate my next move. Leaving Theo isn't an option. I know that for sure.

Without warning, the alarm stops. The sudden silence actually startles me. My ears are accustomed to the blaring. Hallelujah. And now Theo's short, quick, panting breathing becomes evident. He sounds like he's about to sob.

"Theo? Theo! It's Sheldon. I've got you, buddy."

His eyes remain shut, and he doesn't budge.

"I've got you. Baby, I've got you."

The moment it comes out of my mouth, I realize Theo will most definitely detest being called "baby," but right now, I don't care. Seeing him like this petrifies me, and I need him to know he's cared for. A loud sigh releases from Theo's nostrils, like a trapped animal escaping from peril, and when I brush the hair away from his forehead one more time, he slowly cracks his right eye.

"There you are. It's me. Sheldon. You're safe. I've got you. I'm not leaving you."

Carefully, his other eye opens. He still hasn't moved a muscle other than his eyelids.

"Brodie pulled the alarm. Everyone's outside. The firefighters are here. There's no fire. You're okay. We're okay. I've got you."

And I do. Literally. His head cradled in my lap, somehow, I manage to hold the most significant human I know in my little hands. His shining eyes, now fully open, lock on my face, and if nothing else, I know Theo sees me and understands I'm here. With him.

Noises begin to intrude, and before I know it, Kent and three rather hunky firemen crowd the small closet.

Squatting down and poking his head under the table, our principal, with a calm firmness, says, "Theo, it's Kent. I'm going to take you home, okay?"

There's no response.

"Do you think you can cover my class? I think he might do better with me," I say.

The need to stay with Theo overtakes me.

Kent glances at his watch, undoubtedly thinking over the rest of the day. There are only a couple of hours left, and right now, Theo needs to get home safely.

"Okay. But I'm not sure he'll move on his own."

The firemen look ready to assist, but I'm unsure if they'll make it better or worse.

"Can you give us a few minutes and come back?"

"Five minutes," says the tallest of the firemen, still a few inches shorter than the man curled up on the floor.

We're alone again, and I return to stroking Theo's hair.

"Listen, we have to get you home. I don't want them to carry you out, and there's no way I can lift you. I need you to get up and walk to my car. Can you do that for me?"

Theo slowly nods, the first movement he's made other than opening his eyes.

"I'm going to get up now," I say, slowly sliding away. He holds his head up, a good sign.

I move out from under the table and stand, bending over to see if he needs me. He slowly unravels himself, stretching his back and lifting his meaty torso off the ground.

"There you go. I'm right here."

Carefully, Theo emerges from under his desk, his eyes on the ground now, and for the first time, his complete lack of communication doesn't bother me one bit.

He's out and upright. "You're doing fantastic, Theo." I step toward him and hold his arm. "We're going to my car. I'm taking you home."

When my hand wraps around his forearm, he bristles but doesn't pull back. I gently tug him, and his feet begin to move.

⁂

"You're safe."

"I got you, Theo."

"You're okay."

He doesn't indicate he's heard me. He's still in a bit of a trance but appears to be reemerging from wherever his mind went when the alarm blasted. When the map on my phone brings us to Theo's building, I find a spot on the street, not even asking him about the parking situation. If I get a ticket, so be it. I jump out and run around to open the door for him, and he stares at me with a confused look.

"Theo, we're at your place. I'm going to walk you inside. Do you need help?"

I extend my hand, unsure what he'll do, and he ignores it. He steps out of my Camry and onto the sidewalk, and when I latch onto his arm, he doesn't rebuff me. We walk up to the front, his limp more pronounced than I've seen it. He leans over and punches in a code, and we're inside. He leads me up two flights of stairs to an apartment on the top floor, and he fishes for his key.

Inside, he drops his keys in a bowl near the door and shuffles toward his bedroom. I close his front door and take a breath. I have no idea what I'm supposed to do.

I walk to the bedroom door. Theo is sitting on the edge of his bed. He looks confused, so I carefully approach, sit, and put my arm around him. Glancing around, there's a large dresser on the opposite wall and a nightstand, but that's it. Like the rest of the apartment, the walls are bare.

"Theo, what can I do to help you?"

Silence.

"Should I call your parents?"

He shakes his head.

I pinch my lips together and plead, "Theo, you have to help me. I don't know what to do."

He pulls out his phone, taps it a few times, and hands it to me.

"Hello? Theo?"

A man's voice asks for Theo, but I have no clue with whom I'm speaking.

"Um, hello. This is Sheldon Soleskin, I work with Theo, and we're ... friends. I'm with him. At his apartment. I took him home. From school. Work. There was an incident with the fire alarm."

"Hey, Sheldon. This is Todd Christian, I'm a friend of Theo's. He's there with you?"

"Christian? From the Army?"

"Yes, we were enlisted together. You can call me Christian too. Can you tell me what happened?"

Christian listens as I explain everything that brought us to Theo's bedroom. He doesn't interrupt or ask questions, but I can hear him breathing, and the occasional sigh slips out.

"… and I don't know what to do."

"Thank you for taking care of him. Are you able to stay for a little?"

"Sure."

"Okay, do you mind putting me on speakerphone so he can hear me?"

"Of course. Hang on."

I reach past Theo and place the phone on the nightstand and then push the button to switch to speakerphone. Christian's voice fills the space, and I study Theo carefully.

"T-Dawg, it's Christian. Thank you for calling me. Buddy, I'm so sorry that happened. I know you must have been scared. You're home now. You're safe. Sheldon's going to stay with you. I want you to lie down, close your eyes. Take something. Sheldon, can you go look in his medicine cabinet? He should have some Xanax. Give him one. It'll help him sleep."

I pop over to the bathroom and open Theo's medicine cabinet. It's sparse as hell. Toothpaste. Toothbrush. Floss. Shaving cream. A razor. A small glass. And a bottle of Xanax. Not a single beauty product in sight. Christian's voice travels, and I can still faintly hear him trying to calm his friend.

"I'm going to call you later. If you don't want to pick up, that's okay, but let Sheldon talk to me. Listen, if you need me to haul my ass up to Portland, I will. I love you, man."

"Found the Xanax," I report, sidling next to Theo with a small glass of water in one hand and the rectangular pill in the other.

"Okay, give him one and let him lie down. But please stay. He shouldn't be alone."

"Got it. Thank you, Christian."

"No, thank you, Sheldon. You're a good friend."

Christian hangs up, and I hand the pill to Theo. He swallows it before taking the water, but then gulps the entire glass down in one go.

"Theo, do you need help getting your clothes off? Or do you want to sleep in them?" His clothes are soaked through from sweat. He can't want to sleep like this.

I'm not exactly sure how I'd help him get undressed, but I'd do my best if need be. The uniform he's wearing today is one-piece and zips up the middle. In order to take it off, he'll have to do most of the work. Theo stands but doesn't do anything.

"I'm going to unzip you, okay?"

He nods, and I move in front of him and carefully begin to undo the jumpsuit. He stares straight ahead, and when his white under-shirt comes into view, I focus on that instead of his face.

"All right, can you help me a little?"

I do my best to hold the sleeves. He pulls his arms out and steps out of the pants section and I gather the massive bundle of damp fabric in my arms. Theo, in his white T-shirt and white boxers speckled with blue dots, turns to his bed. All I want is for him to feel better, but I'm unsure what else to do for him. I pull the covers back, and he crawls in. Before I leave him to sleep, I sit on the edge of the bed and lean over, slowly rubbing the thick muscle on his upper arm. Like a stray dog finally ready, Theo succumbs, allowing me to offer him a small amount of affection.

"I'm going to be right in the other room. On your couch. I'll check on you, but if you need anything, Theo, holler."

He doesn't speak, but when I try to remove my hand, he grabs it. He clasps my fingers, and without making eye contact, without uttering a syllable, Theo speaks volumes. With that small squeeze, we connect, and my body relaxes before he releases my hand and rolls over.

"Sleep well, baby."

There are a few dirty dishes waiting in the kitchen sink, probably from breakfast, and I wash them up. Staring out the window, I rinse. The overcast skies have become a full gray blanket. I may not be a native Mainer, but if I were a betting man, I'd say snow was in the air.

By dinnertime, Theo is still out cold. Not wanting to disturb him or offend his culinary palate, I order a large cheese pizza to satisfy my grumbling stomach. After tipping the pizza delivery person, I settle in on Theo's couch. I ordered an extra-large because I figure Theo might be hungry whenever he finally wakes up. Sitting on his sofa, I pull out my phone and text Naomi.

> Sheldon: Had an emergency at school. At Theo's. May need to stay the night.

> Naomi: You okay?

> Sheldon: I'm fine. Didn't want you to worry.

> Naomi: Thank you. Love you. I'm here if you need anything. Looks like snow.

The last thing I want to do is wake Theo up, but it's almost nine o'clock, and I'm exhausted. I tiptoe in and check to make sure he's breathing. He's out cold. Poor baby. He's thrown the covers off, but the room feels chilly, so I carefully cover him back up. When I pull his comforter up to his neck, he turns and opens one eye.

"There's my Theo. You sleep. I ordered pizza if you get hungry."

I'm not sure he'll like it, but I don't care. I lean over, push the curls out of his eyes, and give him a soft kiss on his forehead. My mouth is still on his damp forehead when his arm appears and wraps around me.

"Do you want me to stay?"

Both eyes are now open, and even in the dark room, I can see they're wide and glistening. The poor man looks petrified. He nods twice. I don't speak but lie on top of the covers and do my best to wrap this man in my arms.

He rolls over and rests his head on my chest. The weight of his skull almost crushes my small frame, and I do my best to stroke his hair and soothe him. After a few minutes, his hand comes up, reaches over, and grabs my waist. He's clinging to me, and it feels like he's attempting to crush me against his body. With his size and strength, I don't even consider resisting.

"I got you, baby," I whisper over and over, attempting to quiet whatever demons rage inside Theo Berenson.

EIGHTEEN

Theo

My eyes fly open to find pitch-black. The quietness feels heavy, almost too silent. I crane to see the time and notice I'm not alone. Limbs, long and lanky, twist around me like vines climbing a tree, and the faint smell of something … fruity brings it all cascading back. Sheldon.

When the alarm assaulted, my brain jerked me to another time and place. Sirens. Mortars. Machine guns. Smoke. And then it shut off. Completely. The rest feels like trying to remember a movie you've seen through fog and too much whiskey. But then he was there. Holding me. Stroking my hair. Driving me home. Staying with me. Kissing my forehead. Calling me baby. Baby. I've got to be the largest baby in existence.

Having him this close, my body reacts. Blood heads south toward my groin, and I know that's not helpful. Carefully, I remove Sheldon's arms and slide out of his grasp. He lets out a sharp breath and rolls over. I stand and grab my phone from the nightstand. It's two in the morning, and my stomach lurches with hunger.

Pissing takes a minute because I have to wait for my dick to soften enough so I don't make a mess, but eventually, I'm able to get it all out and head to the kitchen in search of sustenance. A pizza box sits on the counter, and when I lift the lid, only a single slice is missing. One-Slice-Sheldon. I grab two slices, stack one on top of the other, and devour them.

Christian. He called. Or maybe Sheldon called him. Or maybe I did? But I remember his voice, and the urge for him to know I'm all right overtakes me. I grab my phone from my pocket and thumb him a quick text, hoping it doesn't wake him or Anna.

> Theo: I'm OK. Will call later when the sun is up.

Standing at the kitchen sink, I notice it's spotless. All the dishes have been washed and dried. The sink itself scrubbed. Why did he go and do that? God, not only is he adorable, but he does dishes too. And now I know he's cuddly. He's so short. And razor thin. He's damn wiry. He was gripping on to me like a monkey clinging to its mother. And his lips on my forehead. Soothing and soft. Sheldon Soleskin is a fucking human sparkler.

I'm zoning out and suddenly realize two things. First, it's snowing. Not light snow, but full-on blizzard conditions that will require plow trucks and shoveling and salt. Second, I'm rock-hard. From thinking about Sheldon, not the snow. I do love snow, purely in a platonic way. If I'm going to return to bed, a bed with a sleeping Sheldon, I need to take care of this. I begin plotting how I might jerk off in silence.

"Theo?" A whisper from behind me. Fuck.

His startling me scares my cock limp. Mostly. Sheldon's right there. Inches from me. He's wearing a black T-shirt and navy briefs that leave very little to the imagination. Lord help me.

"Are you okay?"

I hold up my half-eaten second helping of double-stacked pizza.

"Oh, you're eating. Good. You must be starving."

He reaches out and rubs my arm. When his hand makes contact, my belly flips, tossing the half-digested pizza and causing my dick to lurch against my boxers.

I finish chewing and swallowing what's in my mouth, raise the pizza, and say, "Thank you."

"I was worried about you. Shoot, I never called Kent."

"Call in the morning. Look," I say and nod out the window.

"Sarah Jessica Parker, it's snowing. It's so beautiful," he shouts, way too loud for the current time, and does a spin. "Oh, Theo, I'm so sorry that happened to you, and I know you're probably annoyed I'm here, but look at the snow. Maybe we'll have a magical snow day together?"

"God, I hope." The thought of going to work today makes my head hurt. Spending the entire day with Sheldon? In his T-shirt and underwear? Oy.

Sheldon's eyes meet mine. "You eat up."

And then his eyes travel south, and for fuck's sake, he's noticed.

"Oh, well, somebody's excited," he says with a smirk. "It must be the pizza."

My face flashes hot, and a tingling begins at the base of my neck and slowly overtakes my cheeks. I turn back to the window.

"Don't be embarrassed. I don't mind. You had a tough day. But you're safe now." He yawns and says, "I'm going back to sleep."

"I'll be right there," I mumble through a full mouth.

When I return to my bed, Sheldon looks so peaceful. Like a sleeping angel. I peel back the covers and do my best not to disturb him. As soon as I settle, his arm flies around me, pulling himself closer, up against me. The little bugger spoons me. I grab his hand on my chest and squeeze it. My body relaxes, my breathing eases, and with Sheldon's entire length plastered against mine, I drift off.

It's just after four a.m., and Sheldon is hard. Rock hard. And pressed up against me. The soft snoring in my ear lets me know he's fast asleep, and my lips turn up, wondering what he might be dreaming about.

"Sheldon?" I whisper.

He attempts to pull me back toward him. I'm no physicist, but even I know a Chihuahua can't move a Saint Bernard.

"Sheldon?"

With a little more force, his heavy breathing stops, and he propels himself away from me.

"Um, sorry, I, well, the friction, and ..." he mutters.

I turn around, and he's sitting up, facing away from me. I reach over and gently grab his waist, tugging him back. Close. Warm.

"It's okay, Sheldon. You were asleep."

He buries his face in the pillow, and I have the sudden urge to pick him up and kiss every inch of him. This can't be good.

"I was," he yells into the pillow and then picks his head up. "Asleep. Completely. I would never, Theo. I swear. I know we're just, well, whatever we are. And after yesterday. Never."

The sight of Sheldon Soleskin. On my bed. In those navy briefs. His creamy thighs. I speak before thinking.

"You could, um, take care of it. If you wanted."

He turns to me, his face scrunched, the freckles smashing together. "Excuse me?"

My mind replays him holding me. Brushing my hair. Calling me ... baby. So infantile and irritating. Why would he call me that? God, I hope he calls me baby forever. And the thought of him curled around my body. So warm. His sweet breath on my face. My cock brushes the fabric of my boxers, and I'm speaking again.

"I mean, only if you wanted. I could, um, watch."

Sheldon's eyebrows take off like fireworks, and he leans in and tilts his head.

He takes my hand. His fingers feel so small against mine. They're warm and soft. I want to grab him and gather him up close, feel his little hot-water-bottle body next to mine.

"Theo Berenson, you want to watch me?"

He rolls over, and the tip of his cock peeks out from his waistband.

I shrug.

"I mean, clearly, I'm, well," he says, nodding to his briefs. "But after yesterday, I don't think we ..."

"Please."

This isn't me. I don't do things like this. But Sheldon on my bed like this, so close, fuck I want to lick him up and down. Pepper every freckle on his body with a kiss. But I need to pace myself. Baby steps.

He leans over and kisses my forehead, and every atom in my body screams for him to stay.

"This okay?" he asks.

I nod carefully.

Continuing to stroke my hair, he moves his face. He's kissing my cheek. So close I can feel his warm breath on my nose. Like that Sunday night. Practice kissing on the cheek. His lips wet and sweet.

"This okay?"

Again, I nod.

He kisses my cheek over and over, and his mouth moves the slightest bit toward mine. After every move, only millimeters, he pauses and asks, "This okay?"

His lips now straddle my cheek and mouth, and he pauses to ask one more time for consent, but before the words come out, I shift enough so our lips connect, and the immediate heat from his kiss shoots a jolt of pleasure to my core. All the light and joy contained in Sheldon Soleskin pours out of his mouth and into mine. And then, to make matters worse, he brings his hand to my chest. My heart thuds so hard. I hope he feels it. He must. His hand, tender but firm, moves over my chest and falls to my stomach. My immediate reaction is to suck it in, but the sad fact is that's not possible.

"Theo, you are so freakin' hot."

And that makes me laugh.

He pulls back, and his eyebrows shift down.

"What? You are."

His hands now circle my stomach in a figure eight motion. He lifts my T-shirt up, and his palms, slightly damp, get lost in the motion over my stretched belly.

"That day we met, in the basement, when you were on the ladder and reached for the chairs, your shirt lifted up and your body, so fuzzy and soft and damn ..." Tipping back in, his mouth finds mine. More assertive, his tongue pokes at my lips, I let him in, and the fucker bites my lower lip.

"Ow."

"Sorry. Too much?"

I pull back and pause.

The urge to grab him and bite him back rushes over me, but I don't. Not yet.

"Can I just … watch you? Please?" I ask.

He stares at me with that sweet as honey face, and I start counting freckles. "I mean, I'm all worked up. From you," he says, and I glance down and see, yup, his navy briefs are still stretched to the max and a flush creeps across my face. He's hard. So fucking hard. With me.

"I don't know, Theo. Are you sure?" he asks.

"Fuck yes."

And for all that's good and mighty, never breaking eye contact, Sheldon Soleskin slides his underwear off, tossing his briefs to the ground like yesterday's news.

"Just watch. You don't have to do a thing."

My eyes go wide because he's fucking beautiful. His flawless skin is completely hairless except for the patch of bright red fuzz above his cock, which shoots straight up and seems to taunt me. And lord help me, I want him. Every inch. But for now, watching him will suffice. I take a deep breath and lean back against my pillows.

Sheldon scootches to the bottom of the bed, leans on one hand, and begins stroking himself. My eyes, glued to his body, scan him up and down. I can't commit to one spot, so I continue studying him. My heart races. I can feel it chugging. Thumping like a damn bass drum. How is this happening? Here. Now. With me. If I had a dictionary and looked up "perfection," it would be Sheldon Soleskin, in his black T-shirt, jerking off on my bed.

Fingers wrapped around his scorching cock, he tilts his head back, and his neck stares at me. His tiny Adam's apple poking out, I want to wrap my fingers around it and suck him like a vampire. And then, because he's Sheldon Soleskin, he starts talking. Lower. There's a gravel in his voice I haven't heard before.

"I'm so horny. My dick is throbbing," he says, lifting his head to look at me. Our eyes meet, and a jolt of electricity rushes through my entire body. I can't help the reaction in my boxers. I want to jump across the bed and devour him, but not now. Not yet.

"You like watching me, Theo?"

I nod.

"You like seeing me stroke my hard cock? It's hard because of you. So hard. Mmmh." He rubs his thumb over the tip and points his dick at me. "When you're sweet to me, it drives me wild. You're so damn sexy."

I'm probably supposed to say something here, but what the fuck? Words are a struggle for me under normal circumstances, and there's absolutely nothing "normal" about what's happening.

"Do you want me to take my shirt off?"

Um, sure, why not. There are probably more freckles. Yes. Yeah. Definitely yes. I nod quickly.

He pulls his shirt over his head and throws it at me. Lean, taut muscle stretches over his thin frame, and I'm not sure I've ever seen anything more delicious in my life. Seeing him completely naked, yup, there are definitely more freckles. Fanning out across his porcelain skin, they're everywhere. On his chest. On his shoulders. They're like constellations in the night sky, and I want to study and explore each and every one of them.

I want to smell his shirt, smother my face with his scent, shove it in my mouth. But I simply place it next to me. For a moment, he sits motionless, his hard cock standing straight up, taunting me.

My eyes practically have their own orgasm from examining him this way, and then he asks, "What do you want me to do, Theo? Put on a show for you?"

My blood sizzles, and every inch of skin covering my body feels alive. He's so close. Unhinged. My pulse quickens. There's so much I want to see. To do. But this requires me to speak, and I'm not sure I can. So I glance at Sheldon and then push the unruly curls out of my face.

"Do you want me to keep stroking my cock for you?"

I nod. Sheldon grabs his dick and starts up again. His hands glide up and down the shaft, the tip bright and luscious. Fuckity, fuck, fuck.

"How about my nipples? Do you want me to play with them?"

I nod, and he sticks two fingers in his mouth to wet them and then circles his left nipple. It perks up, and he opens his mouth and moans softly. The quiet noises coming out of him create the most beautiful soundtrack to accompany the show he's putting on. My dick aches against my boxers, and I wonder if it's possible to come from simply watching Sheldon Soleskin's performance.

"You like that, Theo? It feels good. I'm thinking about you. Your hands. So big and strong. All over me. Every inch of me. Would you like that?"

I nod, and I can't help it. My hand hovers over my boxers, rubbing the head of my cock through the thin fabric. The nerves spring to life, my thumb sliding back and forth over the tip, the cotton adding more friction and making my dick hungry. Sheldon doesn't break eye contact when he leans over and spits on his cock. There's something in his eyes I haven't seen before. A rawness. He spits again, and a small grin fans over his lips. With the sudden wetness, his hand speeds up, and slick noises fill the room.

"If you want to take it out, Theo, I'll watch you too. But it's totally up to you. Whatever you want," he says, his dick pointing right at me in his hand. "Do you know how hot you are?"

My lips curl up slightly, and I stifle a laugh. Me? Hot? Whatever. But I'm not arguing with him now. No way. This isn't stopping.

For all that's good and holy, Sheldon leans back and lifts his leg onto the headboard. Still stroking away, he's changing positions, and fuck, fuck, fuck, I'm done for.

"Want to see my ass?"

"Please."

I've never spoken so quickly in my life.

"You do? And you're so polite. I love that."

Sheldon, never taking his right hand off his cock, the tip pink from attention, reaches down with his left hand and grabs his ass cheek, tugging at it. And there it is. His gorgeous, beautiful hole.

Right there. On my bed. Two feet away. If this is how I die, I'll go with a smile on my face.

I have a choice to make. Sit here and watch, my cock desperate for some attention, or do something about it. Once I cross this line, there's no going back. But Sheldon is here. Naked. How much self-control am I expected to exhibit? I undo the single button in the front of my boxers, allowing my dick to pop out. My shirt and boxers are technically still on, my cock, finally free from fabric, throbs, and I'm unable to keep my hands off it.

"Yes, baby, stroke it. Wow, your dick is so thick and gorgeous. Mmmh. I want to watch you stroke it. Nice and slow, not too fast, Theo."

My mouth falls open, but I quickly shut it, not wanting noises to escape. Sheldon on full display makes my heart race. My eyes greedily engulf him, and I try to imagine what it might be like to touch him. Everywhere. To run my hands over every inch of his body. Feel his cock. That ass.

His hand moves from his ass to his mouth, and he sucks on three purple-painted fingertips before returning them and slipping his index finger into his hole. My eyes have adjusted to the low light, and I can perfectly see him finger himself. He's sending me over the edge. The precum on my cock drips, speeding up my own stroking.

"You like that. I'm imagining your fat cock inside me," he says, adding another finger, and fuck.

"Mmmh," slips out of my mouth.

"Are you close? Stroke it. Come for me, Theo. All over, I want to see you shoot everywhere."

Sheldon's words initiate my impending orgasm, and I feel it rising slowly and overtaking me. My chest caves in, and I start to tremble. It's too much, but I can't stop. My body tenses up, and Sheldon stops pleasuring himself and inches toward me.

"I won't touch your dick, but can I kiss you while you come?"

I nod because saying no to Sheldon makes no sense.

His lips find mine, and his tongue enters my mouth. The air from his nose, hot and swift. Kissing Sheldon while I jerk off makes my insides melt like a marshmallow in boiling hot cocoa, and I fear

I may vanish into a puddle. My breath quickens, and he breaks the kiss and nibbles on my lower lip.

"Come for me, Theo. All over, I want it. You."

And that's it. I can't hold back anymore. With a few more strokes, I erupt. I haven't come in weeks, and the buildup shows. Long, thick ribbons cover my hand and shoot up to my belly, drenching my shirt and plastering Sheldon's arm and stomach.

We lie still for a moment. Silent. And then, for all that's holy and sacred, Sheldon takes his left hand and wipes my cum from his arm. He slathers it on his own cock, stroking it as he moves in to kiss me more. I lay there waiting for him to finish, but wishing he doesn't and we stay like this forever.

"You ready for my cum, Theo? You want it?"

He bites my upper lip, and I nod just enough for him to feel it without shaking him loose.

Sheldon's face begins to tremble. It's slight, but the way we're connected, I feel the twitching as he shoots all over my stomach. The warm thick liquid blasts out and covers me, instantly making my skin tingle.

I want to run and grab something for him to clean up because, as usual, I've made a mess of things. Literally, this time.

"I'm sorry," I say.

"Sorry? For what? That was cumtastic."

"Excuse me?"

"Cumtastic. Cum and fantastic. Cumtastic."

Once again, Sheldon's rendered me speechless. He doesn't seem the least bit bothered by the substantial amount of bodily fluids. Our loads, mixed together, create something new. Sticky, salty, and auspicious. That dimple returns when he smiles, and he leans over, and for the first time, his hands land on my face. They're covered in, well, us, but I don't care because he's kissing me. Again. Letting a huge sigh out, I'm not sure what comes next, but having Sheldon right here, his lips on mine, wanting me, of all people, I almost forget to be scared.

NINETEEN

Sheldon

Everyone assumes I'm innocent. Squeaky clean and living my best Mister Rogers life as a first-grade teacher. But the truth is, while anonymous hookups may not be my thing, I enjoy sex. A lot. I simply prefer it with someone I actually know better than from a bathroom stall. The more connected I feel to someone, the more I let go. This morning, with Theo, I was pretty close to full throttle, and I can't figure out why. The man has erected a barrier around himself that rivals the Great Wall of China. But searching for those tiny cracks, trying to lodge a sliver of myself inside his fortress, turns me on.

I grab my phone from the nightstand. It's almost seven, and I need to be at school by seven-thirty. This is a total I-have-to-be-on-the-mainstage-but-I-haven't-even-started-my-makeup moment.

I dart out of bed and quickly remember I'm naked. Scanning the dark room, I can't find my underwear ... right, I popped it off last night. Before popping off myself. Well, time to face the music. The giant, cuddly bear music.

Walking into the living area, Theo stands in the kitchen, facing out the window over the sink, eating more pizza. His shirt rides up just enough for me to get a peek at his belly fuzz. I want to lick it until he begs me to stop. Not now, Sheldon. I need to find my underwear. Exhaling, I center myself. Theo's safe. Eating. If I want to avoid a walk of shame, I need to get dressed and jet home before school.

I turn to head back into the bedroom to search for my underwear, but Theo's voice interrupts as I hunt for my skivvies.

"No school."

"Words? From Theo? Without being prompted? Has Santa come early?"

"I'm Jewish. Santa skips me."

"I know. You're a big tasty kosher bear."

He stifles a laugh, and pleasure washes over me, knowing I can elicit even a little joy from him.

"You're naked."

"Yes, I realize that. I can't find my underwear, and I'm freezing. Did you hide it?"

"Not on purpose."

And Theo winks at me, sending a flush over my naked body.

"Did it snow much?" I ask.

"Come look."

Theo nods toward the window over the sink. Abandoning the need for my briefs, I move closer to him. His eyes are glued to the floor, and I quickly realize he's staring at my feet. As I approach, they travel up until our eyes meet. I brush past him and lean over the sink. My peering out the window gives him a clear view of my ass.

"We got walloped."

"No school."

"Yeah, you said. So, what are we doing today?"

I turn to face him, keeping my distance.

"We? Don't you want to go home?"

"Not really." I move a few inches closer. "My car is buried. There's no rush. Unless you want me to leave," I say, quickly patting his arm. "I need to text my sister. And Kent. He'll be worried about you."

Theo gives me a dazed look and opens his mouth but quickly closes it.

"Yes, Theo, I want to hang out with you. That was, well, a lot of fun this morning. Or whatever time it was. Like, the most fun I've had in a long time. Was it fun for you, Theo?"

I reach over and take his hand, gently tickling his fingers with mine.

"Yeah," he says, once again lowering his gaze.

"Good. That makes me happy. You're a sweet guy, Theo. Truly."

"Can I ask you something?" he says, eyes on the floor. He pulls his hand away and walks to the couch. Needing to find some kind of warmth, I follow. "Why are you being so nice to me?"

I sit next to him and snuggle up close, attempting to both comfort him and pilfer some of his body heat.

"I think the better question is, why don't you think you deserve someone being nice to you?"

He ducks his chin, and with the quietest voice I've heard from him says, "I had someone."

"Someone?"

"Overseas."

"Christian?"

He laughs, and the loudness overtaking the quiet space of our soft tones startles me.

"Fuck no. Christian is straight. Pin straight. He's like a brother." He stares down at his hands and says, "Ricky. His name was Ricky."

"Oh." I take his hand, and the warmth immediately makes my shoulders drop. "What happened?"

He shakes his head slowly. A small sob escapes his mouth.

"Oh, baby."

I crawl into Theo's lap and tuck a loose curl behind his ear before wrapping my arm around his neck.

"I've got you, Theo."

After we sit silently for a few minutes, he takes a deep breath and says, "I'm hungry."

"You know what? Me too. Ravenous, actually." My belly growls at the idea of food.

"Was that you?"

"It was. My stomach is feeling feisty."

"Sit here." He heads into the kitchen. "I'll make us something."

He's not ready to talk about Ricky, but I'm patient. If I can wait for Hollywood to release a quality queer rom-com, I can wait for Theo. I take his cue and change the subject.

"I'm not the biggest pizza-for-breakfast fan. Do you have anything else? Cereal or toast?"

I wrap myself in a super-sized knit blanket, lie on the sofa, and call Kent.

"Sheldon! I was worried about you boys."

I look over at Theo. He's cracking eggs, whisking, pouring, making a huge mess, but there's such an intensity to his movement. His limp almost disappears as he walks from one end of the kitchen to the other in constant motion.

"Theo's fine. He's making me breakfast."

"You're still there?"

My ears burn knowing I've just accidentally spilled a huge pitcher of tea to my new boss.

"His friend asked me to stay. It's fine. I'm on the couch," I say, covering my naked legs with the blanket.

"Ah, well, there's no school."

"I heard. And saw."

"Are you okay there? Theo's a great guy, but, well, he can be a bit of a ..."

"Beast? Yes, I'm fully aware. He's being a complete gentleman."

"All right then. Well, enjoy your day. Stay safe, and I'll see you both Monday."

The most incredible aroma assaults my nostrils and my stomach grumbles like Santa starving for milk and cookies. Walking over to the kitchen, I see Theo has made the most elaborate, gorgeous breakfast.

"Ready to eat?" he asks, my blanket now acting as a robe. He's made a spread fit for a king. Or a queen. Plates of scrambled eggs, waffles, fresh-cut melon, strawberries, and condiments and sauces I don't even recognize greet me.

"Theo. You really can cook."

"It's nothing."

"Um, sir, this is most definitely something. What other tricks are up your sleeve?" I ask, crawling my fingers up his arm.

"Dig in," he says, handing me a plate.

After loading up with a little bit of everything and pouring maple syrup on my waffle, I spot what appears to be butter, except it almost resembles a golden mousse or pudding, so I ask, "What's that?"

"Whipped butter."

"You whipped butter?"

"Yes, Sheldon. I whipped butter. With orange zest. Try it."

"Theo, you are full of surprises. Have you ever thought about being a chef? C'mere." I tug on his shirt, cueing him to lean down. I plant a soft kiss on his cheek and whisper, "Thank you, baby."

"Baby," he says in a low, almost inaudible voice.

I'm unable to decipher from his tone whether he likes this term of endearment or not.

"Is it okay if I call you that sometimes? You know, it's good practice for when we're around other people. Boyfriends always have cute little nicknames for each other."

"I guess."

"Would you like a nickname for me?"

He shrugs.

"Well, you think about it. It's up to you. If you need some suggestions, let me know."

"Eat."

"Okay, okay, I'm eating."

With no table, we take our packed plates over to the couch and settle in to eat. Theo's food not only looks amazing but tastes like something you'd get at a gourmet brunch. The orange butter on my waffle creates the perfect mix of creaminess, citrus, sweetness, and crispness.

"Theo, this is incredible," I say as I chew. "Having you for a fake boyfriend will do wonders for my mouth!"

I laugh at the unintended innuendo, and Theo's ears turn pink. He shoves a forkful of eggs into his mouth and darts his eyes away from my face.

"You know, you're a really good kisser."

He shrugs.

"Who have you been kissing, Theo Berenson?"

"Just you."

His eyes stay on his plate.

"Theo, with a handsome face like yours, I know you've kissed other people."

"Only Ricky."

He shifts, and I know I'm treading on thin ice. He looks down, his chest expanding. Using the same strategies I utilize with apprehensive students, I ask questions to try and pull him along.

"Did you meet in the Army?"

Theo doesn't speak, and I worry I've upset him. Again. Putting my hand on his forearm, I gently squeeze the tight muscle with my thumb and rub my fingers around the light hair on his arm.

"Baby. It's okay. It's just me. We don't have to talk about it."

Without looking up, he softly says, "I'll tell you."

"I'm right here." I put my plate down.

"When I enlisted, I knew there was a really high chance of being deployed. The war was raging, and joining meant your ass would be on a plane to the Middle East. I kept to myself during basic training. Only spoke when spoken to. I was cordial. Don't Ask, Don't Tell was about to be repealed, but the Army is a petri dish of toxic masculinity. I wasn't trying to make my life harder."

I take his hand and begin massaging the center of his palm with my thumb. I don't know what else to do to soothe him, and this feels like the bare minimum.

"They crammed us on a plane like sardines. It was definitely not first class. Fuck, it wasn't even coach. The whole plane reeked of wood and musk and, well, locker-room sweat. We sat three across on both sides. You just filed in and sat. I got a middle seat. Me. In a middle seat. What a joke. I watched the window because I thought looking out would calm my nerves, but the cards weren't in my favor. Except they were," he says, the hint of a smile sprouting on his face. "When I sank down and saw the boy in the window seat … He wasn't really a boy, but he had such a baby face, looking back at me with eyes that were more scared than my own."

"And that was Ricky?"

He nods softly.

"He was barely twenty, but his baby face made him look more like sixteen. Over the almost twenty-four-hour flight, we talked. By the time we stepped onto foreign soil, I knew Ricky was gay. I also knew he needed protection. Maybe it was being dumped into a warzone. Or how he looked at me. I told him I'd keep an eye on him. And I did. Right up until the end."

His voice breaks. I can feel the tension in his body. His shoulders hunch forward, and he's not looked up at me the entire time, but there is wetness on his cheeks. My heart breaks for him. I remove my hand from his and gently lift his chin, forcing our eyes to meet.

"Why don't we stop? At least for now."

He slowly nods, my hand still under his chin. I wipe a tear away with my thumb, wishing it was as easy to erase his pain.

"Come here," I say, pulling him closer, "I can only imagine how hard it is to talk about this. But you know what? When you talk about him, I can hear how much you love him."

"I really did. Do. I mean, do."

I lean over and give Theo a tender kiss at the corner of his mouth. He lets out a rumpled sigh and leans forward, places his plate on the coffee table, and buries his head in the spot where my neck and shoulders meet. I curl my arms around his torso and do everything in my power to wrap him in my arms and hold him close. This isn't practicing. This isn't fake. This man, in my arms, might be the most real I've ever felt. Without words, I try to let him know I've got him.

TWENTY

Theo

Cleaning up, Sheldon insists on washing, so I dry. Between yesterday, early this morning—um, whatever that was—and talking about Ricky, my eyes feel heavy, and my body's not far behind.

"I need to lie down."

"Okay. I'm going to call my sister. I'll only be a minute, and then I'll join you. Sound good?"

His hazel eyes, currently a goldish hue, peer at me deeply, and the contents of my stomach get a kick. But my body can't meet the request. Not now.

"Sheldon, I'm tired."

"Me too."

I nod, pat his shoulder, and return to bed. Crawling under the covers, I reach for my phone before closing my eyes. A message awaits.

> Christian: You OK?

> Theo: I'm OK.

> Christian: I was worried.

143

Theo: I'm sorry for worrying you.

Christian: It's what we do. Sheldon seems cool.

Theo: He's all right.

Christian: He sounded cute.

Theo: What do you know about cute?

Christian: I know cute. Gotta run. Anna's ragging me.

Theo: OK. Chat later.

Returning my phone to the bedside table, I roll over and stare outside, watching the snow continue to blanket the giant oak near my bedroom window. I've never really had a boyfriend, so what the fuck do I know? But this whole pretend schtick with Sheldon makes my chest feel like a rubber band being pulled taut. Maybe I'm over-thinking it. But how he kissed me. How he looked at me last night on my bed. My dick couldn't deny the temptation of Sheldon Sole-skin. And after, he clung to me in bed as if his life depended on it.

Even from the next room, I can make out most of Sheldon's conversation with his sister. Because even his whisper really isn't anything like a whisper.

"I think so. He seems to be ... No, no, we're only practicing. For the wedding. Of course I want his parents to adore me ... He's actually a sweet guy ... Naomi, I know, I know, I will ... don't worry ... I am ... Yeah, this afternoon. If something changes, I'll text you. Okay, give Janice a smooch for me ... I know, just pick her up and do it. And tell her I love her ... Yes, I love you too."

Only practicing. Of course we are.

His feet move closer, and I roll over and close my eyes. The covers shuffle, and there's some hesitant movement. And he's next to me. The heat of his naked body inches from mine. Oy.

"Baby?"

I keep my mouth still, and his arm slowly wraps around me,

barely reaching over my torso. He smashes his entire body against me and slowly moves his arm up and down mine. His neck burrows into my back, and his breath, close and sweet, somehow thaws my popsicle heart. The little bugger is actually trying to be the big spoon.

"I got you," he whispers and softly kisses the back of my neck.

I exhale gently and close my eyes. Right now, I succumb to whatever spell Sheldon Soleskin casts, letting his warmth and tenderness lull me to sleep.

I wake up and am completely trapped. My body begins to seize. I remind myself to take air in. Forcing a deep breath, I slowly get my bearings. The world comes into focus. Sheldon's limbs, all four of them, are wrapped around me. He's taking cuddling to another level, and even though part of me wants to shove him off, he's so fucking adorable. He's like a tiny baby bear clinging to its mother for dear life as she lumbers through the woods. Except I'm the mama bear.

His eyes are closed. He has freckles dusted across his cheeks. My fingers twitch. I want to touch them. Start my inventory. I don't want to disturb him, but my bladder has other ideas. I lean over and give him a light kiss on the forehead.

He groans and attempts to plaster his body even closer to mine.

"Sheldon? I need to pee."

Gradually, his arms begin to loosen their grip, and he rolls off me. The moment contact breaks, I miss the small furnace of his body on mine.

"I'll be back."

As I prop myself up, he murmurs, "Okay, Terminator."

It takes a second to register his joke, but the corners of my lips turn up as I head to the bathroom.

At the sink, washing my hands, I glimpse myself in the mirror. My head looks like a potato. My mother always tells me to cut my hair. "You were so handsome with that short army buzz, Teddy.

Don't you want boys to see your sweet face?" But when I look at myself, I see nothing anyone might find sweet.

When I return, Sheldon is curled into a ball. He's so fucking precious. The urge to scoop him up and carry him around in my pocket sweeps over me. When I slide back into bed, because he's facing away from me, his ass greets me, and fuckity, fuck, fuck. I need to ask Abba if there's a prayer to resist temptations because Sheldon's smooth, creamy body cries out for attention. Doing my best not to disturb him, I scoot myself underneath the covers, keeping a few inches between us.

"Chilly. Cuddle. Practice cuddle," he murmurs, sounding half asleep.

"It's past lunchtime."

This newsflash causes Sheldon to turn over, pop open his eyes and say, "Are you hungry?" I cock my head and raise an eyebrow. "Noted."

"Did you really want to stay in bed all day?"

"Maybe," he purrs, sliding closer, his face resting on my pillow. His breath tickles my ear.

"Do we really need this much practice?"

"Maybe."

"Okay. C'mere," I say, pulling him next to me.

He plasters himself to my side, and we stay like that until we drift off.

When I wake up, Sheldon's not in bed, but I hear him in the living room. The guy really cannot whisper. That is, his "whisper" can be heard through doors and walls.

"Yes, sir. Kent, sorry. I will. Take care."

I can hear his footsteps getting closer, and then he's next to me, clinging on for dear life.

"Everything okay?"

"You're up," he says. "I wanted to check in with Kent again. He was really worried about you. He's a good guy."

"He is. Always has been. You know, he's Jewish. He worries a little too much. We all do. It's a Jewish thing."

146

"Well, I think it's sweet. And what are you so worried about?" he asks, poking my chest.

"Pretty much everything."

He doesn't reply but looks at me, puppy dog eyes in full effect. He squeezes me even tighter, and my stomach replies with a loud growl.

"Let's get some food. All this snuggling makes me hungry, too."

He scoots out of bed and bends over to pull his underwear on, and that ass …

That *ass*.

I'm doomed.

TWENTY-ONE

Sheldon

We huddle on Theo's sofa, nibbling the gorgeous Mediterranean spread he whipped up.

"Opa! This baba ghanoush is incredible."

"I smoke the eggplant. It's a game changer."

"You really never thought about being a chef?"

He pulls his lips in, and I'm suddenly worried I've said or done something to upset him. I know I can be too much for many, and Theo, for all his brute size, clearly is a delicate soul.

"What is it?" I ask him.

"Earlier, when you were on the phone with your sister, you said something about her kissing Janice."

"She doesn't like to do it. Hates it, actually. She and Janice have a very love-hate dynamic." Theo moves his head, and his hair swoops down to cover his eyes. I reach over and brush it aside. "Technically, Janice is *our* cat. Though when Naomi brought Janice home two summers ago, she simply texted, 'Little brother, I have a surprise.' And I hate surprises that don't end with candy or sex."

"Noted."

"Naomi popped out two minutes before me, and she'll never let me forget it. What she jokingly refers to as the best two minutes of her life. She's only teasing. Mostly. We adore each other beyond measure. She knows me better than anyone. She knew I'd melt when the tiny kitten's soft fur touched my hands and those bright eyes blinked up at me."

"You do seem like a sucker for cuteness."

"Why do you think I like you, Theo?"

His ears burn pink, but he doesn't turn away or avoid my eyes, and I reach over and rub his forearm.

"That's sweet. About Janice."

"Hey, creatures adore me. Small and big," I say, rubbing his knee and glancing around his rather barren apartment. "You know Hanukah starts next week, and you have literally no decorations up."

"We don't decorate for Hanukah. Here's a menorah. Done."

"Well, that's no fun. Plus, we need some Christmas decorations."

"For what?"

"If your parents are going to believe our fake interfaith fantasy, their son would at least have some mistletoe up for his boyfriend, right?"

"I guess."

"It will help our believability."

He rolls his eyes, and my face cracks with a huge grin at his sassiness.

"What? It's true. We can be the gay Ashton and Mila."

"Who?"

"Ashton Kutcher and Mila Kunis. She's Jewish. He's not."

"I don't know who either of those people are."

"Oh, Theo. I have my work cut out for me. Anyway, we're stuck here for the time being. What do you have for crafting?"

Another eye roll. This time he ends with a slight head dip, adding drama, and my chest puffs with pride.

"I'm going to tickle you if you don't stop being so darn cute."

I make a move toward Theo's side. When my fingers get close to his gorgeous belly, I pause and then stop, not sure if tickling would send him off the deep end or not.

"I don't craft."

"Well, lucky for you, I'm a first-grade teacher. We're about to have a massive Martha Stewart moment up in here."

We stand at the pantry. A converted closet, Theo's pantry mirrors him. Large, intense, packed, and stacked. There appears to be some sort of organization, although I'm not sure about the methodology. Scanning the shelves, I search for a few items we can use.

"Let's see … aluminum foil, these colored paper napkins, cupcake liners, this … um, what is this?"

"Parchment paper."

"Perfect. Parchment Paper. Where's your recycling?"

"Here," he says, opening a cabinet holding a large bin.

"Grab any cardboard," I instruct. "'Now we need scissors, tape, markers, glue if you have it …'"

"I might have superglue."

"We'll make it work."

He returns from his bedroom with the supplies, and we huddle around his counter.

"I want your parents to walk in here for the first-night dinner and be blown away. It will earn me big points."

"We're not really together. You don't need to earn points with them."

"I want them to like me, for you. Even for one night."

I trace two large menorahs on the parchment paper with a black marker and hand him one to cut while I handle the other. They'll be our templates to craft them out of cardboard, blue and white napkins, and foil.

"What about your parents?"

Theo's question catches me off guard. My hand tenses, straining the scissors. They become stiff and achy. I take a deep breath.

"What about them? I told you. We don't talk."

"But why? You're great. I don't get it."

I continue cutting, hoping to get lost in the process as I talk.

"You think I'm great?" I say, leaning over, my lips inches from Theo's stubbly face.

"My parents are gonna kvell when they meet you. Seriously."

"Kvell?"

"Eat you up. Pinch your cheeks. Want to kiss you."

"Oh. Well, they can kvell away."

"So your parents are … assholes?"

"Pretty much. When I was about six, maybe seven, Naomi got a bottle of pale-pink nail polish as a favor at a friend's birthday party. The color was so pretty on her fingers. I wanted mine painted like hers so badly. One afternoon, in our room, she indulged me. I remember loving the feeling of cool liquid gliding over my nails as the intoxicating sweet, pungent smell overtook our room. It literally never occurred to me that there was anything wrong with what we were doing. After we were finished painting each other's nails, we danced around our small room, blasting the radio and waving our arms dramatically to try and get the slick polish to dry quickly." I flail my arms, hoping he can envision it. "When my mother came in to ask us to turn the music down, she took one look at me, curled her lip, and snarled at me with cold, flat eyes. She grabbed my wrist tightly and barked, 'We have to get this off before your father gets home.' That was the moment I knew it wasn't okay to be me."

I've told that story many times, and it never gets easier. I didn't do anything to elicit that reaction. That was the beginning of being shunned for being myself. My heart aches from missing my parents sometimes, but I know this is how it needs to be.

I sigh and look at the ceiling.

Theo reaches over and takes my free hand. His eyes glisten, and he blinks a few times before he says, "I'm so sorry, Sheldon."

"Thanks. I mean, it stinks, but really, it's for the best. I have to take care of myself. And Naomi. And Janice. That's my family now."

He gingerly squeezes my hand. "I love your nails," he says, rubbing the smooth purple polish between his fingers. "Fair warning: I'm pretty sure my mother will want to adopt you."

"Really?"

"Oh yeah. Sylvia Berenson will try to cram you in her purse and take you home. She can be a smidge … overbearing at times, but it all comes from a place of love."

"You're lucky."

He drops my hand and says, "I guess."

"Come on, let's start taping these menorahs together so we can decorate. Your apartment is going to be the most amazing Chrismukkah showplace, and the Berensons are going to adore it. And me."

I poke his chest and grab the crafting supplies.

TWENTY-TWO

Theo

Two menorahs, four giant dreidels, and too many tiny Star of David snowflakes later, my halls are completely decked. Sheldon really knows how to make something beautiful out of crap. Sugar to add sparkle to the snowflakes? I'd never have thought of that. He promises to bring some mistletoe over next week. For practice kissing.

All this pretend affection. The kissing. The hand-holding. The getting off together. It's starting to fuck with my head. I probably should say something to him about it. But I also don't want it to stop. Because having Sheldon as my fake boyfriend, even for a few weeks, is better than the alternative.

He's on the couch now, doing this thing where he sits with his legs underneath him like he's almost trying to make himself smaller, which seems impossible. Maybe he's cold. Maybe I could warm him up.

"Any idea when the snow's going to let up? I mean, I have no clean clothes here."

He laughs, and his dimple beckons. I want to grab him and kiss all the freckles that dot the landscape of his face. For practice.

"It's slowing down. I'll head out in a bit and clean your car off."

"Theo, you are such a gentleman. You know that?"

He carefully crawls into my lap, situating himself so our faces are inches apart.

"How did you get so damn sweet?"

"Me?"

"Yes, you."

I shrug because in my entire life, I don't know if anyone besides my mother has called me sweet. And I'm pretty sure she was projecting.

"Do you like all this practicing?" he asks.

I don't like it. I love it. I nod and rest my forehead on his.

"Me too."

He wraps his arms around me and brushes his lips to mine.

"This okay?"

Instead of nodding, I kiss him. Not pretending. Not practicing. But with my heart. I close my eyes and imagine a world where someone as magnificent as Sheldon Soleskin might actually like a lug like me. And I wonder if he feels it when my mouth falls on his. My breath a little deeper. I gather him up so easily, and he's moved one hand from my back to my head. He tangles his fingers in my shaggy waves, and when he presses his tongue to my lips, my soul soars.

Sheldon pulls himself up, and my hands move to cup his ass. Fuck. I don't want this to get out of hand, but my fingers can't stop. Each cheek, the most precious gift in my palms. This sure doesn't feel fake.

Breaking the kiss, Sheldon pulls back and whispers, "Hey, baby."

"Hey."

"I should take a shower. I'll wear my dirty clothes. But I'm a mess and can't go home like this."

My heart gallops. I want to beg him. Please. Don't go. Stay here. Stay in my arms. Hold me. Kiss me. Tell me I'm sweet. Please. But instead, I mutter, "Okay."

In the bathroom, I give Sheldon a clean towel. Before I leave, he flings his briefs off and hops into the steamy shower. One last glimpse at the perfection of his body. I want to rip my T-shirt and boxers off and jump in there with him. Wash his body for him. Soap him up. Scrub every inch of him. Kiss him the entire time. But that's not me. That's not us. So, I get dressed, put my winter gear on, and head outside.

Snow still falls but it's slowed considerably. My landlord shoveled the four steps and walkway, but Sheldon's car looks like an avalanche fell on it. Between the actual snow and the push-off from the plows, he got hammered hard. Fuck. Now I'm thinking about his ass again.

Holding the shovel we store in the entryway for this purpose, I pop my earbuds in, fire up my Queen playlist and get to it. "I Want to Break Free" begins, and the orchestra plays me to Sheldon's car. When the drums and guitar kick in, I'm fully invested—hacking at the snow around the base, throwing it as far as I can onto the front yard. Freddie sings about falling in love and knowing it's real, and god knows this isn't good. This isn't love. This isn't even real. This is fake. This is practice. Complete mishigas. Sheldon needs a date for his ex's wedding. I need to convince my parents I don't need a fucking yenta. That's all we're doing.

But he was naked. And he kissed me. On the lips. And he got off in front of me. I may have never had a boyfriend outside a war zone, but I felt something. Something in my stomach. And not indigestion or heartburn. Fireworks. But silent. Safe.

When the song ends, and the opening piano chords of "We Are the Champions" overtake my ears, my breath catches. I steady myself on the shovel and shut my eyes. Christian's raspy yell cuts through the warm air of the barracks, "Yes! This is my jam. Crank it up!"

Harris increases the volume on our cheap boombox, static and feedback screeching through the air but nobody cares.

"Queen. Freddie. Fuck yes!" Harris jumps on the table meant for meals, but in this moment it transforms into a stage. He grabs Doyle's hand and yanks him up, and the two of them sing. Loudly. Horribly. But nobody cares.

"Get up here, Pooter!" Doyle shouts, and poor Pooter, all limbs and bones, scurries up. His ears burn red, and his chin dips, the enthusiasm of the other guys not sparking him.

"God, I love Queen," Ricky whispers. We play rummy on the freezing ground, only a small tarp shielding us, waiting our turn to cover rounds, when the magic of Freddie triggers the impromptu sing-along.

"Yeah? Well, go on then," I say, picking myself up and yanking his arm. It's beyond cold. Even bundled in our gear, our breath can be seen when we talk, and there's no heat. No hot water. No comfort.

"Get up here, Joven," Christian shouts, taking Ricky's gloved hand from mine and tugging him up.

The four of them clap and stomp to the music, almost drowning out Freddie and his mates with their howling. I watch Christian—so carefree and fearless—lead them, offering a small piece of his courage and bravado. And Ricky. God, Ricky. Watching him get pulled into the magic of the music, the moment, my eyes glisten a little because since we met on the plane six months ago, we've grown close. His precious face, the sweetest punim I've ever seen. Something about him, he glows.

Christian knows. He caught us necking outside the latrine in the middle of the night.

"Dude, I couldn't give a rat's ass," was all he said.

"Theo. Hello? Theo?"

That's not right. My brow furrows. That voice doesn't belong here.

I blink my eyes open, and confusion overwhelms me. Sheldon's there, looking about as confused as I feel. Fuck. How long was he standing in front of me, watching me zone out? I pop my earbuds out and hold them up, "Sorry, the music," I say and shove them into my coat pocket.

"You okay?"

I lift my chin and nod.

"You didn't have to clean my car off for me. That was kind of you."

I shrug, Ricky's ghost still swirling shadows in my head.

"I'm going to get going. Walker's on call. Naomi's been alone this entire storm, and Janice is starting to revolt."

"Okay."

"You going to be okay on your own?"

Please don't go. Please stay. Please come back upstairs and take off your clothes and get under the covers with me. Let me hold you. Hold me. Or attempt to. But don't drive away and leave me. I nod. "Yeah, I'm fine."

"Hanukah starts in"—he puts his fingers up and counts—"six days! Yikes. When do your parents arrive?"

"Wednesday. They stay here." I nod at my building.

"But you only have one bed."

"Yeah, I take the couch. It's all good."

He wrinkles his sweet brow and then says, "We should probably see each other this weekend. I mean, if that's not too much for you. But we've got to plan the dinner. I know, I know, you've probably got a whole menu planned, but I should know about it. And I want there to be some Sheldon Soleskin flavor. It will make us more believable. Maybe I can come back over tomorrow night? Or, better yet, why don't you come over to my place?"

"Um, sure."

"Awesome. I'll text you tomorrow morning."

Sheldon opens the door and, before getting in, grabs my coat and tugs me toward him.

"See you tomorrow," he says with a wink and, standing in the middle of the street, gives me a kiss right on the lips.

Dear Lord, creator of the universe, thank you.

TWENTY-THREE

Sheldon

"Kitty girl!" I shout as Janice leaps into my arms, purring, and immediately starts head-butting my chin.

"Nice to see you too," Naomi says from the couch, snuggled under a large purple and pink fleece blanket.

Cradled like a baby, Janice flips her head, chin up, and I pepper her with tiny kisses.

"I missed you too, baby girl."

"Yeah, she was not amused you were gone. She stayed by the door most of the night waiting for you. I attempted to give her some attention, but she swatted at me."

"She's sensitive."

"She's nasty. Except to you, of course."

I join Naomi on the couch and pull some of her blanket over my lap before setting Janice down. Naomi and I melt into each other, and I wonder if all twins do this. Phantom memories of the womb, being so close, our bodies once in constant contact.

"How was work?" I ask.

"The usual. I'm training a new girl, and she couldn't find a patient's vein. Like at all. The poor guy looked like a pin cushion. I was calm and patient and deserved a medal. Or cake. It was a bitch getting home, but it only took me about ten minutes longer than usual, so I'm taking that as a win."

"Oh good. Also, now, I want cake. What have you been doing stuck inside? You didn't happen to bake a cake?"

"You mean besides getting the constant stink eye from Janice? Catching up on sleep while Netflix glows in the background. If I had the ingredients and skills, we'd be swimming in baked goods. We really should keep a few boxed mixes stocked for emergencies. But more importantly, how is your custodian?"

"Theo. His name is Theo. And he's coming over tomorrow night."

"Oh, is he? What time? I'll be home by four. Walker is babysitting his nephews. I promised I'd go over around seven to help."

"We didn't decide on a time yet, but I think I'll suggest seven."

"Bean, come on. I want to spend some time with you and your new man."

"He's not my man. We're just helping each other out. His parents arrive Wednesday for Hanukah, and Timothy's wedding is the following weekend. We don't have time to dillydally."

She dips her chin and cocks her head. I know my sister better than anyone in the world, and I know her you're-full-of-shit look.

"So, all this practicing is working out for you?"

"Yes, we're getting to know each other. He's actually a sweet guy. Did you know he can cook? Like not heating up frozen food or making ramen ... he whipped butter for me. With orange zest. It was something else."

"Sounds like the butter might not be the only thing whipped."

"Hush. It's not like that. We have to convince his parents, Timothy, and all his guests. The only way to accomplish that is to go in hard."

"Go in hard? Exactly what happened last night?"

"A lady never kisses and tells."

She slams a throw pillow at me, sending poor Janice fleeing for cover. I grab her legs under the blanket and yank her down, lie on top of her, and tickle her sides. We both laugh, and tears dot the corners of my eyes as we tussle.

Lying in bed, I stare out the window at the building next to ours, close enough that if I were a smidge taller than an elf, I could reach out and touch it. Theo could grab the neighbor's window, open it, and jump in for a cocktail. I thought Theo would be a tough nut to crack, but maybe my charms are softening him.

When I was little, one of my mother's nicknames for my father was Grouchy because, well, he had a propensity toward testiness. Apparently, being superconservative and married to an ultracontrolling woman will do that to you. Imagine that? Not knowing any better, I heard him referred to as Grouchy so often that I started calling him "Grouchy" long before anything resembling "Dad" came into my lexicon.

"Not Grouchy, Daddy, say Daddy," my mother would implore.

But my dad never minded. He actually smiled when I shouted "Grouchy!" running after him as he plucked every last weed from the backyard. My mother was not amused that her attempt at jibing him was stolen by me and transformed into a term of endearment. And I think he enjoyed it. Maybe even loved it.

I don't know why my father had a soft spot in his heart for me when I was little. What causes a hardnose meanie to take a shine to one person over another? My mother resented our bond immediately. It caused a wedge in our already fractured relationship. Naomi, ever my protector, actually connected with Dad over his affection for me. In hindsight, I think the three of us were simply trying to survive my mother. Naomi and I escaped, but Dad wasn't as fortunate.

Exhaustion creeps in, and my eyes struggle to stay open. Before turning my light out, I shoot Theo a quick text.

> Sheldon: About to go to sleep. Hope the rest of your day was OK. Why don't you come over at six tomorrow?

That will give Naomi a little time without scaring the poor man silly. There's no reply, so I place my phone on the nightstand next to my rosemary candle and take some deep breaths, hoping the sweet smell will help me get some sound sleep. Even with Janice purring softly beside me, my double bed feels extremely large and cold.

Janice lays on my chest, slowly making biscuits. Her nails, needing a trim, poke through the sheet, and if I don't stop her soon, she'll leave a mark.

"Come here, sweet girl."

I grab her and plop her down next to me, belly up, and begin rubbing.

"My friend Theo is coming over tonight. Are you going to be a good girl and be sweet to him?"

Janice swings her softball head around and bites my hand. Answer received.

"Well, he's nice. Mostly. And I like him, so maybe try to give him the benefit of the doubt." Janice squints her eyes at me. "Well, at least don't attack him, okay?"

She begins gnawing on my knuckles.

Removing my hand from her jaw, I grab my phone. Theo replied at three fifteen. Yikes.

> Theo: OK. Should I bring anything?
>
> Sheldon: Just your handsome face. We'll order something when you get here.
>
> Theo: 👍

Ah, the thumbs-up emoji. The least romantic emoji in existence. It says, "affirmative," but nothing else. I suppose, given his fondness for silence, Theo's limited texting game shouldn't surprise me. The fact of the matter is, it's been less than twenty-four hours since I've seen him, and I kind of miss the guy.

Theo falls into the "it's complicated" category. He's not like most guys I've dated. Not that we're really dating. I know I'm a lot for most people. For someone like Theo, I'm like extra cheese on top of the extra cheese you already ordered. And you happen to be lactose intolerant. The thing is, I'm actually looking forward to seeing him tonight, and I'm not sure if that's prudent.

⚓

"I'll get it!"

When our buzzer rings, I'm still wrapped in a towel from my too-long shower to get every spot on my body sparkly clean. Naomi's voice pierces the bathroom door, and my stomach drops at the thought of Theo alone with her. Whipping off my towel, I spray myself with my jasmine and sandalwood body spritz and sprint to my bedroom to get dressed.

"... so this guy grabbed my ass when I turned around to adjust his heart monitor. I'm thinking, sir, you just had a heart attack. Maybe you should simmer down a bit. But I really do love being a nurse. Most people are so grateful, and I know I'm helping during a stressful time."

Naomi shoots me a wink as I walk into the living room. Theo towers above, well, everything, standing in the entryway with his coat on, rubbing his chin. I wonder if he'll open the door and bolt.

"Theo! Let me take your coat," I say, rushing over to his side.

He begins to remove it, and I help him by peeling it off and hanging it in the small closet near our entrance.

"I'm glad you're here," I whisper, pulling him down to give his cheek a little peck and point above his head. "The mistletoe."

Theo exhales sharply, his breath minty and sweet, blowing my hair as Naomi watches us with curious eyes.

The three of us stand in our small entryway, Theo the much larger side of the triangle we make, and for maybe the first time in recorded history, there's silence in a room occupied by the Soleskin twins.

"So," Naomi says.

"So," I say.

"I brought snacks." Theo lifts a plastic bag, holding it up like a trophy.

"Come." I take his arm and lead him to the kitchen.

Our kitchen, much like Theo's, defines basic. Technically, everything exists if you wanted to cook, which neither of us do. It has big cheapest-appliances-that-barely-function energy. The counters are laminate, while the cabinets are a light "oak" facsimile from the nineteen eighties. We do a lot of heating, reheating, water boiling, microwaving, and grilled cheesing. There's more frozen food and takeout in our refrigerator than would be advised by a nutritionist.

"You didn't have to bring anything, Theo. I told you, just your handsome face. We were going to order dinner."

"Just snacks," he says, placing the bag on the counter.

As he unpacks, I quickly realize Theo hasn't brought chips and salsa. There must be six or seven containers of varying sizes, and I can't help but wonder how much of his day Theo spent making all this.

"Theo, what did you do?"

Naomi wanders over, her stomach prompting her to join us.

"Did you make all this?" she asks.

Theo nods, and for the first time, his lack of speech doesn't bother me. When he nods, his lips curl up the slightest bit, and his eyes sparkle. Unlike me, Theo Berenson doesn't feel the need to fill every silence with sound. He's not being difficult or rude, only carefully choosing the time and words to speak.

"Naomi, he's got magic hands."

I take his hand in mine, rub it gently, and then hold it up for her to inspect.

She raises an eyebrow. "Oh, does he?"

"Hungry?" Theo asks.

"Always," Naomi and I both say in unison.

Theo pauses from his unpacking and gives us a quizzical look.

"We do that," we say again in unison.

"Often," Naomi adds.

"It's a," I begin, and she joins me with, "twin thing."

166

Theo dips his head and smirks, and I'm tickled at how he tries to hide his amusement.

"What did you make?" I ask.

"Well, you asked if I could make Japanese, so ..." He begins uncovering dishes and sauces. "Gyoza, tsukune, and sweet and spicy soy-glazed edamame."

"Whoa," Naomi and I say in unison.

My heart warms thinking about him in his kitchen, orchestrating the ingredients.

Naomi grabs some plates, and we start loading up.

I loop my arm around his and whisper, "Thank you."

Naomi pops a caramel-colored meatball in her mouth and, while still chewing, asks, "What in god's name is this? Because it tastes like heaven exploded in my mouth."

"Tsukune. It's made of chicken. The glaze makes them ..."

"Sinful," she garbles with a full mouth.

"Come, let's sit," I say, motioning to our small kitchen table. We have it pushed up against the wall to save space, but when we have guests, it pulls out to accommodate two or three extra people.

"Okay, Theo, please don't take this the wrong way," Naomi says, and I wince at what might follow, "but how are you not a chef?"

I search Theo's face for a clue about how he takes her question, and he wrinkles his forehead and shrugs. I know I can be a lot. Naomi can be a lot. The two of us together might be too much for poor Theo.

"Theo's great at his job. People think all custodians do is clean, which they do, but it's so much more, especially in a school. I couldn't have survived these last few weeks with Brodie without Theo's help."

"I've thought about it," Theo says.

"What?" I ask.

"Being a chef."

"I mean, I'd be eating at your restaurant. Often," Naomi says.

"But I enjoy my job. Being a custodian. Cooking is a hobby."

Theo does this thing where he pulls up half his mouth into a grin, almost like he's afraid to let a whole grin break free. I wonder if he's uncomfortable with this combination of praise and questioning his current job, so I swoop in.

"Theo's parents arrive Wednesday for the first night of Hanukah. It's going to be my first real Hanukah dinner."

Naomi shoots me her I-know-you're-changing-the-subject-brother stare but, thankfully, doesn't question me.

"What does that entail exactly?" she asks, and we both look to Theo.

"Food. Candles. Prayers. In Hebrew," he says with a shrug.

"And it's just the first night?" she asks.

"First and last. The rest …" Theo shrugs.

"Well, I cannot wait. Plus, I get to win his parents over."

Naomi gives me a smile, and I know exactly what she's thinking. Parents. Our parents.

"Well, speaking of parenting, I have to run to Walker's. He's on uncle duty, and well, if I leave him alone too long, the kids will be covered in chocolate and nacho cheese," she says.

Because he's a gentleman, Theo pops up when Naomi stands, and not wanting to appear rude, I follow.

"Theo. Thanks for the food. And letting me crash for a little. I can see why my brother has been smiling so much lately."

Her teasing tone nips at my heels.

"Anyway, have a wonderful night, and hopefully, I'll see you again soon," she calls from the front door, where she's wrapping herself in a deep burgundy coat that beautifully coordinates with her hair.

Theo nods, and with the click of the door, we're alone. I scan the table. All the gorgeous food he made. Japanese food. Because I mentioned it in passing. Standing at the table, in the wake of Naomi's exit, Theo begins to sit, but I stop him.

"Wait," I say.

TWENTY-FOUR

Theo

Standing in Sheldon's kitchen, with the remnants of the huge spread I spent all day preparing, nervousness creeps in. The fluttering in my stomach makes no fucking sense. We were alone for almost twenty-four hours in my apartment. He was naked for most of that time. We did things. Crap, now I'm thinking about Sheldon naked. Heat flashes on my face, and I'm sure he notices. He has too. But he doesn't say anything. For once, Sheldon is quiet.

He takes a step toward me. My body wants to flee, but I'm up against the wall, and I'd have to push past him, so I stand perfectly still and wait.

"Baby, you did too much," he says, motioning to the table.

I shrug because he's right. I spent the entire day shopping and cooking. But I wanted to make it. For him.

"Can I thank you?"

My eyes squint, and I search his face for clues.

"Look," Sheldon says, pointing to the archway between the kitchen and a small hallway. The cheap, plastic-looking mistletoe once again goads me. "Mistletoe."

"It's fake."

"Yes, but it's still mistletoe. Can I?" He steps closer, and his breath tickles my chin.

"Oh. Okay."

I grab his sweatshirt and tug him close. When his nose nears mine, I close my eyes and wait.

His lips brush mine cautiously, tenderly, almost like he's asking permission. And this tentative Sheldon feels strange and new.

I begin to move my lips to kiss him back, and he wraps his arms around me, pulling himself up onto his toes. God, why does kissing him feel so right? Part of me wants to sweep the food off the table and throw him down and ravage him. Feel him. All of him. This fake dating shit continues to fuck with my head, and maybe we should talk about it. Except Hanukah is Wednesday, and this might actually work. I can't mess it up.

Sheldon breaks the kiss and says, "There. Thank you."

He starts moving plates and containers to the counter, and I help because, well, it's my nature to try and clean messes.

"Go relax on the couch. I'm going to pack this up and be right over."

"Okay," I say and feel my stomach gurgle. The gyoza sauce was spicy, but this is something else. He wants to talk. About us. Fantastic.

Sitting on the couch, I study the entertainment center. The TV sits in the middle, and there are books and knickknacks on the other shelves. A small statue of a cat dressed like a warrior stands guard. Against what? I have no clue. And the photos. Only a few photos of Sheldon and his sister dot the shelves. In every single one, they're together. Smiling. Laughing.

"All set. Your containers will be dry to take home before you leave. And if not, I'll just dry them. Thanks again. For bringing all that deliciousness. You're delicious too, Theo."

He sits next to me. Like right next to me. Even though we have the entire couch. When he leans in a little, I wrap my arm around him and gather him up. Having Sheldon close feels like a warm bath. With bubbles. And a beer.

"Before we talk about this big dinner and what I need to know, can we talk about, well, how this"—he motions between us—"is going? For you."

"Fine," I say.

"Good. And all the … touching and what we did the other night?"

I nod.

"Good. Obviously, I don't know them, but I think your parents are going to believe we're a couple. All this practice, well, practice makes perfect."

Practice.

"Sure."

"And we can keep practicing. If you want."

"I mean, yeah. I guess."

He reaches over and kisses me on the cheek. Then again, closer to my lips. He crawls into my lap, and I pull him closer, wishing I could tuck him inside me forever.

Sheldon's mouth on mine, his tongue in my mouth, holding him, all of his weight on me, the room begins to spin. My skin crackles like dry sand has crusted over it, and I need a breath, so I pull back.

"You okay?"

"Yeah, it's just …"

"What is it? You can tell me."

His eyes. Like giant bright pools of glass. I want to dive in and drown. He blinks his blondish auburn eyelashes at me, and I swallow hard. There's a dull pain in the back of my throat. The need to tell him, to release even a sliver of it, overtakes me, and I blurt out, "Guilty."

"Guilty? About what? Us?"

"Not us."

"Well, what then?"

My chest feels tight. I almost let go of Sheldon to check my heart, make sure it's still there, but I don't dare release him. I've only told this to my parents, and obviously, Christian knows because he was there. But something inside me screams to tell Sheldon.

"Baby, I'm right here. You're safe."

He reaches up and cups my face with his hands. I draw in a deep breath, count to seven, blow it out, and prepare. Closing my eyes, the entire scene flashes in my mind, but I need to say it. All of it.

"Ricky."

Curled up in my lap, Sheldon's weight, even though he's small, grounds me. He rests his head on my chest. I think he knows. Maybe because I've closed my eyes. I can't look at him while I say this. I can't look at anyone.

"My parents were the reason I enlisted in the first place. Having the most liberal parents on the planet, I could do no wrong. It was the only way I could think of to rebel. Nothing I did upset them. You're gay? Let me find you a nice Jewish boy. Don't want to go to college? Awesome! You're voting Republican? I'm sure we can talk this out."

Sheldon perks up and stares at me.

"I never did. But that's how desperate I was to push their buttons."

He snuggles back into my chest. A little hot-water bottle warming my heart.

"I knew joining the Army would get under their skin. And I had no direction. With such freedom, I craved boundaries. Routine. Discipline."

Sheldon rubs his cheek into my chest with tiny circles of affection, and goosebumps fan out over my neck.

"We were clearing trees. Me, Christian, Harris, and Ricky. It was part of the gig. We had to chop down the trees to eliminate insurgent hiding spots. Our sergeant ordered chainsaws for us, but they didn't work, and nobody could figure out why. Seven chainsaws. Not a single one worked. He was livid. But the trees still needed to go. We used hand axes. It was brutal work."

I let out a big sigh, and Sheldon rubs my arm all the way up and down, squeezing a little near my shoulder.

"Trying to lighten the mood, Harris was telling jokes. Cheesy jokes. What did the fish say when he swam into a wall? Damn. The worst. Dad-joke-level material. But when the sun's beating down on your already sunburned neck, and it feels like the desert has migrated inside your mouth, you laugh to keep from crying. We laughed at every silly joke."

A sound falls out of my mouth, remembering. Half laugh. Half sob. Sheldon lifts his head and kisses my neck.

"The tree cover was thick. We spread out enough to cover small areas and stay within earshot of each other. Hacking away at the trees by hand, the blisters, the heat, laughing like childish school-boys, Ricky was about fifteen feet from me. We were playing a little game, trying to see who could fell the next tree first. It wasn't really fair. I clearly outweighed him. But he was all muscle, and he swung at those trees like a man on a mission.

"By that point, we'd been kissing, so much kissing, my lips would tingle just thinking about it. Christian knew, the other guys probably suspected, but even with all their teasing about anything they could find to tease about, they let us be. I'm still grateful for that. Ricky and I positioned ourselves to sneak peeks at each other between swings. It was a silly diversion. The trees, tall and prickly, only gave a modicum of shade. And Ricky had beaten me the last three trees. Each time he'd finish and stand, staring at his watch, fake yawning, taunting me with his beautiful face. I was determined to be victo-rious on the next one. Focused on my hand, the axe, the damn tree, I went to town. Not looking up, not watching over him."

Sheldon turns his face inward, and his lips are on my shirt. My chest. My heart.

"And then it came. Out of nowhere. The sound was like someone pulled the lid off the world. Everything shifted to screams and smoke and dust. Blinded by debris, I knew exactly where he was in relation to me and ran to him. When I found him, he was on the ground. My entire body went numb. I could barely see him through the soot, but the moment I touched him I felt dampness. The rusty smell of blood. My heart trumped my brain, and I, I just picked him up ... I didn't know what to do, who to cry for, where to take him, I knew, I-I knew, I knew ..."

"Oh, Theo."

I'm done. My lips part, but only a small whimper spills out, and even though Sheldon sits in my lap, he's holding me. The tears well up, and when they spill over, showering his head, he simply holds me closer. Tighter.

"I got you, baby."

TWENTY-FIVE

Sheldon

I open my eyes. The sun pokes through my shade, illuminating the gentle giant I'm currently attempting to swaddle. After his confession last night, Theo was in no state to do anything but sleep, so I brought him to my bed, tucked him in, and held him close until gentle wheezes filled my room. Janice was not impressed with this new intruder in her space, but she quickly found a nook next to my pillow and snuggled in for a little warmth.

With all I've dealt with in my life—school bullies, my parents, the constant stress of walking through a world meant for a certain kind of man and being, well, me—nothing I've dealt with compares to Theo's experiences. I know he needed to tell me. Maybe this is why he's so damn grumpy all the time. All I know is I want this beautiful lug of a man to feel safe. Happy. Loved.

Theo stirs under me, rolls over, and nestles his nose near my neck. I take a deep breath, overtaken with emotion, and the lightning bolt realization hits me over the head like a frying pan in an old Saturday morning cartoon. This isn't fake. This isn't practice. Theo and I have something. Or at least we're starting to. Or at least that's how it feels for me.

But then that voice, that bitch of an inner saboteur, creeps in.

You're too much. Too small. Too gay. Too femme. And then the words of my mother. "Nobody will ever love you."

Theo's the opposite of all that. Why on earth would he want me for more than a sham boyfriend to appease his parents? Once he realizes all he has to offer and I help him gain a little confidence, he'll wonder why he even needed to pretend with someone like me.

"Morning …"

Theo opens one eye, and our faces are close enough that his long eyelashes brush my chin.

"Hey, how'd you sleep?"

"Really well. I've got my little teddy." Theo grabs me and pulls me against him.

"Excuse me, if I can't call you Teddy, there's no way you can."

"How about if you keep calling me baby, and I get to call you Teddy? But only until I think of a better name for you."

"Um, okay. Sure."

I worry I can't hide the nervousness in my voice, and my body begins to retract, slowly pushing away and moving to get up. But Theo has other plans. His large paw wraps around my waist and hauls me back.

"Where are you going?"

"I have to pee."

"Oh. Well, come back, okay?" Theo asks. "I want to talk to you about something. And then eat."

Standing at the bathroom sink, staring at myself in the mirror, my stomach feels tight and uncertain. What the hell does Theo want to talk about? The dinner? His parents? How soon we can forget about all this nonsense? Naomi would yell at me for being so worried. And crap, Naomi. I heard her come home late. Once she realizes Theo's here, the jig will be up. I splash some cold water on my face and head to her room.

When we were babies, my mother kept us in a single crib, and once we graduated to beds, we snuck into each other's most nights. Maybe it was being so close for nine months in my mother's belly, or maybe it was my desire to feel close, safe, and I knew, even then, she was my one true protector in this world.

Cracking Naomi's door, I sneak in, crawl under the covers, and snuggle up behind her.

"Naomi?" I whisper.

She lets out a low groan and then proceeds to fart right on me.

"Okay, you're up."

"What?" she mumbles.

"I need to talk something out."

"Now?"

"Yes, now."

"Can't it wait?"

"No, it can't. It's about Theo. Who's in my bed right now."

This gets her attention, and she whips over, facing me.

"He's here?"

"Yes."

"You slept together."

"Yes. Slept."

She cocks her left eyebrow.

"We did more the other night."

She darts up, props her pillow against the headboard, and gets comfortable.

"Bean! I thought this was all a sham. What's going on?"

"I don't know. He was so ... sad, but also hot, and I, I ..."

"Wanted to help," she finishes for me.

"Yeah."

"Do you like him?"

"I don't dislike him."

"Bean."

I sit up so we're facing.

"Maybe."

Naomi reaches over and grabs my nose, twisting it enough until it pinches.

"Okay, I do. But come on. Look at him."

"What?"

"Look at me."

"Sheldon Soleskin, I am your twin sister, your soulmate for life, and I need you to listen to me," she says, moving her hand from my

177

nose to my chin, holding it firmly so we're eye to eye. "You are a gem. A catch. Gorgeous. Inside and out. And I'm not just saying that because we're practically identical. I need you to put aside all your insecurities and understand what a beautiful soul you are. Can you accept for one second the man in your bed might actually like you?"

In one of those extremely rare instances, I don't know what to say. My eyes dart to the mattress, and I take a large breath in, fearful the answer might crush me.

"He likes you, bean. I saw the way he was looking at you last night."

"How?"

"Like he was on a seven-day juice fast and you were a piece of birthday cake."

A loud cackle escapes my mouth, and Naomi pokes my chest.

"Go," she says. "Talk to him."

"I love you, Naomi."

"I know."

When I enter my room, Theo's sitting up, looking at his phone, the sun from my window casting a soft glaze on his beautiful sandy curls. Janice lies on my pillow. Theo's presence doesn't seem to bother her one bit. Theo immediately turns his attention to me, and his lips turn up, revealing that goofy smile. He's starting to share more, and, lord, I'm in trouble.

"Hey," he says.

"You hungry?"

"Yes, but come here first."

He opens his left arm, a mammoth invitation to curl up in the curve of his torso. I close my eyes and dive in, getting lost in his solace and warmth.

"I wanted to talk to you about something," he begins.

"Okay."

"About Wednesday. My parents are going to love you. I have zero doubts. I'm worried my mother may go overboard because, well, she tends to do that. She's going to want to see you more, I know it. And then there's dinner on the last night too. I know we only agreed to the first night and Timothy's wedding, so I'll make up an excuse for why you can't come. I can say you have a meeting for school or something. Maybe something with parents."

"Oh. I mean, I don't mind."

"Don't mind what?"

"Seeing them more. The last night too."

"You don't? But that would mean you doing two events to my one for you."

"Yeah."

And now I'm talking in as few words as possible, and this is not who I am or want to be. My chest feels heavy, and it's not Theo's meaty bicep lying across it.

"Really? You don't mind?" he asks again.

"Theo, I don't mind. I, I actually would like it."

"You would? You might feel differently after you've met them."

I chuckle at the thought of his loving, overbearing parents wanting nothing more than their son's happiness.

"Theo, I have to be honest with you about something."

"Okay."

I close my eyes and take in a deep breath. Placing my hand on Janice, I bite my lip and spit it out.

"All this pretending, practicing, well, I know we barely know each other, but, but, well, I like you."

"I like you too."

He leans down and kisses my forehead. Not in a corny grand-motherly way, either. His lips linger a little longer, and I need to make sure he understands what I'm saying.

"I mean, I think I like you more than, well, more."

"I like you too," he says with a nod.

"Theo, listen to me."

Propping myself up, I take his strong chin in my hands and force our eyes to lock.

"I don't just like you. I'm starting to *really* like you. As more than a friend."

"Oh."

"I get it. I'm not most guys' cup of tea. I'm so, well, me. And you're, well, this." I wave my hand over his torso like I'm scanning him at airport security, and Theo's face remains unmoved. "You drive a truck, for god's sake. And not some cute little truck. A monster truck."

"Actually, monster trucks are massive. Like four times the size of mine."

I give him my best are-you-kidding-me-right-now teacher look, and he pulls his lips into a thin line. "And tough guys typically go for, well, other tough guys. But I've been enjoying our time together. More than I should've let myself. I don't expect anything, truly. I just hope we can still be friends, and if you're uncomfortable, that's understandable. I'll still come to your Hanukah dinner and then take Naomi to Timothy's wedding, no strings attached. I'm sorry, I didn't mean for this to happen, but you, well, you were so ..."

Theo's massive mitt of a hand blankets my mouth. I let out a huge breath, and he catches every air molecule in his palm. He bends closer, moves his fingers, and his lips brush mine. Slowly at first, then with more pressure, his tongue begins to lick my bottom lip. A tenseness overtakes my stomach, and I pull back, breaking contact.

"Wait, but what—"

His index finger comes to my mouth, pressing my top lip to the bottom.

"Shh. For once in your life Sheldon, please just listen. Okay?"

It feels like Santa's sleigh, at the beginning of the night, with all its presents, has landed squarely in the middle of my chest.

Heeding Theo's instructions, I simply nod.

TWENTY-SIX

Theo

"Sheldon, you talk too much. So much talking. All the time. How you don't lose your voice has to be one of the great mysteries of the universe. Right now, I need you to not be a royal pain in my ass for a minute."

"Excuse me?"

Of course, I've gone and said exactly the wrong thing. Sheldon likes me. Really likes me. Tears sting my eyes because the idea of someone so damn adorable and kind and sweet actually thinking I might be more than a bumbling oaf makes my head woozy.

"No, I mean, just, just, don't talk. Please. Let me get this out."

Sheldon opens his mouth, and a huge sigh escapes, his warm breath reaching my neck. I close my eyes, take my own deep inhale, open my eyes, and speak.

"Sheldon, you, I … I never thought anyone like you would even consider seeing something in someone like me." He opens his mouth, and my eyes go wide, attempting to serve him my own version of his teacher look. "Let me finish."

He nods.

"All this fake stuff, I don't know, yes, it's leading to, well, real stuff. If I'm being honest, it scares the shit out of me. The last time I felt this way about someone, he went and died in my arms. The thought of something happening to you, it, it—"

Sheldon launches himself at me. His arms engulf me, and his face buries in my neck. A wave of cold washes over me, and the words get caught in my throat. I focus on some deep breathing. The scent of Sheldon—not any of his products, but him, the sweetness of his skin, his essence—becomes part of my centering breath. The tears start, and not wanting him to see, I hold him tightly, hoping he never lets me go.

"Theo, I've got you."

He's squeezing me so tightly, every muscle in his body clings and grips me, and I want to stay here, in his bedroom like this, clutching each other in the quiet morning light.

"Theo?"

So much for the quiet.

"Yeah?"

"I'm starving."

I laugh, and he pulls his head away, joining me so our chuckling becomes one.

"Baby, are you crying?"

I nod because there's no denying it. Sheldon reaches up and wipes the tears from my cheeks and then kisses me right underneath each eye. His lips glisten from the wetness.

"I'm okay. I just. I just … I'm not used to being vulnerable. I'm afraid people will think I'm weak."

"Theo. You're literally one of the strongest people I know. Inside and out." He places his palm on my chest.

Wanting him close again, I pull him toward me, until he's crawled into my lap.

"Theo, how did you get so sweet?"

I can't think of a reply. So I kiss him. The moment my lips fall on his, I feel a small tinge of calmness creep in. How does he do that? Make me feel at ease. At home.

His hands are on my face, cupping my cheeks, and when he deepens the kiss, my cock comes to life because Sheldon's tongue has that effect on me. With his ass on my lap, there's no hiding my excitement.

"Oh, well, hello, there," he whispers into my mouth.

"It's you. You do it."

"I thought you were hungry?"

"I am. For you."

Sheldon's tongue begins dancing with mine. His hand reaches between his legs and settles on my cock, pushing my boxers to the max. My dick tingles at the friction, and once again, I find myself wanting Sheldon Soleskin. All of him.

"Okay?" he asks.

"Sheldon, stop asking me if it's okay and jerk me off." His eyes go wide, and I blurt, "Please."

The single tug at the hem of my boxers is all I need. I lift my ass and pull them down in a flash, causing a chuckle from Sheldon.

I lie back, in only my T-shirt, and my dick sticks straight up, and Sheldon stares and then says, "You really *are* horny."

"Do you mind?"

"That you're horny? Jerking you off? Are you kidding me?"

His hands wrap around my cock, and he immediately begins stroking it. He's sitting with his legs crossed, and my eyes never leave his face. He rubs the tip of my dick with his thumb, the precum adding a slickness, and I wonder if I can arrange it so Sheldon never takes his hands off my cock? I start counting freckles, and by the time I reach thirty-three, he leans over and spits on my dick. I fidget for a second, and he pauses.

"You really have a gorgeous cock. I mean, it's stunning, really," he says.

"You really like it?"

"Theo. I want to worship your beautiful dick."

I exhale. Sheldon's hands stroke me, throbbing, pulsing, as his eyes shine. He really does love it. His grin widens, his white teeth shining as his hands bob up and down. Occasionally, his thumb glides over the head, and he lingers there, and my body trembles, the intense pleasure almost too much. Almost.

"Yeah, baby. Your cock is so gorgeous."

"Fuck, yes. Don't stop. Make me come, Sheldon. Please."

"Yes, sir."

He returns to stroking and spitting, and little grunts escape his mouth. Damn he's precious. He leans over and, feeling brave, I reach around and cup his ass. Filling my hand, I squeeze the muscle.

"Okay?" I ask.

"Theo, you can do anything you want to me. Anything."

With permission granted, and overtaken by the moment, I slide my hand under his soft pajamas. My fingers dance close to his hole, the skin thin and tender, and that's it. Between him jerking me off and the thought of doing more, fingering, licking, fucking, I can't hold back any longer. He's launching me into space.

My cock throbs in his grip, his beautiful purple nails wrapped around it, and the sounds of him working me over fill the room. My heartbeat syncs with the rhythm of his strokes, and I tilt my head back, trying to take it all in. This must be what heaven feels like.

"I'm close. Fuck, Sheldon, watch out."

And I can't hold back. He's jerking me so fast I shoot all over my leg and the bed. I'm not even sure where it all lands. After the last spurt escapes, he's still going at it, determined to pump every last drop out of me. My body shivers at the sensation and I stammer, "Okay, okay, I'm done."

He leans over and plants a wet one right on my mouth.

"Theo Berenson. You are so hot."

Before I can respond, my stomach growls.

"Let's go see if we can make something for breakfast," I say.

"Theo, all we have is cereal. And I'm not even sure we have milk."

"Let's go out then. Should we invite your sister?"

"You wouldn't mind?"

"Your sister coming to breakfast? Of course not. Go ask her."

"Picture it, seven-year-old Sheldon, a towel wrapped around his head, forcing the entire family to watch his choreographed dance to 'Sleigh Ride.'"

"Wait, wait, slow down," I say, sitting across from Naomi as Sheldon folds his arms on the booth's table and buries his head in his nest of limbs. "'Sleigh Ride?'"

"The Ronettes version," Sheldon mumbles from his hiding spot.

"It's faster," Naomi adds.

"For the choreo," Sheldon says.

"Exactly how did your parents not know you were gay? Are they conscious?" I ask.

Sheldon's head pops up like a jack-in-the-box, startling me.

"Listen. They thought I was … dramatic."

"And they weren't wrong," Naomi says.

Sheldon glares at his sister, his teacher look evolving into its next form. He's fucking adorable.

"It's a classic. And begs to be choreographed for a Christmas morning extravaganza performance."

"But did you need the towel?" Naomi asks.

"Yes. The complete Ronettes fantasy includes fabulous hair."

"Obviously," she replies.

Sunny Side Up is a funky breakfast place that's open all day, with outsider art plastered everywhere, unmatched tableware and glasses, and a large copper statue of their mascot, Mr. Egg, near the door. The decor has gone festive for the season, with garlands and small twinkle lights weaved through all the regular knickknacks. Mr. Egg wears a Santa hat, and the utter ridiculousness of a giant copper egg wearing a Santa hat makes me chuckle.

The booth clearly seats four, but Sheldon ignores the space and smooshes up against me anyway. His entire side connects to me, and my shoulders relax as his hand squeezes my forearm while he and his sister chat away. Watching their banter and obvious affection for each other, I'm incredibly grateful they have each other but also angry at their parents for missing out on such incredible humans.

"You two are …"

"A lot," they both say in unison and then immediately begin cracking up.

"Walker literally says that all the time," Naomi says.

"Walker. Her own McDreamy. Wait, McSteamy. Strike that. McPerfect."

"He's definitely not perfect," Naomi says.

"I was going to say lucky," I say, finally able to speak. "You two are lucky."

Naomi and Sheldon give each other a glance. They don't say a word, and it feels extremely strange to have silence with the two of them nearby. Sheldon scootches over a smidge, and he's almost in my lap. Looking up at me with massive eyes, he says, "What do you mean?"

"You have each other, and there's clearly some magical bond between twins. I'm an only child. I only have my parents."

I cringe the moment the words come out of my mouth. Parents. My hand instantly jets to scrub my face, and why the fuck did I say that? When I peek at Sheldon, his eyes widen, eyebrows furrowed, and he grips his pinkish-orange sweatshirt.

"I need to pee." He scoots out and is gone in a flash.

"I'm sorry," I say to Naomi, wishing I could rewind and have a do-over.

"Don't be. Listen, Theo, this is never going away, but it will hurt less for him as time passes."

"How long has it been?"

"Let's see, it was right after Mother's Day ... six years ago."

"Six years? Fuck. Sorry, excuse me."

"Don't apologize. You're good. And yeah, it's kind of mind-numbing."

"And you don't talk to them at all? Ever?"

"Nope. For a few months, they kept trying to call me. My mother said, 'We're not upset with *you.*'" I shake my head because I can't think of anything to say. "To which I replied, well, I'm upset with you."

"You really are lucky. Both of you. To have each other. I can't imagine him going through that by himself."

"That would never happen. Sheldon is … I can't explain it. My heart." She covers her heart with both hands. "We're like two pieces of the same soul."

Sheldon returns with a fresh, reddish hue to his face. I'm fairly certain cold water was splashed on his sweet punim. His freckles sparkle, and the moment he plops next to me, I move my hand under the booth and place it on his thigh. Without looking, he moves his hand on top of mine, and I feel the adrenaline flowing through my veins as my heart drums against my chest. After our chat about the F-word (feelings), I'm trying not to overthink things. I tend to let my mind spin and create problems where they don't exist. Even if we just hang out until dinner with my folks and the wedding and then remain friends, I'd be okay with that. I don't really have any gay friends. And Sheldon has to equal at least three gay friends.

"You okay?" I ask, squeezing his leg under the table. He nods but doesn't speak, and a silent Sheldon almost makes me lose my appetite. Almost.

Thankfully we're interrupted by our server. "Hi, I'm Alex, They/Them, and I'll be helping you today. Can I start you off with any drinks? Juice, coffee, tea, me?"

When Alex says "me," they wink at me, and there's a prickling on the back of my neck. I'm fairly certain they're simply being friendly, but I'm not used to attention like this. Sheldon's fingers wrap around mine, and he says, "Coffee for me. What do you want, *baby*, some juice for your blood sugar?"

"Coffee for me too. We both take it black," Naomi says, nodding to Sheldon.

"Two coffees and a juice. Is that orange, sugar?" Alex asks, and I nod.

"I'll be back in a jiff with those and to grab your order." They're off like a bolt, and Naomi's eyebrows dance on her forehead in a way that makes her look so much like her brother it's frightening.

"Well, Alex seems to want a piece of Theo pie," she says.

"What?" I ask.

"You. They were totally flirting with you," she teases.

"No, they weren't," I say. "People don't flirt with me."

"Well, Alex was, and they're definitely 'people.'"

"All right, enough," Sheldon says. "Alex can flirt all they want, but he's mine. Sort of. At least until Christmas."

Naomi rolls her eyes, and a frosty wave washes over me. Hanukah is Wednesday. The wedding is the following Friday. The dates swirl in my mind, and I try to make sense of them all, but my head feels light and dizzy. This mishigas between Sheldon and me expires in two weeks. Why I thought this was a good idea eludes me.

After breakfast, we pile into Sheldon's car. Naomi climbs in the back, giving me the front, "for your long legs," and we head to their apartment. When we get there, I open the car door to head for my truck, and Sheldon says, "I'll be right back," and pops out to join me.

He does that thing where he wraps himself around my arm and, without looking up at me, he says, "She likes you."

"You think?"

"Oh, for sure. But it doesn't matter if she likes you because I like you. Wait, that's a complete lie. Not about me liking you, totally do," he says, and his fingers find mine. "About it not being important if she likes you because it totally matters."

We reach the door of my truck, and I turn to face him. His beautiful eyes look up at me, and the bridge of his nose, dotted with freckles, scrunches up before a smile overtakes his face. The final assault? That dimple.

"I'll see you Monday at school," he says.

"Okay."

"Text me if you want. I'm just going to do some planning."

"Okay."

"Theo," he says, rummaging in his coat pocket.

He produces a small twig of mistletoe and waves it as high as he can. It barely reaches my nose.

"Can I give you a little kiss?"

"But your sister," I say, nodding toward the car, where she waits and most definitely watches.

"I don't care."

"Oh. Okay."

I lean down, and he pops up on his toes, and when I'm not quite close enough, he reaches up, grabs the sides of my face, and gently tugs me further. My eyes close, and I wait because the more I get to know him, the more waiting for Sheldon makes my chest expand with a tiny sliver of the sunshine he's constantly radiating. Except, there are clouds there too. Dark clouds. I need to figure out how I can roar loud enough to blow them away. Forever.

When I sense Sheldon's lips near mine, I crack my left eye, and there is his beautiful skin, dotted with enough freckles to fill my soul with joy, and goosebumps overtake my body. They start on my face and expand until my pinky toe finally joins the parade. The kiss is soft. Slow. Short. But his lips, right on mine, even for a brief moment, make me believe, even momentarily, maybe there's hope. For him. For me. For us.

TWENTY-SEVEN

Sheldon

"Yes, Kylie, that's it," I say, patting her on the back as she finishes her math problems. In first-grade, double-digit addition feels monumental, and even for my adult brain, teaching it can be a head-scratcher. I sit at the kidney table by the window, the December sun doing its best to warm us as the average temperature drops with Christmas approaching. Kylie swings her feet under the table, and Brodie sits next to her, closer to me, because he just does better when he's closer to me.

"Can I see yours?" I ask, and Brodie slides his paper over.

"Brodie. This is it. You grouped the ones and tens, and your name … look how much neater it is. You can totally read it."

He stares up at me, a wide grin overtaking his face, and my chest swells at the progress he's making, both academically and socially. I'm unsure if spending time with Theo is the reason or if he's just settling in with strong routines and procedures, but I don't care why. I'm simply relieved we seem to have found a way to get through our days without any major histrionics.

"All right, friends, it's almost time to pack up. Five more minutes to finish."

Brodie takes my hand as we walk to the bus.

"You had another fantastic day, friend. You should feel proud," I say, squeezing his fingers.

"I do."

"Good. It makes my heart so happy when we have good days together."

"Me too."

A voice catches me by surprise. "There's my guy." Theo. I'm not sure if he's talking to me or Brodie, and I'm not asking.

"Theo!" Brodie shouts. He releases my hand and bolts to him, doing his best to wrap his arms around Theo's thighs.

"How was the rest of your afternoon?" Theo asks him, pulling Brodie's chin up with his finger.

"Good! Right Mr. Soleskin?"

"More than good. Excellent." I give Theo a soft smile as I catch his gaze.

"Go with Mr. S. You don't want to miss the bus," Theo says, and Brodie gives him one more squeeze before clutching my hand. The way he's burrowed into my heart, it's hard for me to believe I've only been his teacher for a little over two weeks.

I return to the classroom after delivering my students to the bus, and Theo is standing inside the door. Rubbing the back of his neck, he gazes down, and I have the urge to tackle him with kisses.

"Mr. Berenson, that was a lovely surprise."

"I wanted to see Brodie. He's a good kid."

"Only him?" I ask, walking up and resting my hand just below his chest, where his belly begins.

Theo jerks away, eyes wide, and whispers, "Someone might see."

My hand gravitates toward my hip, and my head cocks, "Excuse me, are you embarrassed to be seen with me?"

He swerves around me and shuts the classroom door. When I turn toward him, he's there, right there, in front of me, looking down, inches from my face. My palm hasn't moved from my hip as I await his answer. Without speaking, he lifts my chin, leans down, and softly kisses me.

My entire body relaxes as his lips brush mine. This man can be so gentle, so tender. With his hand still supporting my face, the tingling in my chest grows, and I wonder if kissing Theo Berenson might be like getting everything you ever wanted on Christmas morning.

When he pulls back, I'm left standing with my lips out, like some cartoon animal waiting for the hero's kiss, my heart shrinking two sizes.

"So, tomorrow," he says.

"Is Wednesday."

"The first night of Hanukah. My parents arrive mid-afternoon. I always take the day off to prep and cook. I have it down to a system, with time to mentally prepare for their arrival." As Theo talks, I move my hand up his arm, rubbing over his uniform, wishing it were softer. "So about tomorrow." He pauses to chew the inside of his cheek. "Do you think you can come over a little before five? You need to arrive before sundown."

"Absolutely! I can come right from school if you want me there earlier. Wait, what should I wear? Something like this?" I glide my hand over myself and do a quick spin, showing off my jade khakis and purple tartan button-down. "Or something less ... colorful? You tell me, Theo. Wait, do I need to wear a tie? Regular? Bow? And my nails?" I hold them up for his inspection. "Should I remove the polish? Probably, right?"

"No. Don't you dare change a thing," he says, taking my hand in his and massaging my nails softly.

"Will there be a yarmulke to coordinate? Should I buy one, or do you have like a secret stash? Oh my god, where do you buy a yarmulke anyway? Wait, is it offensive for me to wear one? Being a ..."

"Goy?"

"I was going to say redhead, but yeah, goy."

"You don't need one. Although you'd be very cute in one." He runs his fingers through my hair, and my scalp tingles at his touch.

But then my ribs feel tight and constricting. Theo's playing the game, and I'm happy we're getting along, but clearly, this is temporary. This is about obligations and appearances.

"Oh, okay. Wait, why not?"

"The Berensons are what my mother calls 'culturally Jewish.' Which basically means we love all the food and traditions but rarely go to temple."

"And you complain a lot."

"Now you're getting it. Although, we'd say kvetch," he says with a hint of that smile that makes my toes tickle.

"Theo, you have to stop talking Jewish to me. It gets me all worked up."

Once again, my cheeks are in his sturdy hands, but this time there's no kiss. Only Theo's eyes on me, scanning me. His eyes grow large, and he's looking at me like he hasn't eaten in a while. And I'm a Christmas roast.

"Sheldon, how is my better half's better half?"

Walker sits on our couch, legs spread wide in that way straight men do, letting the world know he's here, he's straight, and that's great.

"I'm good. Well, fine. I'm fine. Why are you all gussied up on a Tuesday night?"

Naomi usually spends time with Walker at his place, and when he does come here, he's almost always in scrubs or clothes that resemble scrubs. Tonight, he's dressed to the nines. The man is wearing a gorgeous gray suit with a teal accent in what I'm guessing is Italian wool. He looks ready for his close-up cover shoot moment.

"It's a freebie. We both have the night and tomorrow off."

"And you're not going to veg on the couch and head to bed at eight thirty like a normal human being?"

"No. We're going out to dinner, but we'll be home by nine and then will promptly resume vegging if that meets the approval of my lady's guardian."

"What requires my wombmate's approval?" Naomi says, walking into the living room as she fastens an earring. She's wearing the most stunning off-the-shoulder dress. The black fabric is peppered with small flowers in shades of pink and blue, with their stems providing green accents. It's one of her few fancy dresses, and I know this one well. We bought it two years ago for our thirtieth birthday party. And by party, I mean Walker took us out for lobster.

"Absolutely nothing, but if he needed it, he'd have it. Permission permanently granted," I say.

"I appreciate that," Walker says.

"Where are you off to?" I ask.

"Another new restaurant. A patient who owns it invited me to be his guest. I suppose after dislodging his left foot from the spokes in his bicycle, a free meal is a sweet gesture," Walker says.

"It's the least he can do," Naomi adds. "You saved both his foot and the bicycle. Well, he'll probably need a new wheel, but still."

"Well, you two have fun. I'm putting on my PJs, snuggling on the couch with Janice, and doing a little studying." Hearing her name, Janice saunters in from my bedroom, where she was most likely sleeping. She walks over and rubs her entire body against my shin.

"Studying, what in bloody hell for?" Walker asks.

"For Hanukah," I say, holding up my copy of *Judaism for Dummies*. "Well, for Hanukah dinner. With parents."

Walker scratches his temple and tilts his head.

"Don't hurt yourself, baby," Naomi says. "Sheldon's boyfriend's parents are coming for Hanukah, and he wants to make sure he doesn't make an ass out of himself. Well, a bigger ass than usual."

"Boyfriend?" Walker's hand moves from his head to his chin, struggling to keep up.

"Fake boyfriend," I say, my mouth dry and crackly.

"Fake parents," Naomi adds.

"Technically, they're all real. We're just pretending," I say.

Walker heads to the closet by the door. Once he's retrieved his and Naomi's coats, he says, "You two. Always getting into some sort of nonsense."

"Mishigas," I blurt.

"Excuse me," Walker says.

"It means nonsense. In Yiddish." I hold *Judaism for Dummies* aloft.

Walker's eyebrows pinch together.

"Walker, sweetie, you go warm up the car, and I'll be down in two minutes."

"Two actual minutes or two Soleskin Twin minutes?"

"Go," she commands, and he slips on his coat, waves at me, and leaves.

Naomi sits on the couch and pats the space beside her. "Sit."

"Someone is feeling her bossy self tonight."

"Tonight?"

"Walker is waiting. What's up?" I ask, scratching the back of my neck.

"What's up? What's up with you?"

"Me? I'm fine."

"Bean, don't play games with me."

A lump forms in my throat. If I had to measure it, I'd say it's relatively avocado-pit sized. I have to swallow hard to push the saliva in my mouth past it. With Naomi sitting here, looking like a goddess, about to spend the evening with her gorgeous boyfriend, and my night planned reading up on Hanukah traditions and watching a (gasp) hetero Hallmark movie on the Jewish festival of lights, I don't have the time or energy to investigate it.

"Really, I'm fine."

"Sheldon Sawyer Soleskin." Naomi's use of my full name sends shivers up my spine.

"I'm just anxious about the dinner with his parents tomorrow. I want everything to be perfect. For him. Now go have dinner with your hot boyfriend. Go, leave me, leave me alone. Janice will comfort me."

She puts her arm around me, pulls me close, and kisses my cheek.

"Bean, you will always live right here," she points to her heart. "Always."

"Until Walker proposes, and you move out."

"Someday, I hope, but not today. And even when that happens, you're never getting rid of me. Literally. Never."

On the couch, with *Judaism for Dummies* open to the page about why fried foods abound for eight days (it's celebrating the oil, ah), Janice purrs in the nest of my legs. I wrinkle my brow thinking about Naomi and Walker. I know it's just a dinner, but they've been dating for a while now. Years. We're thirty-two. Well, Walker is thirty-four, but still, they've got to want to get married at some point. And what's stopping them? Me. Me and my unhealthy attachment to my sister. Me and my not having anyone but her.

My stomach suddenly feels unsettled, and the thought of finishing the leftover pizza in the fridge makes it worse. No appetite is not a good sign for me. I bite my lip and grab Janice, who immediately begins purring. Sweet Janice never asks for much except for her food bowl to be full and constant attention from me.

Tomorrow night I'll head to Theo's to meet his parents. It sure doesn't feel fake. All these feelings. All the affection. All the kissing. It can't be fake. Yes, we started this to help Theo get his parents off his back. To avoid a yenta. So I can save face at Timothy's wedding. What happened?

Theo. His big handsome face. His big, tender heart. His big, gorgeous cock.

Janice crawls up my chest and nuzzles my chin. Tears sting the corners of my eyes, but she doesn't stop, pushing and pressing her tiny soft head on my face.

This has to work. If Theo's parents like me enough, maybe this won't end. My heart gallops like I'm about to lip-sync for my life. I head to the bathroom to grab the nail polish remover and cotton balls.

TWENTY-EIGHT

Theo

"There's my gorgeous son."

Sylvia Berenson never fails to let me know how handsome she thinks I am. Of course. She's a Jewish mother, it's required in the Torah somewhere. She scrambles into my apartment, and my father follows, carrying the one small suitcase they somehow share for over a week. My mother will wash items nightly. In my bathroom sink. Clothes hanging everywhere. Including her unmentionables. Oy.

"My son," Mom says, hands on my chest before the words escape her mouth.

"Teddy, you look good," Abba says, his flannel peeking out from under a heavy sweatshirt and parka.

"Abba, can I take your coat? We have heat in Maine, you know."

My father's hands land on my cheeks and pull me down. "I know. My old bones are just chilly. Now, give me your face. Abba needs to kiss this face."

And he does. Right on the lips. A big, wet kiss. For as long as I can remember, my father has kissed me on the lips. Far too often.

"Quit hogging the boychik, Adam." My mother pushes him off me and replaces his hands with hers. Now, my lips are not only wet but smothered in bright, ruby lipstick. Awesome.

"Mom."

"How is your leg?" And because Sylvia Berenson has absolutely no boundaries, she reaches down and grabs the back of my left thigh.

"Mom!"

"Teddy, I'm your mother. I was at your bris. I wiped your tuchus when you were little. I can check the injury you sustained while fighting for our freedom."

"I'm fine, Mom. Same as last year. Same as the last time we talked. Same as I'll be the next time I see you."

"And the physical therapist can't make it go away?"

"Me having an artificial femur? No, Mother."

After the attack, it turned out I needed a total femoral replacement. That would include my femur, hip, and knee joint. I'm lucky I only walked away with a limp. I close my eyes because my mother touching the area of my injury somehow kicks up memories. Smoke. Fire. Ash. Wood and oil.

"Well, I just want you to be able to walk."

"I literally just walked to the door to let you in."

"I know, sweetie. I meant walk, well ..."

"Normal," Abba says.

"I'm fine. People barely notice. Nobody cares. Except you."

"Nobody cares about you?" Sylvia says, and I cram my eyes shut and wince because today is the first of eight nights of this mishigas.

"What about this new boy? Is he ..." Abba wants to know but doesn't want to sound like it matters.

"A redhead? Yes. A teacher? Also, yes."

My parents steal a quick glance. After being married for forty-one years, they seem to communicate telepathically. Abba raises his eyebrows, and Mom shakes her head in such a small way that you'd miss it if you blinked. I do not blink.

"No, bubbeleh. Is he Jewish?"

"Abba, I told you already." My mother's head juts out. "He's not Jewish."

"Not even a little?" Abba asks.

"How is someone a little Jewish?" I say.

"Like those celebrities who study kabbalah and wear the red string. I mean, it's not much, but it's something," Mom says.

"No, he's not. Not even a little. But speaking of little. He is short. And gay."

"I'd hope so," she says.

"No, he's gayer than me."

"Wait, is there a scale?"

"No, I mean not really."

"Gayer than you? Like that RuPaul? Teddy, are you dating a drag queen? Because if you were, that would be fine with us, right, Mommy?"

As the story goes, when I began speaking, mimicking what I heard, I called my parents Sylvia and Adam. Hoping to stop it, they began calling each other "Mommy" and "Abba." Over thirty years later and they still do it. It's kind of ridiculous but also sweet. My folks definitely have a deep affection for each other.

"No, Sheldon isn't a drag queen. He's just, well, very gay."

"Sweetie, you're gay. We'd expect your boyfriend to be gay. Or bi. Or pan. You know we don't care about any of that stuff," Mom says, waving her hand at imaginary nonsense. "We can't wait to meet him. Jean is on call. She's a top-notch yenta. She found Myriam's daughter a wife. A doctor, no less," she says, dipping her chin.

If Sheldon and I can convince them we're actually an item, perhaps she'll stop this ridiculous talk of hiring a yenta. I'm feeling fairly confident we can pull it off. If nothing else, we've become friends. I mean, surely at least friends. Maybe friends with … benefits. That's what Christian called it.

"I have no doubt she's capable. But no need for that," I say.

"And look at your apartment. So festive. The decorations. I'm plotzing. Who did this?" she says, running her hand over one of the giant menorahs taped to the wall. "Surely, not you."

"I helped. Sheldon did most of it. He's very creative."

"Clearly. What time will this craftsman be here?" Abba asks.

Right on cue, the buzzer blares.

"That'll be him. Now listen, be nice."

"Be nice. Us? We will be nothing but nice," Mom says.

"Don't embarrass me. Please."

"Who would embarrass you?" Abba asks as he lifts his shirt up, scratches his hairy belly, and makes a loud fart noise with his mouth. Deep breaths.

My mother immediately wraps Sheldon up like hamantaschen. He's in there somewhere, beneath the sparkly blue pashmina she wears every year for Hanukah. Of course, he succumbs, melting into her, and Abba and I share a look.

"Mrs. Berenson." Sheldon's voice is muffled. "It's so fabulous to meet you!"

"Sylvia, call me Sylvia."

"Mommy, let the boy breathe. He'll suffocate in your bosom."

Sheldon's fiery hair comes into view, and then his sweet face and he says, "Yeah, not really used to being buried in a woman's bosom."

Abba lets out a deep laugh. "Oh, he's a comedian, this one."

"Now let me look at this punim," Mom says, grabbing Sheldon's face for a post-embrace inspection. "Freckles. So many freckles," she says as if Sheldon didn't know.

"Yeah, they're my personal, built-in, always there glitter."

My mother reaches out, and her fingers get close to Sheldon's face. "May I?" she asks, and I swear, by god in heaven, Sheldon doesn't speak a single syllable. He nods.

With his consent, Mom gently brushes Sheldon's cheeks and slowly moves up toward the bridge of his nose, where his freckles blossom into a glorious pattern. His eyes close, and a wistful smile overtakes his face. He looks like a sweet puppy being petted for the first time.

"This is a good punim. That's face, dear," she says, moving her hand to his chin, holding him in place. "May I give you a kiss?"

For the briefest second, Sheldon's eyes go wide, and then he says, "I'd be honored."

And in the grand tradition of Jewish mothers everywhere, Mom plants a gentle kiss right on Sheldon Soleskin's lips.

"Teddy. This one is a keeper. Mamaleh knows."

Sheldon shoots me a quick look, and his eyebrows dance at the mention of my parents' nickname.

"Let Abba have a turn," my father says, walking over and standing beside Mom. He doesn't dare intrude on their moment but gives Sheldon the once-over.

"Yes, yes, I see it. He's definitely a mensch." He purses his lips, a telltale sign of deep thought, opens his arms, and then shouts, "Welcome to the mishpocha!"

"Thank you, Mr. Berenson," Sheldon squeaks out.

"Mr. Berenson? Who's that? I'm Teddy's Abba. You call me Abba."

"All right, all right, enough," Mom says, clapping her hands. "The sun is setting. Let's get cracking."

I've spent the last few nights preparing. Challah was braided, and I premade the latkes mixture so we could simply fry them together. Abba and I stand back as my mother walks Sheldon through the process.

"The oil is burning hot. Splattering will happen. This is why we wear cute aprons," she says.

"Yes! I love a sweet, Martha-does-Hanukah-makeover moment," he says, and my mother laughs as if she's just heard the funniest joke in existence.

"Teddy, why didn't you tell us Sheldon was this hilarious?" she asks through tears.

"I don't know," I say.

Sheldon interrupts me with, "Sylvia, Theo just has a less developed sense of humor. But, trust me, he adores me."

"How could he not?" Abba asks.

Abba and I finish setting the folding table I borrowed from school, his favorite job, while Mom and Sheldon pat the latkes dry. I put the brisket on the table, and my father reaches in and pinches off a piece and pops it in his mouth.

"Abba, we have a guest," I say.

"Sheldon, do you care if Abba takes a pre-meal taste?"

"I encourage it!" he shouts.

With the table set and ready, Abba grabs the menorah and candles from the mantle.

"Now, Sheldon, each night, we take turns lighting the menorah. It's a mitzvah to have all the members of the family take a turn, and since it's the first night and you're a new member, why don't you do it?"

Sheldon bites his lip and blinks at me, and I try to think of what to say to throw him a lifeline, but my mother, sensing his nervousness, jumps in.

"Teddy, you help him. Like Abba used to help you."

A slow smile overtakes his face, and Sheldon's hand reaches out. My heart pauses. His nails. They're naked. Bare. The polish erased. Why?

I've seen Sheldon do this with his students. They hold the pencil, and he takes their hand and guides them in writing or drawing. I take his hand and guide him through, first lighting the shammes and then the first night's candle. My parents and I sing the prayer, and when we reach the v'tzivanu, Sheldon joins in. I almost drop the candle, starting a giant blaze, but Sheldon's holding on tightly. He gives me a little wink, and my stomach goes tumbling.

"Beautiful boys," Abba says before kissing my mother.

Sheldon perks up on his tippy toes and kisses my cheek. My mother's mouth falls open, and she clutches her chest. We're doing it. They're buying it.

"Abba, my charm bracelet. I left it in the car, come with me to get it," Mom says.

"Your bracelet? It's in the bedroom. Come, I'll show you," Abba says, his voice bubbling with frustration.

"No, it isn't," she says sharply, her eyebrows flying up. "Come with me," she reiterates as if we can't all see through her ploy.

"We'll be right back," Abba says with a sigh, slipping his coat on and grabbing his keys from the bowl by the door.

"It's going great. Your parents adore me. I mean, I think they do. They seem to, right?"

"Sheldon, it's been an hour, and my mother is obsessed with you. Clearly."

"I thought so, but you know, I'm not trying to be a Valentina."

I shake my head, knowing this is probably a Drag Race reference I don't know, and then jittery excitement blossoms in my chest because now I know the references are to Drag Race, and what does that mean?

"What happened?" I ask, taking his hand in mine. He looks at me, eyes wide, and lowers his voice. "Your nails. Why did you take the polish off?"

"I didn't know, and I just wanted everything to go smoothly."

"Sheldon. I like you." I poke him gently in his sternum. "All of you. The way you dress. The dancing. Your nails. All of it. I don't want you to change anything."

"I know, it's just one night. And it's working, baby. Wait, am I allowed to call you Teddy now?"

"No."

"Okay, we'll work up to it." My face twists and bunches, but then he's there. Right next to me. His hand reaches for my face and pulls me toward him. "Theo, this is working. They're totally buying us."

"Yeah, they are. I guess we're fooling them," I say, my throat throbbing as the words choke out.

"Teddy bear, we're not fooling them," he says, his bright eyes shining up at me. "Now, I might act my way to an Oscar one day, but you, my friend, couldn't act your way out of a paper bag. What your parents are buying is this." He moves his hand between us. "Us. It's real. We don't have to fool them. They know. I can tell. I'm very good at reading people. If I wasn't a first-grade teacher, I was going to be a therapist. Or a medium. Definitely something where you read people."

And even though he's doing the thing where he talks and talks, I don't want him to stop. My eyes are glued to his mouth. I'm perfectly content to watch his lips move and yap away to his heart's content.

"Sheldon?"

"Yeah?"

"My parents are going to be back any minute."

"Okay, good, we'll eat dinner, and I can tell them about how I dragged you to the festival of lights and how we got stuck here in the blizzard together, oh, and how I twisted your arm to make these gorgeous decorations Martha herself would envy, even though you—"

And I kiss him. Not to stop the talking, although stopping the talking is an added bonus. Having Sheldon here, with my parents, making everything brighter, lighter, better, makes me want to kiss him and kiss him and kiss him some more.

"Okay, okay, Abba, maybe you were right," Mom says, barging in. I break the kiss with Sheldon. But he doesn't pull away. He's still right there, in my arms.

"I told you it was in the bedroom, but do you ever listen to me? No. The answer is no."

Without stopping, they bicker right into my bedroom. Sheldon looks at me, eyes wide with amusement. His face cracks into an enormous grin before bursting into laughter. My heart fills with light, and before I know it, my own face beams right back at Sheldon, still in my arms, his silly laugh filling the room, making everything right.

TWENTY-NINE

Sheldon

As Sylvia says, Theo's brisket really does "melt in your mouth like butter." It's sinful. There's challah, which Theo braided and baked himself, glazed carrots, and horseradish potatoes. I didn't even know horseradish potatoes were a thing, but Abba assured me they are most definitely a thing, and now I see why Theo needed the day off. The latkes are crisp and salty, and even the few I let cook a tad longer than needed aren't ruined. "I like the burned parts. They remind my mouth not to get cocky," Abba says.

With the table cleared and cleaned, Abba's eyebrows gather, and he pulls a small wooden dreidel out of his pocket. Theo taught me the basics last weekend, and I'm ready to win some nickels.

"Sheldon, sweetheart, you sit next to me," Sylvia says, patting the spot next to her on the sofa.

Abba carted a giant jar of nickels from Florida to Maine. Theo explained that this is a Berenson tradition. They play. They laugh. And at the end of the game, all the nickels go back into the jar for next year.

"Teddy, you sit here," Abba points to the chairs, and Theo grabs two and places them on the other side of his small coffee table.

"Now sweetie, dreidel is a fun game for children, but we are not children," Sylvia says.

"No. My family plays schoicket dreidel," Theo says.

"Schoicket. It means cutthroat. We take no prisoners," Abba adds.

And he isn't kidding. They spin that dreidel like we're playing for millions, not nickels. One of Theo's spins actually takes minutes before the dreidel relents on the table. With each spin, piles of nickels grow and diminish, the dreaded shin causing groans and what I assume is profanity in Yiddish. When I finally spin, and the dreidel lands on gimmel, Sylvia yawns and says, "It's kismet. Sheldon has won, and I'm beat. Abba and I drove all day, and we need to sleep."

"Well, it's been lovely meeting you both," I say, not wanting to overstay my welcome and knowing they all must be tired, including Theo, who cooked all day. "I hope I'll get to see you again before you head back south."

"Oh, sweetie, of course you will. Abba and I will just putter around Theo's apartment. We'll walk around town. There's a cute knitting store I love to visit."

I stand to leave, and Abba says, "Well, you boys, have a good night. Theo, we'll see you in the morning or not until after work?"

I rub my chin and glance at Theo.

"Abba, you wake up before the sun. You'll see me before I go to work."

"Teddy, you're staying at Sheldon's. We know the couch is a tight fit for you," Sylvia says, patting her son's tummy affectionately.

"Oh," Teddy says, a flush creeping across his cheeks, making his sweet face even more kissable.

"Yes, of course, Theo's coming home with me. That will give you two some peace and quiet, and yeah, this big guy on the couch ..." I rub his arm and give him a little squeeze. "You wouldn't be very comfortable. Teddy. Come, let's pack a bag for you." I take his hand and lead him to his bedroom.

Sylvia and Abba both nod as small smiles creep onto their faces. These two don't need a yenta for Theo. They are yentas.

"How were the parents?" Naomi asks before I've even pierced the doorway.

"They're amazing, and Theo's staying here," I say, taking my coat off. "For a few nights. Well, eight nights."

"Oh, well, where is he?"

"Parking. He wanted to have his truck and needed to stop to buy a razor. I told him he could have one of mine, but apparently Theo —who washes his face with hand soap—is brand-loyal for razors."

On cue, there's a knock on the door, and Theo enters with his duffel bag over his shoulder.

"Theo, welcome to Chez Soleskin. Mi casa es su casa. And I can stay with Walker if you boys would like some ..." Naomi wiggles her eyebrows and then says, "Privacy."

"No, we're good," I say, maybe a little too enthusiastically.

"Sure you are," she teases as I drag him into my room, coat and all, to escape her as quickly as possible.

"Naomi," Theo replies with a nod. His ears are pink, either from the frigid December cold, embarrassment, or both.

Safe inside my room with the door closed, Theo takes his heavy parka off and bites his lip as he stands holding it.

"Oh, here, I'll take that. I can hang it up."

I grab a hanger from my closet, and as I put his coat away, he lays his bag on the bed, waking a fast-asleep Janice and sending her running into my closet.

"Oh crap, I'm sorry. I didn't mean to scare her."

"She's fine. Or she will be. She'll come out before you know it. Why don't we brush our teeth and hit the hay?"

"Yeah, it's been a day. And a night," he says, scrubbing his face with his palm and shooting me a quick glance.

After we've both used the bathroom—he for five minutes and me for fifteen, hey proper moisturizing is critical in harsh Maine winters—we're in my bed. Theo's wearing his T-shirt and boxers because, apparently, he's averse to pajamas, and I've got my lavender PJ pants on.

"I really did have a nice time with your folks."

"Yeah, they really like you. A lot. They would be polite even if they didn't, but that was way more than polite. That was complete adoration."

"Well, I'm glad they adore me. I'm kind of adorable, eh?" I prop up on my hand, my arm making a triangle to hold my head, and stare at Theo. He's on his back, arms at his side, lying stiff as a board.

"Yes, Sheldon, you're kind of adorable. Kind of."

"You're kind of adorable yourself, you know."

"There's something I want to do before we go to sleep. If that's okay."

I feel movement in my pants at his suggestion.

"Oh. Really?"

He's up, digging in his bag, and back on the bed before I know it, his fingers wrapped around something in his palm.

"When I stopped to get razors, well, that was kind of a lie. I mean, I did need one, but I wanted to get something else."

Theo puts his hand out and unfurls his fingers, revealing a small bottle of blue nail polish.

My mouth falls open, but miraculously, nothing comes out. Dampness dots the corners of my eyes, and how did this man come into my life?

"I thought maybe, for Hanukah, you might like blue."

"Theo. I, I … I'd love that."

I reach to take the polish from him, and he covers my hand with his free one.

"Maybe we could do it. Now? I could help you?"

"Theo Berenson, you want to paint my fingernails?"

"Yes."

I throw my arms around his neck and pepper his face with kisses. Every vein in my body hums with joy.

"Hold, please," I say and run to the bathroom for my manicure kit.

We sit across from each other, a pillow between us, and Theo Berenson, the gentle giant, carefully paints my fingernails. He's slow, cautious, meticulous, and I swear at one point his tongue juts out from the side of his mouth. I want to throw my arms around him and kiss every atom on his face. But I'm still. Calm. Quiet.

When the brush slips onto my skin, his eyes go wide with worry, and this man. God, this man.

I pull a swab out of my kit, dip it in the bottle of polish remover and wipe the error away.

"I'm sorry," he says.

"Baby. You have nothing to apologize for."

Carefully, so not to disturb our setup, I lean over and kiss him softly on the lips.

The sharp smell of polish fills the room, yet Theo's sweetness overpowers it. He's methodical. He's tender. He's everything.

"What about you?" I ask when he finishes my final pinky.

"I'm good," he says with a shrug.

"How about one nail?"

"One?"

"A thumb. Then we can match a little," I say, taking his thumb in my hand, making sure not to disturb my damp nails.

"But your nails are still wet." He takes my hands and softly blows on them, sending my heart leaping in my chest.

"Okay, maybe tomorrow."

"Tomorrow. Goodnight, Sheldon."

"No kiss?"

Theo's face doesn't budge, but with the faint moonlight coming in the window, I see his eyes veer toward me. I move my face so I'm hovering above his, and with my lips almost touching his, I mutter, "This okay?"

Theo's arms wrap around my back, drawing me to him, my entire body resting on his, and he kisses me. And not a peck or a simple goodnight kiss. His mouth devours mine, our lips smash together in a cacophony of teeth and tongues, and when Theo lets out a low moan from his throat, my dick springs to life. There's no way he doesn't feel it.

"Still okay?" I ask him because I want to make sure we're on the same page. Or at least in the same book.

He reaches for my face and pulls me toward him, our lips again kissing, his tongue inside my mouth, deep whimpers escape his throat, and okay Theo Berenson, you're a doer, not a talker.

His kiss tells me everything. Those hands, large and rough, move from my face to my back and then around my waist, tugging and pulling me toward him. Closer. Perhaps the smell of the polish turned him on? I'm not questioning it. His hands migrate to my scalp. Fingers comb my hair. All the while, our lips never part. Theo may not utter a word, but his kiss speaks volumes.

Because he's pulled my body to his, I can feel his dick, thick and stiff, through the fabric separating us. With both our cocks at full attention, my heart needs clarity with Theo, and against my better judgment, I speak.

"So, before, when I told you I liked you …"

"Yeah."

"You said, 'Oh.' And then well …"

"I mean, you're okay," he says with a raised eyebrow.

"Okay."

He's teasing me, and it drives me wild. His breath, somehow minty cool and warm at the same time, tickles my nose.

"Sheldon, listen, here's the thing. When I like someone, it doesn't end well. I liked Ricky. I liked him so much and, well …"

I drop my head onto his neck. I can feel his chin on the top of my scalp and, for a moment, wrap my arms around his sides and squeeze him tightly. My scrawny muscles give out after about thirty seconds, but dear lord, I give it my best shot.

Lifting my head up, our lips almost touch, and I say, "Theo, baby, I'm not Ricky. We're not in the middle of a war zone. Nothing is going to happen to me."

"You don't know that."

"No, I can't guarantee it, but I can tell you, right now, I'm here" —I lift myself up just enough to poke him in the chest—"with you."

"I'm scared," he says, and by all that is good and mighty in this world, he's done it. Said it. He's chipped at a brick in the wall he's erected around himself. It may only be a tiny fissure, but it's a start.

"Of me?"

"Yes."

He closes his eyes, and in this instant, he reminds me of a small child hoping not to see whatever is the cause of their fear.

"Theo, look at me."

He cracks one eye.

"Theo, you have nothing to be afraid of. I'm as harmless as a lamb."

"A lamb? Really? That's the animal you're choosing to associate yourself with?"

"I don't know. They're small. And cute. And honestly, I'm trying to make you feel better so we can get back to kissing."

"You really want to? Keep kissing me?"

He attempts to look away, but my face is so close he can't really escape my gaze.

"Theodore Berenson, I want to kiss you and kiss you and kiss you and then kiss you some more."

His eyes widen, and before I let him speak, I crash my mouth on his. It only takes a second for Theo's lips to part. My tongue enters his mouth while his hands move down my back and land just above my waist.

"You are so sexy, Theo. I really want to do more with you. Like really want to have some mind-blowing sex with you. Are you good with that?"

He purses his lips, closes his eyes, and nods. Finally.

THIRTY

Theo

Lying in Sheldon's bed, his breath on my face, a wave of warmth washes over me. This is really happening. We're going to do this. Something more. Ricky and I never did anything more than jerk off together. I need to focus on Sheldon's voice. Sheldon's face. Sheldon's body. Sheldon's freckles. Sheldon's lips.

I open my mouth, and my voice, choked with tears, says, "I like you."

"You do?"

"So fucking much," I say, my voice warbling. "C'mere."

Sheldon wraps his arms around my shoulders, and his mouth reaches for my cheek. Staying close to my ear, his lips, so soft—how is every part of him so fucking soft?—brush my cheek. The moment he makes contact, I feel my dick pulse in my boxers, unable to ignore the bubbling heat.

I turn my head slightly, our lips make contact, and fuck, kissing Sheldon Soleskin might be the end of me.

We don't move the rest of our bodies, only his face on mine, and carefully, his tongue explores my lips, and I let him enter my mouth. Tongues touching, twirling, I give a low moan, and Sheldon pauses to say, "Okay?"

"Mmmhmm." I pull him closer, hoping he understands how much I never want him to take his lips off mine.

Contact resumed, Sheldon's hand lands on my chest and begins exploring my torso. My chest, my stomach, with only a ratty T-shirt on, unable to hide under my bulky uniform. He starts playing with the hem of my shirt and runs his fingers underneath.

"Gosh, you're sexy," he says, and I can't help but let out a laugh. He breaks the kiss and props himself up on his elbow.

"You think that's funny?"

"Well, yeah. Kind of."

He sits up. All the way up. He takes the bottom of my shirt in both hands and begins peeling it up.

"Take it off. Your shirt. Please."

Sheldon doesn't weigh more than a wet bagel. My reflexes scream for me to stop him, and I easily could, but I don't. My parents adore him. I adore him. So much. Too much. Fuck.

"But, but ... Guys aren't attracted to an oaf like me."

"Well, I'm a guy, and I'm going to tell you something, Theo Berenson, and I want you to listen carefully. Okay?"

I nod.

"This body." His hands explore my chest, move to my arms, and travel down to my right hand, which he takes in his. "You're so strong. Inside and out." He lifts my hand to his lips and plants a kiss on each finger. "You need to understand how sexy you are." With each finger adored, he takes my index finger and pops it in his mouth, gently sucking and tonguing the tip before removing it. "Your body makes my blood simmer, Theo."

I'm lying there. Blinking. My forehead wrinkled, and certainly, speechless. Of course, Sheldon won't allow more than a moment of silence.

"I'm going to take your shirt off and show you how much you turn me on."

Lifting the bottom, he rolls my shirt up until I'm forced to either resist or comply. Without giving it too much thought, my arms raise over my head, and Sheldon tugs to remove my shirt completely. He lets out a few adorable grunts and groans as he seems determined to do it solo. When he's finally removed it, he tosses it to the floor.

My eyes go wide, and I will myself to submit with a single nod.

And for all that's good and mighty, Sheldon leans over and brushes his lips on my stomach. My bulging, fuzzy, fat stomach. Heat flushes my head as he carefully explores every inch.

"You good?"

His words calm me. Sheldon's body over me, his cock growing in his purple pajamas while he fawns over me. Me.

"Mmmh."

"Baby, you drive me freaking wild."

"Sheldon, do you ever swear?"

He pauses, glances at me, and says, "No. I'm a *lady*."

"C'mere, lady," I say and pull him up for a kiss.

He glides his mouth over my chest, kissing his way down, and when he takes my left nipple in his teeth, a growl escapes my mouth. I hurry to cover my lips with my hand.

"Do you like that? Let me hear how much you love it."

He reaches up and pulls my hand down, placing it on the small of his back. Inches from the crack in his perfect ass. Oy.

I'm unsure what's happening, but this Sheldon, the one taking control, makes my eyes glow. More importantly, my cock springs to rapt attention, stretching my thin boxers. There's no way he hasn't noticed.

He weaves up to my neck, kissing and sucking. Breathy noises escape when he comes up for air, until he's back to my mouth. With a short, tender kiss, Sheldon breaks contact, moving his lips to my ear.

"Can I play with you?"

Closing my eyes, I take a deep breath. Of course I want Sheldon's hand back on my cock. I count to five in my head, exhale, and say, "Okay."

He nuzzles my neck, his warm breath making me shudder, and his hand travels down my body until it grazes the hem of my boxers. He slides a finger under, and it brushes the head of my cock, wet with precum, and a tingling sensation starts in my groin, moves to my chest, and finally overtakes every inch of my body.

"Your cock wants some attention. And"—his entire hand engulfs me and simply holds my dick—"Theo, gosh."

He quickly shimmies out of his pajamas and crawls toward my waist. When he moves to slide my boxers off, I peer down. He's positioned himself with his head near my cock and his rear near my head. Smart guy. Sheldon's ass is on full display, and as he twists and turns to remove my underwear, I get a peek at his hole. Since the first time he played with himself, I tried to commit it to memory, closing my eyes, willing the image back. But now I see it again, in the flesh, and my cock throbs even more.

"There we go," he says. "Now I can see you. All of you."

He kisses the scar on my thigh. My legs tremble.

"I want to play with your gorgeous cock."

I release a small laugh. Nobody has ever talked to me like this and I'm not really sure what to make of it.

"Theo. Your dick is a stunner."

My face flashes hot, and I'm sure my cheeks are bright red.

"Breathe. Let me make you feel good."

I do as I'm told. Lying my head back, eyes closed, focused on my breathing, I remind myself I'm safe with Sheldon.

He begins stroking me, slowly. The feeling of his hand on my cock, I'm not sure I'll last very long. I open my eyes to center myself. Sheldon's lying on his side, and even though he's facing my dick, I can see the corner of his lips. He's smiling. Clearly enjoying himself as much as, if not more than, me. My head is light, and before I overthink it, I reach around and pat his ass. It's fucking delicious.

"You like my ass? You can touch me. Anywhere you want. Permission granted. Go for it."

I leave my hand resting where it is and slowly make circles. His skin, soft, smooth, and demanding of attention. Massaging his gorgeous, delectable ass is enough. For now.

He begins to jerk my cock faster, and when I flinch a little, he moves his face close and spits on my dick.

"Theo. Your cock feels like heaven."

The slick, slippery motion high-kicks my orgasm into motion. My balls tighten, the rest of me tenses up, and I know I'm close. Without saying a word, Sheldon picks up speed because, apparently, he's learning to read me like a book.

"Yes, baby, come for me. I want it, Theo. Yes, come for me. Shoot it all over for me."

The release approaches, but it's Sheldon, near, talking me through it, encouraging, comforting, pleading, that sends me over the edge like a boulder falling off a cliff. My orgasm overtakes me, rocking my body while Sheldon never stops stroking. He's using his left hand to cup and massage my balls and fuckity, fuck, fuck. With each pass his fingers make over the head of my cock, I shiver. Even when I've stopped shooting, he continues. The guy is determined to milk every last drop from me. When he finally relents, Sheldon turns toward my face and has the most mischievous grin I've ever seen. He rests his head on my thigh and lets out a sigh.

"Good job," he says.

"Fuck, that was intense."

"You like that?"

"Fuck yeah, Booster."

"Excuse me?"

"I thought of a nickname for you. Booster."

"Booster?"

His face scrunches up, and I want to pinch him.

"Yeah. You're small but mighty. Somehow you manage to uplift a big oaf like me. Booster."

Sheldon's eyes widen, and his face lights up like a glorious sunrise.

"Excuse me, sir, you are not an oaf," he says, kissing my leg. "But I love it. Booster!"

My hand never leaves the smooth skin of his backside. How long will it be before I need to remove it? I catch my breath. As I touch Sheldon, his warm body starts to melt something, and somehow it makes my soul ache with tenderness but also scares the shit out of me.

"And Theo Berenson, I'm not a big label queen, but I'd say you, my friend, are an ass man."

My eyes slam shut, and with his face on my thigh, I'm positive he can feel the temperature of my skin rise.

"Nothing to be embarrassed about. I have a great ass."

"You do."

"My ass thanks you. Now, maybe you can help me a little."

"Help you?"

Sheldon rolls away so he's on his stomach, arching his back just enough so his round, delicious bottom is on full display. Fuck. I'm done for.

"I can get myself off, and well, no pressure, but if you wanted …"

Quicker than a wink and without a sound, my hand returns to his behind, and I'd like to live in some alternate universe where I never need to remove it.

He reaches underneath and begins stroking himself with his right hand. His eyes glow as he takes my hand.

"You've got strong hands, baby. Want to make me feel good?"

"Mmmh."

"Start with one finger," he says, wrapping his hand around my index finger, "and circle right here."

He guides me to his hole. It's damp and delicious. Even though I want this, more than anything right now, my hand pauses.

"You okay?"

I nod, take a deep breath. I'm safe with Sheldon. We're safe. I lock my eyes on his arched back. His rear rocked up. His hand holding my finger. His spectacular ass. And I let him take the lead.

"Yeah, just like that. Slowly. Tease it. Rub around the outside. A little pressure. Yes, just like that. Do you feel that? I'm getting wet. For you, Theo. God, you're making me hungry for it."

Releasing my finger, he lets me take over, guiding me only by voice. I want this. I need this. Him. And Sheldon's showing me the way.

"Now, I don't have any lube at the moment. You'll need to use spit. Okay?"

Without removing my finger from its spot, I gather as much saliva in my mouth as possible and hock it on Sheldon's hole.

"Oh, yeah. My hole is so horny for you, Theo."

Now wet and slick, there's way more movement. Even though I just came, my dick jolts to life. Somehow, it's getting hard. Again. Oy.

"Lord. Theo, you know exactly what to do. Just like that. I'm ready. Slowly ..."

I gently push in, barely, and I instantly feel Sheldon's heat surrounding me, sending shockwaves of pleasure up my arm to my core and racing down to my cock. This fucker is going to do me in.

"Theo, that feels fan-freakin-tastic. Now, deeper, deeper, all the way in. Yes, baby, yes."

I pause, and Sheldon turns toward me. He's simply staring at my hand. Inside him.

"Theo, you okay?"

"You're so ..."

"So what?"

"You're so horny."

Sheldon laughs. "Theo, I told you. My ass is starving. For you. Wanna try another finger?"

"Yes. I mean, are you sure?"

He shifts his hips. His ass is now closer to my face, and fuck. Fuckity, fuck, fuck.

"Beyond."

With that, I spit on his hole and carefully slip another finger in, and honestly, that's enough with my baseball-mitt hands. And now I'm thinking about sports, which should never happen, let alone while I'm finger-banging Sheldon Soleskin.

"Now, Theo, I want you to screw me. With your fingers. Deep. And don't stop until I come."

"Umkay," I mumble because, between Sheldon's orders and my fingers inside him, my mouth's ability to produce coherent words has taken a hiatus.

I do as I'm told, and Sheldon keeps stealing glances at me. My eyes are wide, mouth wide open, and the faintest hint of a smile creeps over my face. I may not have any experience, but with Sheldon's guidance, I'm managing quite nicely. With my fingers sliding in and out, Sheldon jostles back, pushing me deeper inside.

"Oh yeah, that's it. You're hitting my spot."

I'm pretty sure my face looks like I've just opened a huge present on Christmas morning. Make that the first night of Hanukah. No, make it both. Sheldon may be the one getting off, but I am completely over the moon.

"I'm close, baby. Keep going, right there, yes, yes, yes. Don't stop."

Thrusting back, this time, he stays there, my fingers completely lodged inside him.

"Deeper. Theo, deeper. I'm close."

Sheldon's ass convulses around my fingers, hot and delectable. With each pulse, he shoots thick ribbons of warmth all over the bed. I don't move, not wanting to do the wrong thing. His body shudders, and when I think he's done, a quiver runs through him. After he seems finished, he cranes his neck, we lock eyes, and he says, "Theo. That was amazing. Shantay, you stay."

He collapses in the mess he made, and I truly hope he has a spare set of sheets. My hand gravitates to his behind, it's new favorite resting spot. Catching his breath, Sheldon turns over and cuddles up to me, nuzzling my neck.

"That was brilliant. You were brilliant."

I let out a sharp exhale, and Sheldon grabs me, covering my neck with kisses.

"I'm starving."

"Me too, Booster."

"We have leftover Chinese in the fridge. I think there's moo shoo."

"Fucking perfect," I say, gathering him in my big arms. I lock Sheldon in a firm embrace. Maybe if I hold him tight enough, he'll never move from this spot.

THIRTY-ONE

Sheldon

For the next few days, Theo vacillates between our two apartments. On Sunday morning, I find myself wrapped in my warmest burgundy parka, with a complementary hat and mittens in light crimson, meeting the Berensons at Schmear and Far, a small Jewish deli Theo tells me is known for their smoked fish.

"So, these fish, do they smoke cigars, cigarettes, or pipes?" Abba asks as we walk inside.

"Ah, the king of dad jokes," Theo says with an eye roll while his mother lets out a laugh that reverberates against the walls of the small space.

Schmear and Far is a cozy spot just off the peninsula with floor-to-ceiling shelves filled with cute Jewish books with titles like *Your Guide to Finding Love Before Your Mother Dies* and *Haikus for Jews: For You, a Little Wisdom*. I'm slightly tempted to buy them all. Yes, to impress Theo's parents, but mainly to understand him better.

Beyond the shelves, a light wood counter wraps around the space, and there's a case underneath it filled with containers.

"Abba, let's take some whitefish salad home," Sylvia says.

"Whitefish? Salad?" I whisper to Theo, the words catching in my throat because they sound so wrong together.

"It's actually delicious. Just wait until we have gefilte fish."

I wrap my hands around his arm and look at the extensive menu. Every item is served on a bagel, which I can see them making in deep vats toward the back of the kitchen area. So much for going pre-holiday low-carb before Timothy's wedding, which is now less than a week away. Six days. But with Theo by my side, I'll strut in with my chin up.

As much as I hate to admit it, Naomi is right. She knows me better than anyone. Timothy definitely doesn't create a sting in the pit of my stomach anymore. There's just some low-level sadness about how things ended, about being dumped under the mistletoe on Christmas Eve. Walking into his wedding with Theo will be the ultimate survival of the fiercest.

"Now, Sheldon." Sylvia wraps her hands around my shoulder, not pulling me an inch away from her son but joining the affection. "If you've never had lox before, you probably want to start with The Classic. An everything bagel—cream cheese, cucumber, dill, onions, capers, and classic lox."

"Onions? For breakfast?" I ask.

"He has much to learn," Abba says, poking his head into our huddle.

"I'm having The King Henry," Theo says.

I glance up at the menu and see Theo's sandwich comes with pastrami lox and ... horseradish. For breakfast. I reach for my pocket to ensure my pack of mints remains at the ready. We're going to need all of them.

With coffee in hand, we find a small table toward the windows. There's not much seating here, but Abba hovered over a couple he was sure would be finishing soon and grabbed their spot the moment they pushed their chairs out.

"Sheldon, your nails," Sylvia says, sending my heart tumbling. My gorgeous, navy nails, out of mittens and on full display.

"I painted them," Theo says with a straight face.

"Let me see," she says, taking my hand before I can attack my food.

"Teddy, you did this?" Abba asks.

A nod from Theo and Sylvia says, "They're gorgeous. But next time, Teddy, do a cleanup with a little polish remover. You want the cuticles sparkling."

I give Theo a smirk, and a sliver of a smile peeks through when he looks at me.

"Next time. I'll make sure of it, Sylvia. Okay, how do I eat this?" I ask with the open-faced bagel in front of me, piled high with fixings.

"Pick it up and shove it in your mouth," Theo says, demonstrating with his own. Cream cheese smears on his lower lip, and a parsley leaf gets caught in the chaos. I should be mortified. But I'm not. Instead, I lean over and wipe it off with my finger. Before I can wipe it on my napkin, Theo grabs my finger and pops it into his mouth, sucking and licking it clean. My dick jolts awake at the sensation of his mouth around my finger. Thankfully, his parents seem oblivious as they devour their food.

"So tonight, I'm thinking before you head to Sheldon's we can finish the leftover brisket, and maybe you could make those maple hazelnut brussels sprouts you made last year, sweetie," Sylvia says, giving her bagel a break.

"Sure. We can stop at the store on the way home," Theo replies, taking my hand under the table. The warmth of his fingers around my palm, squeezing just enough but not too tightly, makes my chest expand. "Listen, I'm going to stay at my place tonight," he continues. We didn't talk about this, and I feel a slight drop in my stomach. Did I do something wrong? "I need to do some laundry before school tomorrow. Just tonight," he says with another squeeze of my hand.

"And cram on the couch?" Abba asks.

"It's only for one night," Theo says. Again, his hand grips mine, letting me know we're okay.

Snuggled on the sofa with Janice, she does the thing where she's on her back and curls her head under a single paw. I'm not sure what it is about seeing her sleeping like this on my lap, but the cuteness level is off the charts.

Naomi has been staying with Walker all week. Our place isn't huge, and with Theo shacking up here, at least temporarily, I totally understand her desire to fly the coop. Walker has a lovely condo on the East End. It's a block from the ocean and, well, stunning. A definite upgrade from our crowded off-peninsula apartment.

As close as we are, Naomi and I can't stay this way forever. Living as roommates. As each other's only family and support. That's not how it's meant to be. Walker adores Naomi, and I know, at some point, they'll want to at least live together. When we were little, Naomi and I spent hours under the covers, in our pillow and blanket fort, talking about our weddings. We never discussed the people we'd marry; we talked about the clothes. The dresses. The venue. The food. The music. The party.

Naomi will make the most beautiful bride. Full stop. She will rival Princess Diana, with a slightly less gaudy gown. Wearing a gorgeous tuxedo that somehow makes him even more handsome, Walker will be waiting for her at the altar. I close my eyes and imagine the look on his face when he sees her. Chills overtake my body thinking about the magic of it all, but then my stomach crumples. Naomi marrying Walker is inevitable, leaving me with my very own Bridget Jones "All By Myself" moment. Except it won't be just a moment.

I love my sister more than Dolly Parton's "Hard Candy Christmas," and of course, I want her to be happy. But she's all the family I have. I want to believe we'll remain as close once we don't live together, but naturally, it won't be the same. She'll be married. And probably having babies. Which will christen me the most fabulous guncle in all eternity, but still. What if I'm alone in this apartment? Forever.

"Winter Song" by Leslie Odom Jr. comes on, and I know I'm in trouble. It makes me cry on a good day, and lying here, with pine-scented candles burning, looking at our small tabletop Christmas tree and the mistletoe by the entryway, it sends me over. Tears sting the corners of my eyes, and before I know it, I'm bawling. Janice stirs, and I gently pick her up and kiss the underside of her chin. And by kiss, I mean leave my mouth there and smooch on her for a good minute. For all her eternal crabbiness, Janice adores affection when she's in the mood. Her purring grows from a small gurgle to full motor as I pet her head and love on her chin. She starts nibbling at my nose, making me smile. She can be so loving when she wants to be. Janice, my sweet girl.

Which makes me think of Theo. What is it about me and moody creatures? Right now, we're having fun, but there's no way this can last. Once his parents leave and Timothy's wedding happens, what reason would Theo have to keep me around? Does he actually like me for, well, me? All of me. I want him to. I know that. This time next week, it will all be over. But I still have five days with him. I wipe my face on my sleeve and grab my phone.

> Sheldon: What time will you be at school tomorrow?

> Theo: Same time as always.

> Sheldon: Which is?

> Theo: 6.30

> Sheldon: OK. See you tomorrow.

Arriving at school before sunrise must be a crime against humanity. Like a quick drag challenge where everyone throws on makeup and clothes in under twenty minutes and then has to be filmed with HD cameras. Why, Mama Ru, why? But a sudden flush of warmth from my groin spreads outward thinking about Theo. After four nights of him in my bed, I missed him last night. More than I thought I would. More than I wanted to. More than I should.

I spot his monster truck in the alley as I drive past the school to the parking lot. He's here. And the lot is empty. The hallways are silent. It feels like the Sunday I set up my room. Except it's Monday, and within a half hour the building will buzz with staff getting ready for the day. I round the hallway and head straight for Theo, my coat and backpack still on. There's no time to waste dropping them in my class.

When I walk into his closet, he's sitting in his ratty chair, feet up on that grimy milkcrate, reading something on his phone. He doesn't look up until I quietly close the door, the soft click of the deadbolt finally getting his attention.

"Hey, don't close that."

"Good morning to you, too."

"No, really, Booster. Don't close the door."

"Why not?" I walk over and stand next to his long legs, which are stretched out and crossed.

"Someone might need me. I don't close the door. Ever."

"Nobody is here. And right now, I need you," I say, lifting my right leg over to straddle him. "I missed you last night."

"Sheldon, folks are going to be here soon. You're being foolish." He reaches to push me off, but I grab his hand and put it on my ass.

Leaning over, I put my finger over his lips and say, "Remember how you barely spoke when we first met? Can you try that again for a few minutes?" I use my quiet voice. We call it a Level One Voice in the classroom. Only the person I'm speaking to should be able to hear me. I need Theo to listen. "Last night, I couldn't stop thinking about you." I sit on his lap. "In my bed." I begin to rub on him through his pants. "Your cock in my hand." I lean forward, my lips an inch from his. "I want to taste it." I lift up just enough fabric to force my hand down his uniform pants.

"Sheldon, please." Theo begins to protest, his mouth moving against my finger, and as soon as he parts his lips, I slip my finger in.

"The door is locked. I want you to stay just like this. Don't move unless I tell you. Are you okay with that?"

His eyes explore my face, and without speaking, his hands are on my waist, grabbing and hauling me toward him. Our lips crash into each other, and his dick springs to life in my hand. Firm and hot, Theo's hard-on informs me he's more than ready for some quick fun before the day begins.

Removing my hand from his mouth, I quickly unbutton and unzip him, freeing his fat cock from the prison of his pants. With permission granted, I turn around and bend over, slamming it into my mouth. As soon as the tip enters, Theo's body shivers under me, and while I want to go slow and be attentive to him, I also know the clock is ticking. We only have a short time before the sounds of feet on the tile outside his door overtake the silence and interrupt my morning treat.

It's hard for me to take his entire cock in my mouth, but that doesn't mean I don't give it my best shot. Good luck, and don't fuck it up. When I realize gagging on Theo's dick might not be the way I want to start my Monday, I use my right hand to assist, creating a warm tunnel of delight for him. Soft, low whimpers come from Theo. Taking the hint I've given by placing it right in his face, Theo grabs my ass. Over my gray navy pinstripe Italian stretch chinos, he cups, massages, and kneads, and I press back into his forceful grip.

"You like my ass, don't you?"

"Mmmh, fuck yeah," he says, his voice even lower. Deeper. "You wear these tight little pants, and when you walk in front of me, all I can think about is getting up in there." He grabs me harder, his thumb spreading my ass underneath my clothes.

My dick pulses with each low-toned word out of his mouth. Bobbing up and down, slurping, sucking, relishing every inch of Theo's magnificent cock, my own strains against the fabric, and I reach back to unbutton my pants if only to give myself a little relief. As soon as the button's undone, my dick pops out. Theo grabs and yanks my poor pants down around my thighs with such force that my breath hitches. Having him take a little control sends shockwaves of pleasure up my spine.

"Baby, do whatever you want with me," I pant. His hands move and spread my ass wide as he pulls me back. "Theo Berenson, you are just full of surprises this morning."

"This okay, Booster?" he asks. His breath is close enough that my hole shutters from the puff of air when he makes the B sound.

"I told you. Anything."

Before the last word leaves my mouth, Theo's tongue makes contact, and my head tips back as I gasp for air. My brain ceases to function for a moment, and for maybe the first time in my life, I'm speechless. Theo begins to devour me. He's starving. For me. The sensation of his lips and tongue and that stubble, that delicious stubble that shows up five minutes after he shaves, is making me tremble. I lower myself on his legs that are still propped on that damn crate, giving me a better resting spot to get back to guzzling him.

"I'm not hurting you … your leg?"

"Booster, shut up and suck my cock."

Yes, sir. Even harder than before, eating me out has sent Theo into overdrive, and I stroke and suck like a ravenous animal. The small room fills with the sounds of wetness, swallowing, licking, and Theo's low groans are the icing on the cake.

"I want you to screw me so badly, Theo. Your cock inside me, pounding me," I pant. The precum on Theo's dick tastes salty, sweet, scrumptious, and I can tell he's close.

My head buries into him. I do my best to create a continuous corridor of wetness by spitting on my hand, jerking, and sucking him. He seizes my waist and pulls me further back, shoving his face against my hole, tongue fucking me, and this might be my favorite thing ever.

Theo doesn't stop. One hand hangs on to my side, anchoring me in place on his mouth, while the other strokes my rock-hard dick. The dual sensation brings fluttery shockwaves through my entire body. It's almost too much to handle.

"Baby, you're rocking my world right now with your tongue."

He's driving me over the edge, and it doesn't take long for my balls to begin to tighten. The primal itch, deep down inside, crawls up, demanding release.

"Theo, you're going to make me …"

I push myself up, unable to focus on anything but how Theo's mouth and hand coordinate, unhinging me. I brace myself on his fabulous thick thighs as the climbing peaks. Theo pumps me until, unable to contain myself, I explode all over his hand and uniform. The sensation rips through me, and my load exceeds the standard.

We pause for a moment, with only the sound of our heavy

breathing. The stillness in the room buzzes with electricity. We don't have much time.

"Now, come for me, Theo. I want it. All of it."

I resume making a sloppy mess on his cock, using my mouth and both hands because we need to wrap this up now. Theo never stops painting the inside of my hole with his tongue, grunting and pulling me back on him, my ass the perfect excuse for him to be quiet.

His body begins to rise ever so slightly, and when his fingers dig into the flesh around my hips, I know he's close. He's thrusting up now, fucking my mouth like a champ, and his cock throbs until he hauls me back with such force my head pulls up, and I'm left simply jerking him off, spitting, using both hands to cover the real estate from his balls to the tip. His face buried deep, tongue flicking in and out, a low rumble from his throat vibrates into my hole, informing me he's about to come.

And yikes. When it happens, the eruption shoots across the space he's created by pulling me back and lands on my face, covering it like the most glorious glaze on my delighted donut face. His legs shake with the force of his climax, and the crate rocks and slams against the floor, startling us both.

"You okay?" I ask.

"Fuck."

"I'll take that as yes. And Happy Monday, by the way."

"Fuck."

"Theo, you're an artist with that tongue of yours. Thought I was going to pass out for a minute there and have a swoony-collapsing-fainting moment."

I stand and move off him, my half-hard dick dangling with my pants around my thighs. Theo sits motionless. No words. His eyes closed. Crud, I've killed him.

"Theo?"

I move toward his face and press my lips to his, the taste of what we've just done mingling between us. Before I open my eyes, Theo's arms fly around me, clutching me close. He's holding me so tight I'm actually worried something's wrong.

"Baby, what's wrong?"

His face buried in my neck, he mumbles, "Nothing. Absolutely nothing."

"We need to clean up. Do you have anything we can use?"

He releases his hold enough for me to pull back a few inches and says, "You're kidding, right? I'm a custodian, and we're in my closet."

"Oh, right."

He chuckles. His face is a mess, covered in spit, and when I bend down to kiss him again, I bite his lower lip before pressing into a full kiss, chuckling through it because we just did all that. Here. Now. When I saw him sitting there, feet up, not a care in the world, something took over. Bringing Theo pleasure, unleashing something inside him, chipping away at his damn wall feels like a drug, and I'm addicted.

THIRTY-TWO

Theo

Thankfully, I keep extra uniforms on a shelf in the closet. You never know when a backed-up toilet might become a fountain, a kid might projectile vomit all over you, or a Sheldon might erupt like a volcano. Oy.

He's gone, off like a flash after washing his face in the mop sink and using one of my towels to dry off. He grabbed my face, kissed me quickly, and bolted to his classroom, leaving me speechless, blinking, and with a slight tingling in my chest. Sheldon Soleskin has come into my life like a fucking tornado and ripped everything apart.

The way he barged in—fuck that was hot. He was hot. Something about Sheldon makes me forget all the voices, all the awful thoughts. When he's looking at me, with those hazel puppy dog eyes, I'm both lost and found.

And those freckles, so many freckles, I want to dot each of them with a kiss.

But allowing myself to feel this way with him is dangerous. He may think he likes me, but he doesn't understand how much baggage I'm carrying. He doesn't get it. Getting close to me never ends well. I need to figure out a way to stop this nonsense before it really gets out of hand. My parents leave in four days, and I'm chewing my lip. Again.

"What happened now?" Christian asks. The man knows me better than almost anyone. Calling him during my first break on a Monday morning is a dead giveaway.

"Nothing happened."

"Bullshit. You did something."

"No," I lie, watching my feet sway back and forth on the milk crate where Sheldon gave me the blow job of a lifetime a few hours ago. While I buried my face in his delectable ass. Fuck. "Okay, maybe."

My right foot slips off, sending the crate airborne and crashing into the wall.

"What the hell was that?"

"Nothing."

"T-Dawg. I love you, man, but you're a bit of a let's say, lug when it comes to, well, really other people in general."

I'm quiet because he's not wrong, and I wish he were.

"It's that guy I talked to. What's his name again?"

"Sheldon."

"Sheldon. What happened? What did you do?"

"Him," I say and wait for the pieces to fall in place.

"Fucking A, buddy! You had sex?"

"I mean, sort of."

"Hell, yes. You've needed to get laid for forever. This is awesome."

I stand up and close the door. For the second time ever and on the same day, but it shuts me off from the school because if anyone walks by, this conversation is not family-friendly.

"We've fooled around. A few times."

"A few times? Theo Berenson, you sly dog. When were you going to tell me?"

"Now. It's only been a few days."

"Wait, a few times in a few days? Damn, man. He must really like you."

I shift in my chair, the rusty springs squeaking, reminding me to squirt them with a little oil to soothe their crankiness.

"That's the problem. It's all a joke. I mean, not really. It's not funny. We're doing it for my parents."

"What? He wants to have sex, fool around, or whatever you're doing a few times in as many days. I'm not seeing how this is for Sylvia and Adam, man."

I let out a huge sigh, and my ears begin to feel warm, blood surging to my face. Sheldon and me. Me.

"It can't be real because ..."

"Because why?"

A quiver takes over my stomach and my teeth are gnawing on my lip again.

"Don't make me say it."

"Say what?"

"Dude, look at me," I say, my hand gliding over my torso.

"Um, we're on the phone. I can't really look at you."

"No, I mean, you know what I look like. I'm, I'm ... fat."

"You're not fat. You're stocky."

"In the straight world maybe, but in the gay world, this is fat."

"Listen, are you trying to get me to tell you how hella handsome you are on a Monday morning? Because that's just cruel."

"And a lie."

"Is it? Who says you're not? Certainly not the guy you're fooling around with."

My fingers find the keys on my belt and begin fiddling with them, rubbing and flicking the grooves of the cool metal.

"I'm waiting. Tell me."

"Nobody, but ..."

"But nothing. Nobody's said it because it's not true. Do I need to call Sylvia and get her on a three-way chat here?"

"God. Please. No."

Christian and my mother have a weird relationship. Their connection is based on their love of teasing and annoying me.

"Then listen. This guy likes you?"

"He likes fooling around."

"That can be an entry point. Pun intended."

"Stop. Please."

"I want you to do me a favor."

"What?"

My fingers have found their way into my mane, twirling and swirling a strand until it pops off with a boing.

"Go with it. Have fun. Don't overanalyze. Which I know is almost impossible for you. T-Dawg, you deserve happiness."

His words create a frosty chill that starts on my shoulders and travels down my back because I'm not so sure I do.

"Theodore Berenson"—his use of my full name lets me know he means business—"I can hear you thinking. Listen, what happened, what happened to him, it wasn't your fault. You have to stop beating yourself up, man."

"Do I?"

"Yeah, you do. There was nothing you could've done differently. Nothing. I was there. I know."

Unsure how to reply, I close my eyes and take a breath.

"Listen, Anna is packing for her convention. She needs me to get her suitcase from the attic. I want you to relax. You're a catch, brother."

"I'm not a fish."

"No, you're a bear. My big fluffy bear. Now go have fun with your new boy toy."

"You're a pain in the ass. You know that?"

"Yes. And I love you too."

I place my phone on the desk and smile. Christian likes to push me. Stop beating myself up. Have fun. With Sheldon. His face. His eyes. His soft skin and sweet breath. A knock at the door snaps me back to reality. When I open it, Kent stands, fist raised, about to knock again.

"Theo, you never have your door closed. Everything all right?"

"Fine. Just fine," I say and stumble backward, tripping over the damn milkcrate.

"Having a good Hanukah with your parents?"

"Oh yeah, wonderful. How about you?"

Kent is the only other Jewish person I know at Lear, and it's nice to have someone to kibbitz with about the holidays.

He walks over and sits on the milk crate. Sheldon over me. On me.

"Oh, good, all good. Been going to my sister's to light the menorah with her kids. It's been lovely, really. She makes the most amazing challah. And I've won a ton of gelt." He pats his belly. "She buys the good chocolate too. But actually, I do need something from you, Theo."

I move to grab the mop and bucket. "What is it?"

"I love your enthusiasm for cleanliness, but it's not that. I need your opinion on something."

"Oh, okay."

Kent shifts on the crate. It slips under him and almost sends him crashing to the floor.

"I'm good! All good. Uh. Um, well, the thing is, I have a date, and I'm wondering about the restaurant."

"Um, okay, but why are you asking me?"

"You know so much about cooking, and I thought maybe you'd know about the place," he says, then clears his throat and rubs the back of his neck. I open my mouth to speak, but he continues. "Also, the date is with, well, it's with a man."

My mouth falls open, and as I'm aware my lower jaw hangs like a dead fish on a line, I close it quickly. Kent Lester is …

"Bisexual. I'm bisexual. It's kind of new. I mean, I've been bisexual my whole life but never dated a man. Once in high school I, but, um, never mind. Anyway, a date. With a man. We connected online. Well, on my phone. Does that count as online? SWISH, have you ever heard of it?" he asks, his knee bouncing like a pile driver. "And I haven't told anyone. I mean you. And the guy. Obviously." He lets out a few small laughs, and I'm fairly certain I'm supposed to say something supportive and helpful, but I'm slightly disoriented because I truly had no clue.

"But I thought you were married?" As usual, I say the densest thing possible.

"I was. But I've been divorced for a while. Seven years now. I was bisexual the entire time, but when you're married to a woman, people assume."

There's a lump in my throat when I swallow. All these assumptions I had about Kent are false, and they're completely from a place of ignorance. The urge to help him rumbles up from my core.

"Oh. Well, I don't go out a ton, you know, I prefer cooking at home, but what's the place?"

"But you know food. It's that new restaurant, Fourteen, over by the water. Have you heard anything about it?"

Fourteen. A new hot spot. I read about it online. The chef moved from New York City to open it, and the sous chef came from California. Both are big shots. It opened last year, but apparently, it's still hard to get a table. Fancy pants. Not really my style, but I don't want to rain on Kent's parade.

"From what I've read, it seems like a good place for a date."

"Even for a ..."

"A what?"

"A gay date?" Kent's looking at me, and I notice his beard is trimmed closer than before. If I were a betting man, I'd say there's some product in his hair. A gel or pomade or mousse or something. I'll have to ask Sheldon.

"Yes, it's perfect. Relax. You're a great guy, Kent. Anyone would be lucky to date you."

The words come out of my mouth, and I realize I sound exactly like my mother. Kill me now.

"Thanks, I appreciate that. Now, let's hope Vincent feels the same way. That's the guy. Vincent. Well, I appreciate your support."

"I'm actually seeing someone. Well, sort of."

It comes out so fast, and I regret it the moment the words escape my mouth.

"Wait, what? Theo! That's brilliant. Who is it?"

I'm not sure if I should tell Kent about Sheldon or not, but then

I picture his sweet face. Those sparkling freckles. The way my heart melts when he's close, and I blurt it out.

"Sheldon."

"Mr. Soleskin?"

I bite my lip and nod.

"Theo. Why didn't you tell me? Why didn't *he* tell me?" Kent asks, clasping his hands like he's just received the best news.

"I mean, it kind of happened by accident. He needs a date for a wedding. I wanted my parents to think I have a boyfriend."

"You were pretending?"

"Yes."

"And now you're ... not?"

"Exactly. At least, I think not."

Kent reaches around and takes me under his wing. Even though I'm much bigger than him, it's nice to be wrapped up in his soft red sweater.

"Theo. I love this for you. For him. For both of you. Nobody deserves it more." Shifting away, he wobbles and says, "Now, let's hope this Vincent and I hit it off."

"Kent, you're a great guy. Just be yourself."

"Yeah, that's what I'm afraid of. My messy self being on full display for him."

"Vincent, was it?" I ask, and Kent nods. "Vincent is going to have the best time with you. Mess and all."

I put my hand on his shoulder. My chest is full, knowing he feels comfortable confiding in me.

"You'll have to tell me how it goes," I say.

"Will do. All right, have a good one."

Finally alone, I sit to enjoy five minutes of peace and quiet before making my way to the cafeteria. Today's menu: French toast sticks. And I don't even care.

THIRTY-THREE

Sheldon

The week unfolds like a cozy holiday commercial for clothes, coffee, or candy. I talk to my class about both Hanukah and Christmas, mentioning lighting the candle with Theo's family.

"Is Mr. Berenson your boyfriend?" Nolan asks.

"He's a boy. And he's your friend," Brodie says with a smirk.

"Well, that is true," I say. "I mean he could be. Maybe. We are both boys. Men. And we're friends. That's all you need to know."

Right on cue, Theo walks in to teach the class the dreidel game. The children gather around a table, and Theo sits in a chair, Brodie saddled up next to him, helping. I stand back and make sure everyone listens and behaves, but I don't need to intervene. They're captivated. By Theo.

Our holiday concert is this afternoon. The kids have been practicing in music class, but we also take some time at the end of each day to sing through the program. Unsurprisingly, most of the songs are about Christmas. There's a single song for Kwanzaa and Hanukah.

We gather on the carpet before heading down. Brodie sits beside me, leaning on me. I ask the class, "Who can tell me something we've learned about Hanukah?"

"The Jewish people were running out of oil, and they didn't have enough," Martha says.

"Yeah, but then the oil lasted for eight days," Amy adds.

"And that's why they have eight nights," Kaden says.

"And they get eight presents," Nolan says.

"I want to be Jewish," Ruby groans.

Brodie laughs, and hearing his sweet laughter makes my heart swell. In the few weeks since I started, we've really become a cohesive classroom community. After the fire alarm debacle, Brodie finally fell into a rhythm. He earns his half hour with Theo almost every afternoon now, and on the off day he doesn't, he maintains his composure about it. Being the last day before vacation, today was a tougher day for him.

When he doesn't earn his visit with Theo after lunch, I call him over.

"Brodie, do you understand why you won't see Theo today?"

He nods.

"Can you tell me?"

Brodie's eyes go wide and then find the carpet.

"Safe."

"Safe, that's right. You have to be safe. And you weren't safe when you …"

"Hid under the table," he mumbles.

"Right, we don't hide under the table and then ignore Mr. Soleskin," I say, cringing at referring to myself in the third person. "Can you look at me, buddy?"

His tentative brown eyes find mine, and why do the toughest kids always steal my heart?

"I still love you, you know that, right?"

He doesn't speak or otherwise acknowledge my question.

"Brodie, there's nothing you can do that will make me—" I say, but before I can finish, his arms wrap around my waist, and he buries his head into my stomach. We stand there, him squeezing me for dear life, me returning his embrace, and I don't finish my sentence. I don't need to.

At the end of the day, families gather at the back of the cafégy-

242

matorium, and school staff dot the doors and corners of the space. Halfway through the performance, during a cheery rendition of "All I Want for Christmas is You," Theo appears at the back hallway door. We don't look at each other or exchange words, but he saunters toward me. And when the children sing about only wanting you, Theo's hand finds mine, and standing there in the giant room, surrounded by the entire school, holding Theo Berenson's hand, my chest expands, warmth overtakes me, and I try, really hard, to relish the moment.

Finally home with gift bags full of mugs, cards, and ornaments declaring me the Best Teacher in the World, I prepare for Theo's arrival with a hot bath. The water soothes my sore feet. Standing all day teaching really does a number on my poor tootsies. Today was a whirlwind. The holiday concert went off without a hitch. Well, mostly. Brodie stood in the front and didn't sing a single word, but he was safe and even bopped his head and smiled a few times. The children really did their best, dressed in their cutest holiday outfits with bows in their hair and bowties around their necks. It truly was beyond sweet.

As I lie in the tub, Janice perches on the edge, watching my every move. Occasionally, she dips her paw into the water and licks it. I reach over and scratch her chin before taking a deep breath. Theo's parents leave Friday morning to make the long trek back to Florida. Tomorrow is the last night of Hanukah, and our cute little playing-house fantasy will be over.

The door clicks, and I hear Theo's voice. "Booster? You in bed?"

I've been leaving the spare key under the doormat for him. Sure, I understand that's not the safest strategy, but our building's front door has a coded keypad, and we're on the second floor, and so far, I haven't had a scary surprise visitor with a knife.

"In the tub. I'll be out in a minute," I shout as Theo's face appears at the bathroom door.

"Booster."

I use my hands to cover my midsection and feign modesty.

"Excuse me, sir. I'm in the bath. Naked."

"I see that."

"How was dinner?"

"Wonderful." He sits on the closed toilet seat and attempts not to stare, but I never take my eyes off him, and Theo is a horrible actor. "Abba put way too much salt in the potatoes, and Mom was furious. 'Your blood pressure is going to burst through the roof, you meshuggeneh.' I'm happy to be here for a little peace."

"Did you have dessert?" I ask, standing and grabbing my towel from the hook next to the toilet. I drip a little on Theo's sweatpants on purpose. The towel caresses my body in front of his watchful eyes. The stirring in my belly moves south, and my cock slowly stiffens.

"Yeah, just Neapolitan ice cream. Mom adores mixing them all together, which is blasphemy if you ask me."

"I mean, I can see chocolate and strawberry, but all three? What's even the point of vanilla ice cream?"

"Right? I only had a few bites. I wanted to get over here," he says, reaching for my waist and pulling me close.

"You did?"

"Yeah. There's something I want to talk to you about."

My stomach drops, and a wave of worry washes over me. Here it is. Tomorrow night. The last night. His parents leaving. He's going to bail, even before Timothy's wedding. Tears form in the corners of my eyes before I can even catch my breath.

"Oh. Um, okay. What is it?"

Theo gently removes the towel from my fingers and takes over drying. He starts at my feet, softly brushing my skin like he's afraid of breaking something. Breaking me. His eyes stay on my toes as he gingerly rubs between them, causing them to wiggle.

"Booster, after tomorrow night, my parents are leaving."

"I know."

"And the wedding is Saturday night."

"Yeah. We probably should figure out what we're going to wear.

We shouldn't match. I mean, matching a little is cute, but being matchy-matchy will look like we're trying too hard. We don't want that. I know what I'm wearing. Maybe I can look and see what ties you have and try to coordinate colors. Just something to tie us together without—"

His hand finds my mouth, and he covers it with his palm.

"Booster, stop. I need to say this."

My eyes close, bracing for impact. I'm literally naked in front of Theo, and he's about to crush my heart.

"I know you said you liked me, and well, the problem is, well …"

"You don't," I begin, and he moves his hand enough to let the words out, "like me."

"No, Booster. I don't. Like you."

I don't open my eyes because the tears are there, and if I open them, they'll stream down my face, and I can't let Theo see how much his words demolish my heart.

"Booster, I don't like you. I'm falling in love with you."

For a split second, I swear the Earth stops spinning. Or maybe the energy surging through my body causes it to reverberate at the same force as the earth's rotation. I don't know, I'm not Bill Nye the Science Guy.

"Did you hear me?"

"No, I'm not sure I did. I'm going to need you to say it again," I say, wrapping the towel around my waist. "And not when my dick is in your face."

Theo laughs and looks at me. His eyes scan my face as if he's searching. I'm not sure for what, but he's taking me in, all of me.

"I love you, Booster. I wanted you to know. Before my parents leave. Before the wedding. Before all this ends."

"You love me?"

My eyes pop open, and the tears fall. Theo hasn't dried my head yet, and maybe he'll think the tears are just residual water from the bath. I'm not sure, and I don't really care. Theo loves me? Me?

"How … how? How did this happen?" I fumble out.

"How did this happen? I don't fucking know. I don't like it any more than you do. It just did," he shouts. The tiny hairs on the back of my neck stand up, and my eyes go wide. "Booster, I'm sorry. Listen. I don't know how it happened. I only know how you make me feel. My parents were talking about you and—"

"Wait, what were they saying?"

"Mom found a deli that sells fresh gefilte fish. She bought some for tomorrow. For you. 'That Sheldon, with that sweet punim, he has very good taste. I think he'll love it.' And then they asked me what my intentions were."

"Intentions?" I ask, cocking my head to the side.

"Sheldon, I'm thirty-six, single, and Jewish. My parents have the yenta on speed dial. They want me to be married. They want grandchildren."

My eyes, already wide, now gape open, overtaking the top half of my face.

"Oh gosh, no, I'm not talking about marriage. I only meant them asking about you. Me. Us. It made me realize, well, how I feel."

"You love me?"

He doesn't speak but nods, a small smile overtaking his face, and for once, I'm not mad about Theo's silence.

I jump into his arms, wrapping my legs around his waist. The towel falls, and Theo grabs my ass, holding me up as we embrace. My head buries into his neck, and if I could crawl inside his soul, I would.

Theo carries me into the bedroom and lays me on the bed. He begins taking his clothes off, and I watch, my cock letting him know I'm more than ready. When he's down to his boxers, those damn ratty shorts, he walks over to the bed and stands. I may need to buy him some new underwear for Christmas. Am I allowed to get him a Christmas present? I could try and buy them tomorrow for the last night of Hanukah, but would it be tacky to give him new underwear in front of his parents? Sylvia would surely approve, but Theo might be mortified.

"Sheldon, I thought maybe we could …" He joins me on the bed, snuggling up next to me. His hand gently lands on my neck before he smooths it down my torso to my dick. "Do more. If you wanted."

I pop up on my elbow and say, "Are you kidding? Theo, I want you to fuck me so badly. Seriously. My butt is beyond horny for you."

He chuckles. "You said fuck."

"This moment called for it. Sorry."

"Don't ever apologize for saying fuck."

"Fuck. I want you to fuck me, Theo. So badly."

"Well, I don't want to disappoint you."

"I have condoms," I say, reaching past him toward the nightstand drawer.

"Sheldon, I've never, um, done this. I'm pretty sure I don't need a condom. Unless you want me to, and then, of course, I will."

"Oh. I mean, I haven't had sex with anyone since Timothy. That was almost twelve months ago. And I've been tested since. Twice."

"Are you sure?" he asks.

"Yes." I reach down and put my hand inside his boxers. His cock, fat and firm, throbs in my palm. "Let's get these off you. Please."

He lifts his hips with a grunt, and I pull them off. His dick pops to full attention like a wooden soldier, and I'm so ready to crack some nuts.

Overtaken with a wave of emotion, I take Theo's cock in my mouth, licking, slurping, and enjoying every moment of getting him ready. His breathing intensifies, and his hands find my head, stroking and massaging my scalp. The feeling of him filling my mouth with his gorgeous dick makes mine grow even harder.

"Booster, wait," he says, his hands moving to my waist and tugging me toward his head. "C'mere."

I move to my knees and then straddle his face, and again, he pulls me down, right on his face. There it is, his thick tongue on my hole, flicking and flitting, making my already damp opening soaking wet.

"Theo. You and that tongue. You're ... oh baby," I moan as my eyes roll back.

"Mmmh. Fucking delectable," he mumbles into me.

Doing my best to brace myself on the bed as he sends shock-waves of pleasure through my body, I drop my head so I can get at least the top half of Theo's beautiful cock in my mouth. His forearms lock onto my shins, holding me in place, drawing me back onto his face.

My body melts onto Theo's tongue. I don't like to play favorites, but I think this might be my most preferred location in the entire world. Riding Theo Berenson's tongue like a surfer on a wave. Over and over, his tongue darts in, coating my hole with his saliva. With him. As much as I never want this to end, I want more.

"Theo, please. I'm ready. I want your cock inside me. Now."

With all his attention, I'm more than prepared. I'm starving for it. For him. I turn around, planting a kiss on his lips. He tastes like sin and sweat, my ass all over his face like a child eating an ice-cream cone for the first time.

"You're fucking delicious," he snarls.

"We're going to take this slow, okay? It's been a while." I reach for the lube I bought and planted in my nightstand drawer.

Crouching over him, I warm it up between my hands, reach back, and spread slickness on him and then myself. His shoulders shudder when I slather his cock, starting with his balls and making sure every inch is saturated.

"Ready?" I ask.

He grips my waist and nods. I take his dick in my hand and slowly position it on my hole. The head rubs against my skin, and I take a deep, cleansing breath. As my body relaxes, I slowly push him inside, only a tiny bit, before moving him right out.

"Oh. Seeing stars. Give me a minute."

His hands move to mine, and he pulls my face toward his.

"Booster, we don't have to do this," he whispers.

"Are you kidding me? I want this. You. It's been a while, is all. And baby, your dick is fat."

His mouth brushes mine, and I close my eyes. And then, for all that's good and mighty, Theo bites my lower lip. Hard. My mouth throbs from his teeth.

"Ouch."

"Too hard?"

"A little. But also, I love it. Now, fuck me. Hard." I pull myself up and grab the bottle of lube. "You can never have enough," I say, rubbing more on both of us.

My body takes him in as far as he went the last time, and then, with a deep breath, I let all the tension and worry escape and feel Theo thrust all the way inside me. We're connected. Finally.

"You okay, Theo?"

Completely still, Theo's face looks like he might be in a trance. Or asleep. I swear if he falls asleep while we're having sex, I will not be amused.

"Theo?"

Silence. Oh, my lord. What will happen to me if I've murdered Theo Berenson with sex? I'll lose my teaching job and be forced to sell horrible clothes at the mall.

"Theo? Are you okay?" I move toward his face to investigate, and his cock pops out of me.

When I'm close enough to kiss him, his eyes bolt open, and the widest smile I've ever seen plasters on his face.

"I'm fan-fucking-tastic."

I let out a huge laugh because, well, he's so enchanting. "Theo, you scared me." I slap his chest. "Now fuck me."

I move back, and his cock, sticking straight up at attention, glides right in. Having Theo inside me feels like winning the mini and maxi challenges in the same episode and then going on to take the crown. With a deep breath, I say a silent prayer to stay like this forever.

"Oh, Booster, you're going to fucking kill me."

"Not tonight. Please."

With him finally settling in, I slide my legs forward and pull myself into a squat, giving me more control to thrust up and down. Theo's hands reach for my chest and find my nipples. I grab his left hand and suck on his fingers and then return it to my torso. His slippery digits begin rubbing and flicking, and the combination of his dick pounding me and his hands all over me, it doesn't get better than this.

"Fuck me, Theo. Just like that. You feel so good. So good ... so good inside me."

His hands press against my pecs, pushing me down. He's drilling himself into me as far as possible. Each thrust sends a wave of delight through my core.

"Booster, you're glorious."

"You are, Theo. You are."

"Does it feel good?"

His eyebrows furrow, and he blinks with curiosity. "Oh, Theo, yeah. So good. You feel phenomenal."

I reach back and massage his balls, his cock pulsing in and out of me, wanting another touchpoint of our physical connection.

"Can you come like this?" I ask.

"It's not going to take much."

I reach down to jerk my cock, trying to keep up.

"Let me do it. Please," he says, gently pushing my hand aside and taking my dick in his thick palm, immediately taking over.

The sensation of Theo pounding me, my ass slapping loudly against his thighs, his hand on my cock, sends frissons of delight through me. I lift my left hand and put it behind my head, trying my best to absorb the pleasure of the moment. I begin rubbing just underneath Theo's balls. A little pressure and he begins to moan.

"Oh, Booster, look at you." His eyes lock onto mine. "You're so fucking beautiful."

Theo lets go of me and grips the sheets. His body thrusts up, and I feel him pulsating and shooting inside me. Complete euphoria overtakes his face, and I'm tempted to grab my phone and snap a picture to remember him this way. He begins to decelerate and moves to resume stroking me.

"You don't have to," I say, reaching to block him.

"Let me. I want to make you come."

"I'm actually really close," I say, his dick still hard, throbbing inside me.

The surge of his orgasm, the view of his gorgeous face,

completely vulnerable, sends me over. Before he clasps on, his fingers only inches from my cock, it happens. My dick explodes, hands-free, shooting ribbons of cum all over Theo's chest.

Theo's eyes almost pop out of his head, and my cock, on autopilot, explodes over and over as I giggle from the surprise. When I can't control the urge anymore, I grab his hand and place his fingers around my dick. Knowing exactly what I need, Theo slides his full fingers up and down my dripping dick, and the last few spurts flow.

"Lord," I say, collapsing on him. "That's never happened before."

"How did you do that?"

"I have no clue."

"Booster, you continue to blow my mind."

"Awesome. That was exactly the reaction I was hoping for."

"You also continue to make a mess whenever I'm with you."

"Yeah, but it's a good mess."

"No, it's a fucking perfect mess."

After we clean up and are back in bed, snuggled up like two tired elves on Christmas morning, a lightness overtakes me. I guess practice really does make perfect. We fooled Theo's parents. Or, did we? I guess maybe we didn't fool anyone. And the thought of walking into Timothy's wedding with Theo by my side makes my heart swell. I couldn't care less about proving anything to anyone. I want to dress up and have a fantastic time with my, my …

"So, what are we anyway?" I ask.

"Humans?"

"No, I mean us. Are we dating? Boyfriends? Lovers?"

"Um, we are definitely not lovers. That's cringy. Do we have to label it? Can't we just be … us?"

"Okay, not a label queen. Noted. But if people ask, what will you say? Who am I?"

"You're Sheldon."

"No, silly. Who am I to you?"

"You're my Sheldon."

It sounds so incredibly perfect. I can't even argue.

"And what do I say you are to me?" I ask.

"Sheldon, if you'll have me. All this …" He motions to his entire body. "You can call me whatever the fuck you want."

"Maybe I'll call you my Grouchy Bear."

His fingers find my face, rub my cheek, and trace my lips.

"Now, my Sheldon, go to sleep. I'll make you pancakes in the morning if you're good."

I cuddle into Theo's chest and drift off, dreaming of warm pancakes.

The sun shines brightly, attempting to warm the frigid temps outside. Entering my window, it forces my eyes to squint. I reach for Theo, but my hand finds emptiness. And then I remember pancakes. But I don't smell Theo's secret warm apple syrup. And I don't hear the clanging of dishes and pans. I slip on my pajama bottoms to investigate. Theo's keys aren't in the bowl by the door. There's no trace of him. He's gone.

THIRTY-FOUR

Theo

"Booster, it's Theo. By now, you've noticed I'm not there. I hate that you might be worried, but Christian texted just after two. Anna was in an accident. I don't know much. He said she's fine, and there's no reason for me to rush there, especially with my parents being here, but well, ride or die, we're family. I hope you understand. Please call me when you get this, so I know you're okay. I love you, Booster."

My truck chugs along at eighty-two miles per hour. According to Abba, it's the magic speed to avoid tickets. He swears by eighty-two. Never gotten a ticket. The thumping bass, plinky piano, and then Freddie's vocals mixed with Bowie's on "Under Pressure" overtake the cab. By the time the band joins them, I'm flying down the highway like Freddie's voice screaming over the music for another chance. It's a good three-hour drive to Connecticut, and I hope to get to the hospital by sunrise.

Christian's SOS text jolted me awake. My time overseas left me a painfully light sleeper, and the soft ding was enough to shake me, even with Sheldon nestled into my chest like the sweetest little baby bear. I can't believe that happened. Not so much the sex. That I believe, Sheldon's a horny little bugger. God bless him. I can't believe I told him I love him. But I do. So damn much it hurts. The voicemail I left might sound a little frantic. I take a deep breath, eyes scanning over my phone in the holder near the dash, hoping he replies soon.

I thought he might wake up when I gently moved him off me. Well, I hoped he would. Maybe those last days of school did him in. Maybe it was the … other stuff. But Sheldon was out like a brick. I left the message as soon as I got in my truck, and as the sun creeps up, I'm hopeful he's heard it.

Marching into the hospital, the industrial cleaner attacks my nose. Understandably, they are not fucking around with germs here. The floors shine, and I smile, thinking how hundreds of children tramping over them would wipe that sparkle right off.

The sterile atmosphere has been brightened with random holiday decor. A large Christmas tree stands in the waiting area, fully decorated with what I imagine are empty wrapped boxes underneath. There are wreaths on the walls, and I do that thing where I search for something, anything representing Hanukah. And find … nothing. Typical. Annoying, yes, but right now, I'm not worried about holiday trimmings. I need to see my friends.

"Anna Christian, please," I say to the nurse sitting behind the glass.

"Are you family?" she asks, her eyebrow lilting up.

"Yes," I say because I am.

"Sign in here." She pushes a clipboard and pen toward me. "Room 804. The elevator is around the corner."

"Thank you."

I knock softly, and when I crack the door, Christian appears, on his feet with a goofy smile across his handsome face, and pulls me into a bear hug.

"T-Dawg, I told you not to come."

"And I told you I was coming."

"Theodore Berenson, get over here and let me look at you," Anna says from her bed. A bandage covers her left cheek and ear, and there's some bruising near her chin, but otherwise, she's the gorgeous woman who captured my friend's heart.

"Look at me? Look at you. What have you done to that beautiful face?"

"One minute," Christian says, "that's how long it took for him to flirt with you."

"Come here, Theo," Anna says, nodding to a chair beside her bed. Beeps and blips from machines fill the room, and my heart sinks. She's awake, and even joking, but what if it had been worse? My head goes light, and dizziness overtakes me.

Sitting, I say, "Now tell me what happened."

"The car is totaled," Christian says. "But cars are replaceable."

I think about Anna's crumpled car and my stomach wobbles.

"It was black ice. At least, that's what the police think. The road looked fine to me," she says. "It came out of nowhere. I just started sliding, and the next thing I know—"

"In a ditch," Christian says, taking over. "I told her driving to a conference in the city wasn't a good idea. The train would've been—"

"Annoying. Inconvenient. I like driving," she says.

Apparently, when you're married, you don't let the other person finish a sentence.

"So you're not hurt?" I ask.

"Only my pride," she says. Her sweet smile appears, and my chest relaxes a little.

"Now, enough about this nonsense," she says, pointing to her face. "Christian tells me you have a boyfriend?"

I give Christian my what-the-fuck-did-you-say look, and he shrugs.

"I mean, he's not my boyfriend," I say.

"You are staying at his apartment. You're having sex. He's your boyfriend," Christian says.

"Sex? Hold up, wait a minute. Who's having sex? My Theo? Does Sylvia know about this?" Anna teases.

"Um, we are not talking about sex," I say as my heart races and a flush overtakes my ears and face.

"What else do we have to talk about?" Christian asks, sitting across from me on the other side of the bed.

"Anything," I say. "And I'm fairly certain my mother knows as she pressured me to stay with Sheldon while they're in town."

"Sheldon? His name is Sheldon? Okay, that is ridiculously adorable. I need a distraction from all this." Anna motions to the entire room. "Tell me everything, tell me."

"Well, he's a teacher," I say, grateful that the conversation has distracted me from Anna's condition.

"At your school," Christian chimes in.

"Let him talk, mi amor," she says.

"He teaches first grade. He started after Thanksgiving. Well, transferred. I helped him set up his room, and we became friends. I mean, kind of." I remember Sheldon wearing that black tank top in the basement. "He annoyed the fuck out of me at first. He talks a lot. Like all the time. And he's small. A little peanut you can pop in your pocket. And he has red hair. Bright red hair. And freckles. So many freckles everywhere. And well, I like him. A lot. A lot, a lot."

"Theodore Berenson, you most definitely have a boyfriend," Christian says.

"It sounds like maybe you more than like him," Anna says.

"Probably. I told him I love him."

"Wait, what?" Christian asks.

"Oh, Theo," Anna says, taking my hand in hers. She has a tube going into it, and I'm careful not to disturb it. "My entire body is in pain, but my heart is bursting with joy. You deserve this. More than anyone."

I deserve this. Sheldon. My eyes close, and I try to take it in. Accept it. For so long, I've felt like being alone, walking through life with a sour taste in my mouth, was my destiny. My cross to bear. My punishment for what happened. But Sheldon sees me. All of me. And he's not heading for the hills.

"Yeah. I do," I say. My shoulders creep back. I do. I really do deserve this. Him.

"Thank God It's Christmas," my holiday ringtone (much to my parent's chagrin), interrupts us. Hey, Queen never recorded a Hanukah song. I grab my phone and see Sheldon's name and number on the screen.

"Is that him?" Christian asks.

"Yeah, I'll call him back," I say, moving to cancel the call.

"No, you will not. Take it, you oaf," Anna says. "Right now."

I know enough not to argue with Anna on a good day, let alone when she's bruised in a hospital bed.

"Hello? Booster?"

Christian and Anna share a look, and I know I'll have to explain the nickname, but I scoot into the hallway for a moment of privacy.

"Theo, oh my gosh, I just got your message. Are you okay? Is Anna okay? I was worried when I woke up, I didn't know where you were. I thought you were making pancakes, but no pancakes and you totally owe me pancakes and apple syrup, by the way. I mean whenever you get back. When are you coming back? I mean no pressure, obviously, you need to be there. Oh my god, Theo, I really panicked for a minute. I thought you freaked out and ran off."

"Booster. Take a breath," I say and wait to hear his exhale. "I'm at the hospital. Anna's banged up pretty badly, but she seems okay." Her car totaled, the scratches and cuts on her face, and then Booster's porcelain skin flash in my head, and my eyes sting. "I'm not sure when I'll be back, but probably not in time for dinner tonight."

There's silence, and I try to imagine Sheldon's face, and there's most likely disappointment there.

"My mother asked for your cell, and I gave it to her. I hope that's okay. She still wants you to come. I think having you there might help with my absence. But no pressure, I can tell her you can't go if you don't want …"

"No, I'll go. I want to. I'm looking forward to it. And if you aren't there, I mean, being with your parents will have to be my Berenson fill."

The thought of Sheldon at my apartment, with my parents, without me, defines bittersweet.

"Booster, listen to me. You're a mensch, do you know that?"

"I'm trying to be."

My eyes close and I try really hard to send the love I'm feeling for this man through the phone. I'm not into all that existential energy bullshit, but if there's some way I can convey this, through miles, through cell towers, I've got to try.

"Okay, I should get back. Call me before you go to my place if you want. Just text first."

"Sounds good. Please tell Christian and Anna hello. I mean, I know they don't know me, but we'll meet at some point, right?"

"Absolutely. They'll adore you. You're pretty fucking hard not to adore."

"Theo, you're going to make me blush. And you're not even here to see it."

And because right now I can't take chances and I need him to know, I say, "I love you, Booster. Do you know that?"

"Of course I do."

My heart aches from wanting. Wanting him to believe me. Wanting him to feel the same. Wanting him.

THIRTY-FIVE

Sheldon

The first day of school vacation always feels like a fog. My body and brain haven't accepted they don't have to get up and work for ten whole days, and I spend most of the morning cuddling in bed with Janice. Around lunchtime, belly stirring, my phone rings. Seeing it's Sylvia, I pick up.

"Sheldon, we understand it might feel awkward for you to come when Theo's not here, but Hanukah is for family, and you're dating our son ..." There's some commotion, and then Abba's voice comes on.

"If you're dating my son, then you're part of the mishpocha. And if you are, then your sister and her boyfriend are, too," Abba says firmly. "You are all coming. And that's the end of it." Before I can speak, he says, "Make sure you're here before sundown."

And with that, they hang up.

Six hours later, Naomi walks into the room wearing a simple blue dress with pleats on the skirt. "Is this okay?" she asks. "I thought it would be cute if I matched your nails."

"And look"—Walker holds up his pale blue tie with small white and pink flowers—"me too!"

He stands there with a toothy grin, and these two, they really do love me.

"You put a tie on?" I ask.

"For you? Absolutely. But only for you. Or your sister. I'm under this Soleskin spell you two have cast," he says, wrapping his arm around Naomi and giving her a quick peck on the cheek.

"Okay, no kissing. I mean, not now. We're going to be late. The sun is setting. Let's go!" I shout, shooing them out the door.

"Sheldon! And this must be your sister. Abba, look at her," Sylvia says, taking Naomi's face in her hands. "This face. Oy. Such a beauty. And no wonder you look just like your brother."

Sylvia wears a blue and white sequined blouse with a latke man on the front. He's got hearts for eyes, and the words "I Love You A Latke" are encrusted with more sparkles across her chest. It's quite possibly the tackiest item of clothing I've ever seen. And I want one.

I smile because we really do look more identical than fraternal, and Abba says, "But this one is handsome, not beautiful."

"Abba, I'm happy being called beautiful. Or handsome. You can call me whatever superlative you like," I say with a wink.

"Walker Stevens, ma'am." Walker puts his hand out for a shake, and Sylvia takes it and pulls him into a giant hug.

"Now this, this is a punim. Look at him, Abba. And a doctor. If only he were Jewish," Sylvia says, although I'm not sure why it would matter.

"Thank you, ma'am. I'm actually agnostic," Walker says.

"Agnostic? What's that?" Abba asks with a crumpled face.

"It means he doesn't eat meat. No brisket. Only gefilte fish," Sylvia says, still holding Walker hostage. "Sheldon, I found a deli that makes fresh gefilte fish. I bought the good horseradish, too."

"It still comes in a jar, but the glass is thicker," Abba explains.

"Come, come in. Abba, take their coats. We need to light the menorah. It's almost dark."

"The sun waits for no one. Not even my almost son-in-law," Abba says.

Naomi gives me a this-is-interesting-but-you-didn't-even-come-close-to-explaining-it look. I promptly give her a I-had-no-fucking-clue-it-was-at-this-level look as she gently pries Walker's hand from Sylvia, and we head to Theo's mantle to light the menorah.

"Now, traditionally, Teddy always did the last night," Sylvia says, "but since he isn't here, Sheldon, sweetie, why don't you do it?"

My eyes go wide. Sure, I did it the first night, but Theo held my hand through the entire process. My forehead prickles, thinking about Theo's fingers swaddling mine, guiding me through the prayer and lighting.

"But, I don't know the—"

"Nonsense," Abba says, stepping toward me. "I'll help you, son."

My breath catches, and the tears come fast and unexpectedly. This man I barely know, so sweet, so calm and gentle, calling me "son."

"Oh, sweetheart, what's wrong? If you really don't want to do it, Abba will do it himself," Sylvia says, swooping in to rescue me.

"Bean, it's okay. I'm here." Naomi steps forward, and before I know it, Walker is behind her, and I'm engulfed in an embrace by everyone in the room.

"We don't … our parents …" Naomi says, and Walker pulls her close, his lips pulled in.

"Teddy told us," Sylvia says. "About your parents. I don't know that I'll ever understand it. How a mother could …" Her arms are around me, the smell of lilacs and hair spray soothing my emotions.

Abba steps forward, resting his hand on my shoulder. "Sylvia," he begins, his voice having a bite I haven't heard before, "I stopped trying to understand ignorant people a long time ago."

Taking my cheeks in her hands, Sylvia aims my face at hers and says, "If Teddy is in your lives, you're in our lives. We would never try to replace anyone's parents, but also, we'll happily dote on you. All of you." She grabs Walker's hand and pulls him and Naomi toward us. "Even ridiculously handsome goys."

"Okay, let's light the menorah," Abba says, taking my arm and guiding me toward the mantle. The aluminum-foil-covered menorahs and dreidels Theo and I made await the candlelight to sparkle and shine. Sylvia, Naomi, and Walker stand close but give us space. I glance back at my sister, her boyfriend's arm around her shoulder, and tears prickle my eyes again.

"Now remember, we light the shammes and then from right to left. The opposite of reading," Abba instructs. "I know you're a teacher, but I'm going to teach you a thing or two."

Holding my hand, Abba guides me through the lighting, just as Theo did. He smells like a blend of cinnamon and black pepper. His warm breath lands on my face as he sings the blessing. Sylvia's warble joins in, and I do my best to sing with them while Naomi and Walker look on.

"Nice job, son," Abba says, and Hanukah might be my favorite holiday ever.

With candles illuminating the room, we sit around the folding table Theo borrowed from school and feast on the food that Theo and his mother spent all week preparing. Brisket melts in mouths, challah sops up butter, so much butter, matzoh ball soup warms bellies, and then there's the gefilte fish.

"Well, what do you think?" Sylvia asks, watching my every move as I take the first bite.

"The consistency reminds me of a meatball, but the flavor is distinctly … fishy, though not overly," I say between bites. "The horseradish balances the flavors well. I like it."

I take another bite, and a huge grin overtakes my face.

Theo's parents steal a glance, and Sylvia says, "He likes it."

"Bashert," Abba says.

"Excuse me?" Walker asks.

"Bashert," Abba continues. "Meant to be. Kismet. Teddy adores gefilte fish. Since he was a little boy. He would gobble it up until the horseradish stained his lips."

Naomi laughs and says, "Awe, baby fish mouth. I bet Teddy was an adorable little boy."

"Yes, I mean technically he was never really 'little,'" Sylvia says, "but yes, he was beyond sheyn."

"Handsome," Abba says.

"Look." Sylvia grabs her phone from the coffee table and brings up a photo of young Theo. "Look at that punim."

A picture of Theo, maybe seven or eight, standing on a dock. The sky is cloudy, and he wears what I'm guessing are husky jeans and a Florida State T-shirt. He's waving at the camera with a huge smile on his face, so pure and innocent, and I get a glimpse of the boy Theo was before ... before life rocked him hard. I want to pick up that boy and hug him and keep him safe.

As everyone huddles around Sylvia's phone, a message pops up.

> Teddy: Mom stop embarrassing me. Please ask Sheldon to call me.

"Embarrassing? Me?" Sylvia says, her shoulders raising at the thought.

"Go in the bedroom, Sheldon," Abba says. "And close the door. Otherwise, you'll have no privacy with this kibitzer."

"Go, buddy," Walker offers. "Your sister and I will be fine."

Closing Theo's door, I sit on his bed. It's neatly made, the covers pulled tightly toward the top. His parents' belongings sit in a tidy pile. It was exactly two weeks ago that I brought Theo home after the fire alarm and slept here. With him. That day feels like a lifetime ago.

"Booster? My mom told you? I can't believe she let you go for a minute. How are things going?"

"Well, your message popped up right as she showed us a picture of you as a boy. She couldn't really hide it."

"Fuck. The one in the Toughskins?"

"Theo, you were adorable."

"Were."

"Yes, you're not adorable anymore. Now you're handsome. And sexy."

"I mean if you say so. But how is it going? Besides them

managing to embarrass me even when I'm not there."

"Good. I mean your parents, Theo, they're, they're ..."

"A lot. I know."

"No, they're wonderful. They're treating us like family. We only met a week ago. They literally just met Naomi and Walker tonight. You'd think we were actual relatives." I lie back on his pillow, hoping to catch a whiff of his scent. "It's good to hear your voice. I, I miss you."

"I miss you too, Booster. And yeah, they're good parents."

"Good? They're amazing. Your mom made me try gefilte fish."

"And?"

"I didn't hate it. I didn't love it, but it was good."

"And they said it's bashert, right?"

"Yes! How did you know?"

"Because my parents think everything is a sign from the universe."

"Well, maybe it is. Maybe we are ... bashert?"

"Maybe. Listen, I was going to come home tomorrow, but they want to keep Anna in the hospital for a few extra days, and I can't leave Christian now ..."

"Oh."

"I know. I don't think I'll be back by Saturday."

"For the wedding," I say. My heart shrinks.

"I'm so sorry, Booster."

"No, I get it. Honestly, I don't even care about the wedding. Really. I just wanted to have a dress-up, dancing, and party night out with you. And we can do that after you're back. Naomi will go with me. We'll have fun. Not as much fun as I'd have with you, but still."

"I'll make it up to you."

"Promise?"

"Promise."

"I should probably get back," I say, taking a deep breath before standing and heading for the door.

"Booster, I love you."

"I know you do."

THIRTY-SIX

Theo

Sitting on the bed in the guest room, my mind keeps wandering back to Anna. I know she's okay. Or will be. I know this in my head, but my body quivers, and the hairs on the back of my neck lift when I imagine the accident. The car. The ambulance. The lights. Christian rushing to the hospital. Not knowing.

"Pizza okay with you? Loaded?"

Christian walks in, wearing a purple T-shirt and black sweats. Catching the violet fabric, my eyes flash to Sheldon's nails. Sheldon's shoes. I've been here two days. The wedding is tomorrow. I should be back. With Sheldon. My Sheldon.

"T-Dawg? I'm starving, I'm ordering."

"Sorry, yeah, loaded pizza, please. Extra cheese. We need extra cheese."

"Yeah, we do."

"What is going on in that head of yours? I know that face."

I stand and head for the bedroom door, hoping the change in location will snap me out of it.

"My face is fine."

"Yeah, it is, you handsome beast. But stop worrying."

Christian walks to the couch in the living room, and I take the recliner. Settling in, my hand instinctively finds the lever on the side, and I push myself back.

"I'm not worrying."

"Theodore Berenson, I know your worrying face."

"I'm Jewish, my regular face *is* my worrying face."

He chuckles and says, "A truer statement has never been uttered. But Anna's fine. I'm fine."

"I know, but what if …" I don't finish because the words feel like boulders in my throat.

"What if? What if what? Life isn't about *what if's*, buddy."

"But weren't you scared?"

"Of course. I was petrified. But once I got to the hospital and the doctors told me she'd be okay, I chose to believe them. They know what they're doing. They're not in the business of lying. And you've seen her. She's flirting with you. She's going to be fine."

I take a deep breath. He's right. But damn. The thought of something happening to her. To someone you love. My chest tightens and faces flash in my head. Ricky. Sheldon.

"Listen," Christian says, "we're going to smash this pizza when it comes. Then we're going to bed early because tomorrow morning you're going home. To your guy."

"No way. I'm not leaving yet."

"Dude, why?"

"Anna's not home. You're alone here and …"

"And you're afraid."

"Excuse me?"

"You're afraid."

I reach for the lever to bring the chair back to upright so I can get up and walk away, but Christian pops up and stands over me, blocking my escape.

"Dude, what the fuck are you doing? You finally found someone you love, and you're staying here with me? Love is a risk. That's the gig. But you do it anyway because it's also the best fucking thing in the world. Go home, T-Dawg. Sheldon is waiting for you."

"But, what if …"

And then, hovering over me, for once in his life actually taller than me, Christian leans over and slaps the top of my head. Hard.

"What the fuck?" I shout.

"Get it together, Berenson. You're not staying here any longer, avoiding your life because you're scared. Not on my watch. I'm kicking you out. Tomorrow morning, we're going to the hospital. You'll see Anna and say goodbye to both of us. Case closed."

"There's something I need to do first. Tonight. Can you help me?"

"What? Tell me, and we'll do it."

I open my mouth, but the doorbell rings.

Christian turns. "Fucking A. The pizza!"

"Theo?"

Sheldon's voice crackles through the cab of my truck. It's almost two o'clock in the afternoon, but it sounds like he's just woken up.

"Booster, did I wake you? I'm sorry, I can call back."

"No, I mean, yes, you did—I was napping with Janice. Sometimes I join her for catnaps when I'm on vacation."

I picture him, snuggled in his bed, a mess of limbs and freckles, Janice burrowing her way to warmth, and a smile creeps over my face. Yeah, my soul aches for Sheldon Soleskin.

"I'm headed back."

"Wait, now? But I thought …"

"I'll explain when I see you. There's so much holiday traffic. I don't think I'm going to make the wedding," I say, and picture the plaid suit my mother dragged me to buy last week.

"Theo, I don't care about the wedding. I just miss you."

He misses me. Me. A sharp twinge in my chest overtakes me.

"I miss you too, Booster. So much."

"You do?"

"Of course I do. I can't wait to kiss your fucking face." He laughs and then I hear some commotion followed by a thud. "Booster, you okay?"

"I startled Janice, she ran off. Well, text me when you're back. Maybe I can see you after the wedding?"

"Nothing could stop me from it, Booster."

Cruising down the highway, I picture his face. Almost always smiling or smirking, but when he sleeps, so calm and peaceful. He looks like an angel, and the urge to see him overwhelms me. I didn't know love could feel this way. Maybe Christian is right. Loving someone means taking a risk. It's time to be brave.

Carefully pressing the gas, I accelerate to eighty-four miles per hour, slightly exceeding Abba's eighty-two-mile rule.

Freddie's vocals and piano bring me into "Don't Stop Me Now." The bass enters before the rest of the band takes off and I imagine my truck is a shooting star bounding through the sky toward home.

THIRTY-SEVEN

Sheldon

Standing in her emerald-green dress, the hem dusting the floor, Naomi fiddles with her earring, struggling to get the back on.

"Do you need help?"

"Zip, please."

I walk over and tug on the back of her zipper and watch the fabric hug her body. My heart swells. My sister has my back. Always. Even as I'm staring at hers.

"So, what do we think of this?" I ask, moving in front of her and giving her a twirl, thinking "this" would be something to impress Theo. I splurged on a cobalt-blue vintage velvet tuxedo. It's no Klein Epstein & Parker custom suit, but we don't all have Mama Ru's resources. I paired it with a white bowtie and painted my nails bright white to match.

"I mean, you look fabulous, obviously," she says. "But it's a Christmas-Eve wedding. Blue?"

"Well, the idea was to look like a Hanukah fantasy for Theo," I say, fanning my white nails.

"But Hanukah's over," she says, handing me the diamond drop necklace Walker gave her for our thirtieth birthday. It only comes out for special occasions.

"I know. But it's the thought that counts." I pinch the clasp and check it's secure.

"You look like a Jewish elf."

"Is that a thing?" I ask.

"You're asking me? You're the one with the Jewish boyfriend," she teases. "And when exactly is he coming back?"

"Tonight. But late. I don't think I'll see him until tomorrow."

"But tomorrow's Christmas," Naomi says, finally snapping the back onto her earring, "Who wants to drive for hours on Christmas Eve?"

"He doesn't care. He's Jewish."

"And he wants to be home for Christmas. To be your present."

"I hope so."

Naomi and I strategically arrive minutes before the ceremony, so we don't have to make small talk with people. Our plan is to hit the reception, have a few drinks, stay through dinner and cake, and then escape when everyone's distracted by the first dance. It's a solid plan. We've used it at other weddings with much success.

As we take our seats near the back, the lamps in the room dim, accentuating the twinkling Christmas lights cascading down the walls. The eighties synths and snare drum of Wham's "Last Christmas" begin, and Timothy and Dwayne appear wearing matching tuxedos. Traditional black and white. Timothy's hair, clearly with extra product, is poofed and swooped into submission. His bright red tie compliments Dwayne's green one, and they look ... happy. Dwayne stands a good three inches taller than Timothy, and his jacket seems to struggle to contain a multitude of giant muscles. Dwayne and I couldn't be more different, and I can't help but wonder what Timothy saw in me. My body shrinks in my seat, and I feel smaller than I already am. Naomi takes my hand but doesn't speak. She doesn't have to.

They walk down to George Michael singing about giving his heart to someone different. Someone special. The urge to stand and bolt for the door washes over me. Naomi's hand holds me in place. I squeeze her palm with my fingers. It would be rude to talk right now, but I want her to know how much I love her.

Luckily, from our seats in the back, we can't see or hear well. There's mumbling about love and finding your person, and when Timothy reaches for Dwayne's lapels to drag himself up for their kiss, a wave of apathy washes over me. It hits me like a partridge in a pear tree. The way things ended between us may have been less than ideal, but Timothy's not a bad person. He deserves happiness, and if marrying Dwayne, the trainer with a body of a Greek god, does it for him, then more power to him.

Once they kiss, fake snow begins falling from the ceiling, and it's actually magical. Christmas morning is only hours away. The snow from the big storm that stranded me at Theo's has all melted, but inside, Timothy's managed to wrangle a little pre-Christmas cheer. Everyone claps, stands, and moves into the ballroom. Naomi and I linger toward the back, waiting our turn to see our seat assignments.

We end up with a small group from Dwayne's gym. I mean, it's Timothy's gym too, but Dwayne works there. Everyone is buff and fit and towers over the Soleskin twins. When I see Timothy and Dwayne making their rounds, greeting their guests, smiling, looking like the cover of a no-really-we're-not-brothers magazine, my stomach begins to gurgle, and I excuse myself and scurry to the bathroom.

The cool water from the sink stifles the heat of my face. I can do this. Naomi is with me. Theo will be home soon. Timothy looks happy. I should be happy for him. Patting my face dry, I take a deep breath and ready myself to return.

"Shelly! Are you okay?"

Timothy. He's walking with such force he almost knocks me over as I exit the men's room.

"Fine, totally fine. Just needed the loo."

"I saw you leave and wanted to make sure …"

"Timothy, I'm fine, this is your night. Come, let's go back."

He reaches out, puts a hand on my shoulder and does this thing where his fingers trace my entire arm until they find my hand. I used to love the gesture, but now it makes my ribs tighten.

"Thank you," he says.

"For what?" I'm genuinely confused.

"For coming. I honestly didn't expect to see you. Not after what I did. How I ended it. On Christmas Eve. That was a grade-A-dick move."

"Accurate."

"You're clearly the bigger person," he says. His thumb rubs my palm and I want to pull my hand away and bolt from the hotel.

"I mean, I'm not bigger than anyone, really."

"You know what I mean."

I nod gently, my throat temporarily overtaken by an enormous lump.

"I know I've apologized for how things ended but let me say it one more time. I'm sorry. I never meant to hurt you. What I did. Going behind your back. Not being honest." He looks at the ground before locking onto me. "I truly hope you can forgive me someday."

When I look up at him, his eyes wide and soft, it clicks. He actually means it. And sure, his intentions may not have been malicious, but damn my heart was broken. But also, without what happened, there'd be no Theo. Theo who sees me. Theo who loves me. All of me.

"Timothy." I bring his hand up to my face and give it a quick peck before dropping it. "I know. It's okay. We're okay. Or will be."

"What happened to the guy you were seeing?"

"Oh, he had to work," I lie, not wanting to explain the situation. "But you'd like him. He's a mensch."

Timothy chuckles and then opens his arms and comes in for a hug, and I let him. Wrapped in his arms, a wave of calm washes over me. I'm actually glad I came. Not to prove anything to Timothy, but for me. Now I'm sure I'm ready. Because now, all I want is Theo. My Theo.

After being left alone with Dwayne's work buddies longer than she'd probably like, Naomi's face lights up when I return to my seat. The minute I'm next to her, her hand takes mine under the table.

I lean over, nuzzle into her neck, and whisper, "Thank you."

"Love you, bean. Forever and ever, amen."

With the cake cut and served, the DJ fires up Michael Bublé's "I'll Be Home for Christmas," and Dwayne takes Timothy's hand for their first dance. The photographer circles them as they slowly sway. Dwayne's arms wrap around Timothy, and I can barely see him. Everyone's phones are out snapping photos. Dwayne really does dwarf Timothy, and my lips turn up thinking how the roles have reversed.

About halfway through the song, the DJ invites everyone to join in, and couples gradually fill in the parquet floor.

"Shall we?" Naomi asks, extending her hand.

My mouth is full of cake (her piece as I've already finished my own). My eyes widen, and I put a finger up and mumble, "One minute."

She tilts her head and gives me her come-on-little-brother look, and I say, "What? It's a delicious cake. There's a perfect frosting-to-cake ratio, and you know how I feel about vanilla cake with white frosting."

"Come, bean," she instructs, grabbing my hand, forcing me to drop the fork and leave the rest of the sugary comfort until after we dance. "The cake will wait."

Enough couples have joined in that we can remain on the periphery of the dance floor and stay in our own little twin bubble.

"Do you want to lead?" I ask because we've always taken turns, and she honestly does it way better than me.

"Sure. Come here."

I rest my head on her shoulder, wrap my hands around her neck, and we dance like seventh graders under twinkling lights and more Christmas decor than Santa's workshop.

"I know this wasn't how you hoped this night would go, bean, but I'm glad I'm here with you."

"Me too," I say into her neck.

The vocal stylings of Michael Bublé echo in the ballroom, and I close my eyes and cling to my sister. My heart feels lighter than Santa's after a night delivering every last present, knowing she'll always be here for me.

A tap on my shoulder interrupts us, and when I open my eyes and turn, my heart drops through my stomach. Theo stands with a satisfied smile on his face, wearing a gorgeous plaid suit. His hair has been slicked back behind his ears, but a few wild curls break free near his temple. He waves his hands in front of his face, and his fingernails are painted in the same dark navy blue he used on mine. It takes every ounce of restraint for me not to attack him with kisses.

"Naomi. May I cut in?"

Naomi smiles, and her face lights up. I'm not sure if she knew he was coming, but she seems almost as thrilled as I am to see him. She steps back, takes my hand, and places it in Theo's.

"Sir, my brother. Treat him with care."

Theo's face breaks into a grin, and a small chuckle escapes his beautiful lips. "I promise," he says, and my insides melt like hot caramel.

My feet, apparently having a mind of their own, do a little hop. In an instant, my legs do their best to wrap around Theo's waist, and he moves to support me and hold me.

"You ... you came," I stutter, my lips trying to keep pace with my heart. "And your nails." I lift his hand, inspecting the job. "How? When?"

"I did them at Christian's. And he helped."

Theo and his oldest friend painting his nails. I'm not sure my heart can take it.

"Wait, what about Anna? I thought, I thought—"

"She's fine," he says, and leans down and kisses my forehead, nose, and finally his mouth lands on mine. It's only been days but having Theo Berenson's lips on mine makes my soul sing like a choir.

"But I thought you weren't coming back because—" Theo's finger touches my top lip, pausing my sentence. Carefully, he lowers my feet to the floor.

"I wasn't honest, Booster. And I'm so sorry. Please let me explain."

My head feels light. He wasn't honest? About his best friend's wife being hurt? The room begins to spin, and faint ringing slides into my ears.

"You lied?"

Theo closes his eyes and pulls a deep breath in. The fake snow has stopped falling, and Mariah's "All I Want for Christmas is You" takes over the speakers. I'm dizzy as I pull my hands from Theo's and bolt out the door and into the cold December night.

Stumbling outside, streetlights and wreaths adorned with Christmas lights illuminate the stone road in front of the hotel. My brain, fuzzy and unbalanced, searches for a place to sit. I was perfectly content for Naomi to be my date. We actually had a really nice time. She let me eat her cake. She always lets me eat her cake. My head spins with confusion. Theo lied to me about Anna? He told me she wasn't doing well, and he needed to stay. Was there even an accident? I spot a black metal bench near the entrance and sit down, putting my head between my legs and taking deep breaths to try and stop the spinning.

"Booster."

I can feel him next to me. His thigh up against mine. A hand gently rests on my back, and I'm suddenly freezing, and while the velvet tuxedo jacket provides some warmth, it's not enough.

"You're shivering," he says. "Come here."

He pulls me toward him, and I don't resist. There's no resisting Theo.

"Why, Theo? Why?" I mumble into his chest, not sure he's heard me.

"Booster, look at me."

I don't move.

"Please."

I move my eyes north, and when they connect with his, there's nothing dishonest or conniving. Only sweetness. Warmth. Love. My Theo.

"I got scared. Petrified. After I told you I loved you, I don't know, it all became overwhelming. Like mountains-on-top-of-me overwhelming."

I rest my head on his shoulder, the need to be closer overtaking my frustration. I can't see his face now, but I'm listening.

"When I saw Anna in the hospital, I started to spiral."

"But I thought she was okay?"

"Yes, only banged up, but seeing my friend's wife like that, I don't know, it shook me."

"Why didn't you tell me?"

His chubby fingers gather my hands up, and he begins softly rubbing them. "I don't know." He lets go with his right hand and scrubs his face before returning to massaging my cold fingers. "Wait, that's not true. I was scared if I let myself love you, the way Christian loves Anna, the way I loved Ricky … something would, would …"

"Oh, baby."

I lift his hands to my face and kiss his knuckles. They're red from the cold, and my lips do little to help.

"But Christian figured me out quickly. He's no fool." Theo wraps his right arm around me, pulling me toward him, his other hand still holding both of mine.

"Theo, listen, I'm no expert, but what I'm learning is that love is a lot like taking a leap off a cliff."

"Well, that seems like a really foolish thing to do," he says, kissing the top of my head.

"Yeah, but you leap, and a net appears. Love is the net."

"Booster. Come here." He pulls me into his lap. "Do you think a net can catch a big guy like me?"

I lift my head to kiss him. Our mouths meet, and his kiss, soft at first but then deeper, firmer, makes my heart pound. There's intention and passion as he clings to me.

"Theo, I'll be your net."

"I love you, Booster. So damn much."

"I love you, too, Theo. Now stop blabbing and kiss me."

And he does. I'm nestled in Theo's lap, wrapped in his arms, and he shelters me. From the cold. From my fears. From myself. I shift to get a better angle and deepen the kiss. Theo holds me up, his hands under my bottom now, and I'm fairly certain he loves the feeling of velvet in his hands. Or maybe it's my ass. Or maybe it's my ass in velvet. We kiss, our mouths finally quiet enough to let the passion flow, and snow begins falling, dusting our heads with white flakes.

"It's snowing!" I yell, pausing the kiss.

"It is. Merry Christmas, Booster," he says, his painted fingernail tracing my lips. "I'm sorry I didn't get you anything."

"But you did, baby. I got exactly what I wanted," I say.

And I pull his sweet face down for another kiss.

Epilogue

Seven Months Later - Theo

"Booster, you um … honestly, my brain can't find the words."

Sheldon stands before me, wearing the Klein Epstein & Parker suit of his dreams. It's purple, with a purple shirt and tie, but somehow all the purples are different.

"I'm going for a monochromatic look. Plum, lavender," he says, pointing to his suit and shirt and fanning his freshly painted fingers in front of his sweet face, "and crimson."

"Well, you look amazing. Gorgeous. Stunning. Beautiful. Delicious."

"I thought you had no words?"

"Well, I thought of a few," I say, pulling him close and kissing his forehead before tipping his chin up and finding his perfect lips.

"I love these lips," I whisper and then kiss him again. "And I love you."

"You know, technically, you're not supposed to see the bride before the wedding," he teases.

"Booster, you're not the bride."

"No, but she's my twin, which means I'm bride adjacent."

"Bride adjacent? That's not a thing. You made that up."

"Maybe, but my twin sister is getting married, and I'm emotional, so cut me some slack."

"I'll cut you all the slack in the world once we get there. Now let's go before we're late."

Planning Naomi and Walker's wedding outside on the Eastern Prom, overlooking the ocean, was risky. But Mother Nature, often unpredictable and even a bitch, has blessed us with a perfect, glorious July day in Maine. The sun is shining, it's warm but not too hot, and the ocean breeze provides just enough motion for Naomi's dress and veil to blow, something Sheldon was way too worried about, leading up to today.

Cruising down Commercial Street in my truck, windows open, "Flash" blares through my speakers, and Sheldon's wrinkled brow prompts me to lean over and turn the volume down to check on him.

"Booster, what is it? We can listen to something else."

"No, I love wannabe futuristic, sci-fi Queen," he says, laying his hand over mine on the console. "It's just happening. For real."

"Yes, it is. And I'm going to be there. My parents are going to be there. Christian and Anna, too. Everyone who loves and supports both you and Naomi will be there."

"I know, I just, it's just, now everything changes. For real"

"Yes, it will, but remember what we talked about." I flip my hand over and cradle his small fingers. "Change can be a good thing."

We arrive at the Eastern Prom, and there's a flurry of activity on the hill near the big gazebo. Hair blows, fabric flaps, and my mother, spotting my truck, screams—yes, screams—as if she's witnessing a crime.

"Boys! Boys! Where have you been? We're starting in ten minutes," she yells, running over and grabbing us both by the hand. She pulls us toward the folded chairs set up on the grass like we're small children being scolded for sneaking cookies. "Sheldon, your sister is waiting for you."

"You told us to be here at eleven," I say, my limp keeping us from moving as fast as Mom would probably like.

"No, I told you to be here before eleven. Before!"

"Oh," I mumble.

"Sylvia, I'm sorry, it was my fault. I wanted my tie to be perfect. And the Kelvin knot is trickier than you'd think. But look at us. Don't we look stunning?"

Mom pauses and gives us both a quick, thorough scan, something she would have done immediately if we weren't late. The lines on her face soften, and a smile takes over her ruby-red lips.

"My boys. So handsome," she says, patting my lapels. "Teddy, this new suit is gorgeous. You've never looked better. Ever. They were worth every penny."

Not content to let Sheldon and I wear anything in our closets, my parents insisted on buying us both new suits. Sheldon protested until Abba declared, "Sheldon. Let us treat you. You're family now."

Sheldon's purple suit fits him to a tee, while my dark navy suit, white shirt, and light purple—sorry, "orchid"—tie coordinate flawlessly with his ensemble. His words, not mine.

When Walker proposed to Naomi during the New Year's Eve dinner I made, Booster took it surprisingly well. Including Sheldon was Walker's way of getting his approval, and I give him big props for that. The twin connection is not something to take lightly.

"Honey, we're going to be sitting right here," my mother says, cupping Sheldon's face in her hands. "If you need anything, you just give me a look …"

"Thank you, Sylvia. I'm okay. Really. But I appreciate that. And you. And Abba. More than you know."

My mother doesn't reply, only pulls Sheldon's face close and kisses him. My heart flutters, watching her dote on the man I love.

"Mommy. Enough. Let him be. There's a wedding waiting," Abba shouts, and with that, I join my parents, Christian, and Anna, while Booster heads to the wedding party near a tent set up for the purpose.

"T-Dawg, you clean up nicely," Christian says, standing to shake my hand and embrace my folks.

"I mean, I'm no model like you," I reply.

Christian and Anna drove up yesterday for the rehearsal dinner. They really do resemble a couple in a catalog. Christian's wearing a suit but no tie, his neck refusing to be wrangled, even by fashion. Anna's pink dress flutters in the breeze, and with them here, my eyes prickle with tears, knowing my entire family insisted on attending not only for me but for Booster.

The day couldn't be more perfect. Only a few small clouds dot the sky, and the ocean breeze has kept the temps cool. When I hear the small string quartet begin to play, I turn, along with everyone, and see her.

Naomi stands, a giant smile across her face in a dress that's "simple but elegant." She and Sheldon spent a month of Saturdays searching, finally finding the "perfect" dress in a small bridal shop in Boston that "only the elite know about." I know how important helping his sister find the right dress was, and once they locked that down, I felt a sense of relief wash over him. I was also pleased to have my Booster back for extended Saturday morning cuddle sessions followed by pancakes with warm apple syrup. Naomi's face beams. She's focused on Walker, standing at the makeshift altar, only the aisle separating them. I see her steal a breath and then turn her attention for a moment.

Her arm laces in her brother's. The two of them, a fucking vision. Booster's giving her away.

Abba offered to do it, and for a hot minute, I thought that would happen. But Sheldon insisted. "If anyone's giving my sister away, it's me."

Naomi's lips part, and I see her mouth, "I love you" to her brother. From my angle, I can't see Booster's face, but if I were a betting man, he's got tears in his eyes.

The Soleskin twins walk down the aisle, and everyone stands. Sheldon's smile is so wide I can see every tooth in his delectable mouth. He steals a glance at me as they pass us, and I wink at him and mouth my own, "I love you."

And before friends, family, and found family, Naomi and Walker exchange vows, kiss, and marry. Sheldon holds it together, and my lungs expand, full of fresh ocean air, knowing he's letting Naomi have her big moment. When the newlywed couple runs down the aisle, and we throw white flower petals at them, I look at my Booster. He's smiling. Happy. And my heart sings.

The reception will occur at a gorgeous waterfront restaurant a short walk from the Prom. I take Booster's hand as we join the small crowd headed down.

"You did good, Booster."

He squeezes my hand but doesn't say anything and a silent Booster causes an empty feeling in my stomach.

"You okay?"

"Yeah, I … I … I forgot my bag. Can you wait a minute?"

"I can go with you," I say, turning to follow.

"No, I'll run. Just wait. I'll be right back."

I sit on a bench in front of the giant gazebo. Sailboats glide by, and I spot a large cruise ship in the distance heading into port. Closing my eyes, I take in a huge breath, my chest full and my heart happy.

"Okay, got it."

I open my eyes, and Booster stands in front of me. The sun is behind him, casting him into silhouette. I'm tempted to grab my phone and snap of photo of him this way. He looks like an angel.

I brace myself on the bench to stand, and he says, "Wait. Please."

"What's wrong?"

"Nothing. Absolutely nothing is wrong. Everything's right."

"Okay, well, we should get going. You know how my mother gets."

"I know, but give me a second."

And then, my Booster, barely taller than me even when I'm sitting, kneels.

"Theo Berenson, you, you, you're a big bear. A teddy bear, and you've given me the biggest gift anyone's ever given me."

A sob in my throat chokes, and I want to make a joke about my dick, but I don't.

"I don't know much, but I know I can't imagine my life without you. And I'm not saying this because Naomi is moving out, and I will be alone. Which is true, by the way. And I'm handling it surprisingly well. A lot of that has to do with you, Theo. You and I are together all the time already, so it's not that. I swear."

"I know," I eke out, and my eyes widen, surprised I'm able to speak.

"I love you, Theo. So much. You are, you are everything to me. And I'd be honored if you'd consider marrying me."

"Consider it?"

"I mean, will you? Marry me?"

I reach down, put my hands under his arms and yank him onto my lap.

"Are you fucking kidding me? Of course. Nothing would make me happier."

Chills overtake my body, and I'm fairly certain this is what heaven must feel like. Booster's lips are on mine, and we sit there, him gathered in my lap, in front of the vast openness of Casco Bay, and kiss.

He pulls away and says, "Listen, can we not say anything to anyone today? I don't want to rain on Naomi's parade. Is that okay?"

"Of course it's okay," I say, tears streaming down my face. "If we told my parents today, it would not end well."

He reaches up and wipes the tears from my cheeks with his thumb and says, "And I'm sorry if I messed that up. I … I always thought I'd be the one being proposed to, not doing the proposing. I hadn't practiced it enough in my head."

"Booster. It was perfect. You're fucking perfect."

And he is. My Booster. Forever.

Acknowledgments

Grandpa - You came back damaged, with so many stories. Thank you for sharing them and trying your best. I will always love you.

Jake D. - You are a true human sparkler. The light you bring into this world can never be dimmed. Never stop being you. I love you, friend.

Jay Leigh - Your continued friendship and early eyes on my words mean more than I can ever express. Thank you from the heart of my bottom.

Gillian Geller and Zoe Stein - My Jewish girlfriends, your insight and feedback have been invaluable in shaping this story. Please continue giving Big Bubbe Energy!

Alison Cochrun and Steven Salvatore - thank you both for your teaching, patience, and guidance.

A.M. Johnson - my boss lady, small and mighty, leaver of voice messages. Thank you for your friendship and support.

Courtney Kae, Fallon Ballard, Anita Kelley, Kayla Grosse, Alicia Simpson, K. Sterling, Amy Spalding, Max Walker, Ashley Bennett, Chip Pons, Brian Kennedy, Charlie Ariggo, Ruby Barrett, and any author friends I've forgotten - thank you all for continuing to humor and inspire me.

To the entire Bookstagram and BookTok communities - you have welcomed me and lifted my stories, and for that, I owe you the sun and moon. Every post, comment, reel, TikTok, and review means the world to me. Thank you all for helping the world be a more inclusive, beautiful place.

Erika - You listen. You talk. You're simply the best.

Karen (both of you!), Emily, Jillian, Deedee, Maggie, Nate, Sarah, Susan, Patti, Brandon, Jeremy, Ron, Derek, and all my friends - Your encouragement and faith in me continue to buoy me.

Elise Vaz - You continue to lift me up and help me see I'm worthy. I love you!

Manda Waller - You continue to be my favorite magician.

Mom - Thank you for the phone calls and listening to me blab about story ideas and characters, and reminding me I can do it.

Dave - My number one cheerleader. My number one guy. I love you more every day, and that's saying something.

And last, to you, dear reader, I hope you enjoyed Sheldon and Theo's story. I'd be honored if you left a review and shared my guys with the world. Knowing you're enjoying my love stories only multiplies the delight I take in writing them. Stay tuned! I've got more mishigas planned!

About the Author

M.A. Wardell lives near the ocean with his husband and cats. When he isn't writing, he's snuggling those cats, reading all the rom-coms, walking to unravel plot points, and taking long hot baths. *Mistletoe & Mishigas* is the second book in the Teachers in Love Series, and he's plotting to play matchmaker again soon.

For more information, visit https://www.mawardell.com/

Also by M.A. Wardell

THE TEACHERS IN LOVE SERIES

Teacher of the Year - Marvin and Olan's story is available now!

Mistletoe & Mishigas - Sheldon and Theo's story is available now!

Napkins and Other Distractions - Vincent and Kent's story coming June 2024

Husband of the Year - Marvin and Olan's series finale coming February 2025